The Caribbean Conspiracy

LESLIE HOLDEN

HARVEST HOUSE PUBLISHERS
Eugene, Oregon 97402

THE CARIBBEAN CONSPIRACY

Copyright © 1987 by Harvest House Publishers
Eugene, Oregon 97402

ISBN 0-89081-619-0

Printed in the United States of America.

CHAPTER 1

Juanita Martinez still could not make up her mind about whether it would be worth the risk.

She was only two weeks away from her scheduled return to America. For almost a year she had been working as an undercover CIA agent in the office of Guadalupe Bentancourt, Cuba's new Ambassador-at-Large. For two years before that she had worked in Cuba's coastal surveillance section, monitoring the radio transmissions of the U. S. Coast Guard, and also secretly recording data for the CIA about Russian naval convoys coming in and out of Havana.

She had done her duty, and more. There was no reason for her to feel obligated to assist in any last-minute espionage forays. Now she just wanted to follow her original plan to fly to the Bahamas with Bentancourt on government business that weekend and, while there, simply vanish into the crowd one day. By Monday morning she would be in Washington having coffee with her section chief at CIA headquarters.

Yet it was that very section chief—Alma Hammond—who had gotten word to her to make a visit to the Russian consulate in Cuba in order to put a transmitter "bug" near the consulate switchboard. Juanita had handled much riskier assignments, but that had been before she was so close to her time to return to America . . . and to Scott Parker.

Orders were orders. But love was love.

She could pretend she had never received the secret message or that the transmitter had been damaged.

But no, that didn't suit her. Besides, Alma Hammond had a talent for recognizing a lie the moment someone spoke it. Alma needed that talent for the type of work she did.

Juanita rolled the small magnetized transmitter between her forefinger and thumb. Such a little item, yet such a risky undertaking.

She looked at her watch: 12:37. Most of the consulate staff would still be out to lunch. Some would be late in getting back. It would be a good time to get the job done and behind her.

"This is the last time," she promised herself. "After I get through with this one, I'm finished. No more last-minute assignments from you, Alma."

*   *   *

In the days before the Castro regime, Cuban nationals held many jobs on the U.S. military base at Guantanamo. The local people worked as cooks, waiters, housekeepers, gardeners, landscapers, painters, woodworkers, and warehouse helpers. Each morning the workers would arrive at the security gate, show their work cards, and be admitted. Each night they would leave the base and return to their homes.

It was not uncommon for the Marines stationed at Guantanamo to visit these folks in their homes whenever a weekend pass could be wrangled from a tightfisted first sergeant. That was how a lanky Texan named Jim Middleton found himself frequently the dinner guest at the home of Jose "Joe" Martinez. Joe was one of the barbers on the base and Jim was a supply sergeant. The supply room and the barbershop were side by side, so the two men saw a lot of each other.

On his first visit to Joe's house, Jim Middleton became smitten by the beauty of Joe's 17-year-old daughter, Rosa. Though already 26, Jim had never married. He had been a Marine for eight years and planned to put in another dozen, but he didn't want to spend them alone. So with Joe's permission he began to court Rosa. Six months later they were married by a Marine chaplain in a small ceremony on the base.

Rosa continued to live with her parents for another year, since married housing on the base was limited and expensive. Jim was able to get overnight passes several times each week, and on weekends Rosa spent the days with him on the base. During Thanksgiving week of 1956, Rosa entered the base hospital and delivered their first child, a daughter whom they named Juanita. That same week, Jim received his transfer orders. He was being shipped back to the States for a new duty assignment in California starting in January.

Everything seemed so perfect: a new baby and a new posting in America. Jim couldn't have been happier. He made arrangements for off-base housing to be ready for him and his family when they arrived in California. He even secured a visa for Rosa's mother to make the trip with them to help with the baby. Everything was falling into place.

On the evening of December 2, 1956, Jim was getting ready to pick up his overnight pass and head for Joe Martinez's home to see Rosa and their new baby. His plans were suddenly changed, however, when a loud siren sent the base into a security alert. The gates were closed, lights were turned out, and all available troops were ordered to put on combat fatigues, draw arms, and take a position on the perimeter of the base.

Fidel Castro and 81 freedom fighters had made an assault landing that afternoon on a western shore. They had overrun the unsuspecting troops of Fulgencio Batista and had confiscated a cache of arms and ammunition. With reinforcements from island guerrillas, they seized and occupied a neighboring village. After establishing a headquarters with a radio base there, they dispatched patrols inland to dynamite bridges, blockade highways, and loot stores and villas. All of Cuba was in a panic, and so was Sergeant Jim Middleton, who feared for the lives of his wife and daughter.

Jim's fears were justified. One of the target priorities on Castro's hit list was the village of San Pedro de la Azur Mar, where most of the Cuban nationals lived who held jobs on Guantanamo. Joe Martinez and his family lived there. During the night, Castro sympathizers ravaged the village. They set fire to the homes, pressed teenage boys into service as supply toters, and shot anyone who showed the least sign of resistance.

But Joe Martinez was not caught off-guard. Since 1953, when Castro's first attempt at a government takeover had failed, Joe had suspected that Castro, or others like him, would try again. For that reason Joe had begun buying items a little at a time from the PX on the base. He now had a small supply of medicine, food, matches, cooking utensils, and blankets wrapped in a tent and hidden in the jungle area beyond the sugarcane fields outside his village. When it became evident that San Pedro was under attack, Joe quickly led his wife, two sons, three daughters, and one granddaughter away to the cane fields. They made their way into the jungle and crouched by their supplies.

For three hours they sat wide-eyed, watching as the flames from their village grew higher and higher. Rosa was convinced that Jim would try to come to her and Juanita. She had to spot him, tell him they were alive, and show him where they were hiding.

Ignoring Joe's pleas to stay with the family, Rosa gave her baby to its grandmother and then made her way back to the outskirts of San Pedro.

By dawn the raiders were gone, but Rosa had not returned to her family. Joe's anxiety could not be contained. He instructed his wife to keep the children hidden while he went to find Rosa. Cautiously he made his way back to San Pedro. He found his home in ashes and rubble. Many of his neighbors were lying shot in the village streets. The carnage was ghastly. The stench of smoke irritated Joe's eyes and nostrils. Nothing was left standing. Even the cows, pigs, dogs, and chickens had been shot. San Pedro was no more. Castro had taken his revenge on the "American-lovers" of Cuba.

Joe wandered the streets and side paths. Whenever he encountered someone he knew, he asked about Rosa. No one had seen her. They asked him about their loved ones. Joe shook his head. No, he had not seen them. Then, with a horror he couldn't have anticipated, he turned a corner and saw a body he recognized.

Awkwardly, hesitantly, Joe approached the body. He knelt beside it and gingerly reached for its neck. No pulse. Dead. It was Sergeant Jim Middleton. Somehow he had made it to the village. Joe saw three dead Cuban guerrillas lying ten feet away. Jim had gone down fighting.

But what of Rosa? Had Jim found her? Was she shot? Kidnapped? Did she try to go to the base? Had she made it back to the family hidden in the jungle?

Joe spent the next hour scavenging for food. When he returned to his family, Rosa was not there. He never saw his daughter again nor ever learned of her fate.

For the next two years Joe and his family wandered from place to place, trying to locate Rosa and trying to avoid the rebel troops. Joe told everyone that his granddaughter Juanita was his daughter. With anti-American sentiments being what they were in Cuba, Joe felt that Juanita Martinez was a safer name for his daughter than Juanita Middleton.

In 1959, when Castro came to power, Joe knew he couldn't keep running. Sooner or later the Communists would catch up with him. He started to make contingency plans for his family members. He found jobs for Matteo and Diego on a fishing trawler bound for Mexico. He told them to jump ship at the first port they came to and never return to Cuba.

Next, Joe took little Juanita, now nearly three years old, to a Red Cross station in Havana. It was a risky move, since Joe had no papers identifying him as a government loyalist. Still, he knew the city well enough to know how to get in and melt into the throng.

Joe explained that Juanita was the surviving daughter of an American GI and that he wanted her taken back to her

American grandparents in Texas. The Red Cross workers were skeptical of Joe and his story, but subsequent tracing revealed that Sergeant Jim Middleton had indeed married a Cuban national and that their daughter had been born in a military hospital. Truly, Juanita Martinez nee Middleton was an American citizen.

That night Joe was apprehended while trying to sneak out of Havana. A tired security captain was not in the mood to fill out the necessary paperwork for a formal arrest. He ordered Joe to be released; he then shot him in the back. His log entry was "escaping prisoner shot."

Four weeks later little Juanita arrived on the doorstep of her grandparents' home in Galveston, Texas.

*   *   *

Juanita approached the Russian Embassy in downtown Havana.

Her face was familiar to the people here. She and her supervisor, the Honorable Guadalupe Bentancourt, Cuba's Ambassador-at-Large, had come here on business as well as for numerous formal dinner parties and state receptions. Despite her recognizable face, Juanita flashed her identification card for the registration clerk at the door. He smiled and waved her on.

As she entered the building, Juanita felt a chill. It was brought on by the many memories she had of coming to this embassy on the arm of Guadalupe Bentancourt. She despised everything the man stood for, and his continuous advances made her ill. She had been forced to give him some occasional indications of romantic hope—a special smile, a good-night kiss, a gift for his birthday—yet she also kept him at arm's length as much as possible. That Guadalupe wanted her as his lover was only too obvious, but Juanita's love and loyalty belonged to Scott Parker. And soon they would be together forever. There remained only this final assignment. Once she attached the magnetic listening device to the operator's reception board, she could leave and be done with espionage work forever. Eight years in this business had been enough.

*   *   *

When she had been a senior at the University of Texas, Juanita Martinez-Middleton had come to the attention of her political science professor. Professor Gene Phipps had served several times as a consultant to the CIA on matters of national security related to Latin American nations. He had been flown to the White House at the time of the Cuban missile crisis during the Kennedy administration, and he had helped negotiate the Mexican surplus oil transfer during the Arab oil embargo of the Ford and Carter years. From time to time, when a promising student attracted his attention, Professor Phipps would call a private phone number in Washington. Juanita Martinez—a master of English and Spanish, a native of both Cuba and the United States, and an attractive and intelligent woman—was just the sort of unique individual that the CIA was always hoping to recruit. Upon receiving Professor Phipps' call about Juanita, Alma Hammond flew to Texas to meet her.

Juanita accepted the job offer. She wasn't a vengeful person, but her father's violent death at the hands of the Castro rebels and her mother's disappearance made her feel a family obligation to take some sort of stand against the Communist takeover of Cuba . . . even if her part would come many years after the event.

Juanita also carried a fantasy that perhaps by someday returning to Cuba she might learn more about her family. The sketchy information she had been given by the Red Cross and the U.S. Marines left a lot of unanswered questions about her past.

Her training had taken two years. Once she was in Cuba, it had taken her another year to gain a credible background and then two more years as a low-echelon typist in a minor governmental office before she had come to the attention of someone important. At last she was given the job of monitoring U. S. naval broadcasts in Cuban coastal waters. When Guadalupe Bentancourt drafted her to assist in the Scott Parker case, she performed masterfully. The success of the mission, at least to those in Cuba, secured a full-time assignment for Bentancourt as Ambassador-at-Large. He immediately made Juanita his personal aide.

In the year since she had supposedly killed Scott Parker, Juanita had returned to Cuba and had gained access to incredibly important political and military secrets. Her mind was brimming with maps, military rosters, computer codes, and other key data she had committed to memory. Now all she needed to do was complete this final job and head home . . . home to America and to Scott.

*   *   *

Her plan was simple. She would approach the operator at the console, ask directions to a particular office, drop an earring on the floor, stoop to retrieve it and, while kneeling, attach the magnetized listening device to the underside of the ledge. Fast, simple, precise. It couldn't fail. She palmed the transistorized receiver and moved forward. For window dressing she carried a manila folder marked SECRET. Inside were 20 pages of blank typing paper.

"*Perdon*," she said. She waited to see how well the receptionist, a Russian, spoke Spanish.

"*Si, señorita?*" came a quick reply.

"I am Juanita Martinez," she continued in Spanish, "from the staff of the Cuban Ambassador-at-Large. Can you direct me to Captain Derasim's office? I have some papers to deliver."

"Leave your papers," said the woman. "His secretary can come down for them."

Juanita smiled amiably. "If you don't mind, I'd like to deliver them personally. I've never met the Captain, and I'd like to . . ."

In a swift, unexpected move, the impatient receptionist twisted in her chair and made a snatching grab for the file. "I said I'll handle it," she insisted.

Juanita's reactions were quick, but not quick enough. The folder was nearly out of her hands before she closed her fingertips on it. A two-second tug-of-war between the women sent the blank pages flying through the air. Even worse, the miniature listening device was dropped atop the counter. It bounced twice then rolled over the ledge. The receptionist looked puzzled for a moment in regard to the blank pages that had fallen from the file marked SECRET. Hastily she reached down behind her chair and retrieved the listening device.

Juanita knew she could never talk her way out of this predicament. She turned and made a dash for the door.

"Stop her!" yelled the receptionist in Russian. "Don't let her escape!"

*   *   *

Guadalupe Bentancourt had insisted that she not be bound or gagged. When she had been delivered to his suite of offices—after a series of high-level phone calls—Bentancourt had surprised the guards by telling them to wait outside in the hallway. He wanted to be alone with Juanita.

Bentancourt poured a lemonade for himself and one for Juanita. He tolerated no alcoholic beverages in his office. He had no moral qualms about liquor, but he always worried about his image. Liquor was a crutch, and Guadalupe Bentancourt needed no crutches.

"I always said you were the best," announced Bentancourt, handing a glass to Juanita. "But not even I knew how *very* good you were. At least, not until today. I'll admit you had me completely fooled. All these months you had me totally convinced that I had won your loyalty."

Juanita stared hard at Bentancourt, but said nothing. She knew that he was angry, outraged, bitter. Though calm-appearing on the outside, he was a raging inferno inside. She knew his moods. When he was the most disturbed, he worked hardest to put on an air of nonchalance. For in his very calmness he was delivering his most effective revenge on his enemies. By not yelling or screaming, he kept his victim off-guard and squirming, too afraid to relax yet hopeful of a sign of mercy. Like a cat pawing and torturing a wounded mouse, Bentancourt could heighten his victim's anxiety and emotional anguish to levels of personal agony that no rack or bullwhip could equal.

Knowing so much about her boss gave Juanita an advantage that most interrogated prisoners did not have. She decided to frustrate his quasicomplacent interview.

She sipped her drink, then noted, "I like your suit. It's new, isn't it?"

Bentancourt blinked at the remark. He had expected a gushing explanation of what had happened at the Russian embassy. Or perhaps a plea for forgiveness. Or tears. Or hysterics.

"My suit?" he responded. Instinctively he turned to the wall mirror. His reflection was impressive. The pale gray suit was tailored perfectly, and the soft blue tie and matching breast-pocket handkerchief added a dash of Continental styling. His hair was black and combed straight back, and his pencil-thin mustache added a flair of Latin distinctiveness. "Why, yes, it is. My tailor delivered it yesterday."

"You're such a clotheshorse," Juanita chided, with a looser familiarity than she usually used at the office. She winked at him teasingly. Obviously, she wasn't going to cry. And as much as that disappointed Bentancourt, he was nevertheless not going to let her take this discussion lightly. There were other ways of breaking people.

"I've had time to do some thinking," Bentancourt said, suddenly changing his voice to a more authoritarian tone. "You've obviously done a great deal of damage to my career and to the relationship between Cuba and the Soviet Union. For a while that was the only thing that occupied my mind. Later, however, I began to look back at all the projects I had involved you in. I needed to know which bridges would now have to be mended."

Juanita's stomach knotted. She knew the biggest game was over. He had figured it out. She could almost predict his next words.

"Scott Parker is alive, isn't he?" said Bentancourt. "You didn't kill him after all, did you? He's in America right now telling the Central Intelligence Agency everything he knows about U. S. POWs in Vietnam. They are probably just waiting to get you out of here before they put Parker before the public."

Juanita looked away.

"Of course," continued Bentancourt, "if Parker comes out of hiding, our allies in China and Vietnam are going to be very upset. Upset enough, I should say, to ask Fidel for my head on a platter. And I have no doubt that he will be most obliging in that respect."

"The price of diplomacy," quipped Juanita. "At least you'll be missed by one person. Your tailor."

"I shouldn't worry about that," said Bentancourt. "You see, Parker is never going to come out of hiding. I've already dispatched a message to the CIA."

Juanita turned her attention to Bentancourt. Her eyes were full of questions.

"It's a very simple agreement, really," he explained. "If Parker comes out of hiding, I'm going to kill you. If he remains undercover, you'll be kept alive."

"They'll never go for it," said Juanita confidently.

"Who? The CIA? Of course they won't. But Parker will. And that's all that counts. You two are in love, aren't you? Don't bother to deny it. I've known for months that you were resisting all my attempts to woo you. I didn't know what was holding back your emotions. Any other woman in your position would have been overjoyed to earn my favor. But not you. And now I know why. It's Parker. You're a fool. He has nothing to offer you. What could you possibly see in him?"

Juanita stood in a self-assured manner. She smiled wryly and answered, "A whole lot more than just a well-tailored suit."

She walked to the door, opened it, and walked out, fully knowing that the guards were still there, waiting to take her to prison.

CHAPTER 2

"Any news from Austin?"

They had taken a break five minutes earlier, and Scott Parker was ready to play his favorite game. It worried him that Alma was not catching her cue and parroting the lines that had become so familiar to them in the past several months.

"Come on, Alma, what's happening in Texas? Any envelopes? Packages? Cryptic messages?" he prodded.

She ignored his barrage of questions and continued to study the notes on her clipboard. Finally satisfied that all was in order, she penciled her initials on the bottom of the page and jotted down the time: 11:46 A.M. Only then did she turn her attention to him.

"Why don't you sit down and I'll go round up the crew," suggested Alma. "We'll continue taping until around 12:30 and then we'll break for lunch." She started toward the door, but before she could pass him in the narrow church aisle he took a quick side step and blocked her path.

This time his voice was void of playfulness. "First let's talk about Austin."

* * *

They had devised the plan nearly a year ago, shortly after Juanita had left Scott at the Walter Reed Hospital and had returned to Cuba for her final assignment. Neither Scott nor Juanita had wanted the separation, but both had accepted it as inevitable. Scott was facing several weeks of recuperation

15

followed by months of tedious debriefing. Juanita had been notified that a position of trust awaited her when she returned to her native Cuba. After years of being "tested" by the Communists, she had finally earned their confidence. She would be given access to their inner circle. All she had to do was come home.

Scott and Juanita knew all about duty. And patience. Still, a few weeks after they had said goodbye at the hospital, each had contacted Alma Hammond with the same request: *Find a way for us to communicate.* Alma was the link. Since she had orchestrated Scott's escape to freedom, she was assigned to oversee his debriefing. Since she was the section chief responsible for U. S. intelligence efforts in Cuba, she was Juanita's supervisor.

At first she had refused both requests. Too chancy, she had told them. But their insistence worried her. If they were too preoccupied with their feelings for each other, would they be careless in their work? Would Scott be able to concentrate on recalling valuable information about his years as a POW? Worse yet, would he attempt to contact Juanita directly? And would Juanita lose her motivation, drop her guard, and unwittingly reveal her double-agent status?

Alma had struggled with the dilemma for several weeks, buying time from Scott and Juanita by assuring them that she was refining a plan. But what kind of plan should it be? She concocted several, played them out in her mind, and rejected each one. Definitely too chancy.

A telephone call from Professor Phipps at the University of Texas had provided the solution. Phipps reminded Alma that Juanita's American grandmother, now 78, was living in an Austin nursing home, weakened by age and muddled by Alzheimer's disease. As a kindness to Juanita, he visited Mrs. Middleton periodically, doing little more than smiling into her glazed eyes, nodding at her disjointed memories, and opening the occasional card that came from a long-forgotten neighbor in Galveston.

"That's it. Don't you see?" Phipps had suggested when he heard of Scott's and Juanita's request. "The nursing home can be the exchange point for letters between Cuba and Appalachia. If Bentancourt is as thorough as we think he is, he's done a complete security check of Juanita and knows about her grandmother. He surely would understand Juanita's wish to keep in touch with her only living relative."

The plan quickly took shape. For every objection Alma presented, Phipps countered with a logical argument. Letters from Havana to Austin couldn't be sent too frequently, of course, and they would have to be written so as not to arouse suspicion. After all, they probably would be screened by Bentancourt's lieutenants before being allowed out of the country. They would have to read like the correspondence from a loving granddaughter to her grandmother.

Phipps offered to collect the letters on his visits to the nursing home. He would forward them to Alma, who would deliver them to Scott on her frequent trips to Appalachia for debriefing sessions. Scott, after a lapse of several days, would be allowed to respond. His challenge would be greater: Each message and the handwriting must reflect the writer—an elderly woman who lapsed in and out of coherency. Scott would compose the letter, Alma would approve the words, and Bea Mead, in her spidery cursive style, would put them on paper. The note would then be addressed to Juanita, enclosed in a larger envelope, and sent to Phipps' office, where he would strip the first envelope and send the second to Cuba by way of the Austin post office.

Foolproof, they all had agreed. All except Alma. *Foolhardy* was her assessment. In a profession where self-denial was essential to survival, she viewed Scott's and Juanita's need to correspond as a sign of weakness. Only after several successful exchanges had been made did she cease her objections.

Letters from Austin soon became a tool to be used to Alma's advantage. When Scott's impatience surfaced after continuous hours of debriefing in Pastor Mead's tiny mountain chapel,

Alma would hint at the presence of a "reward" in her brief-case. The game would begin. Scott would calm his impatience and dutifully answer probing questions about his 12 years in a series of POW camps. Whenever the harsh lights of the video equipment or the discomfort of the hardback chair caused him to grumble, she would allude to a postcard or a package from Austin and he would submit to more questions, provide more details, and struggle to revive more memories. Officials at the Pentagon, viewing the debriefing tapes that Alma supplied, remarked on Sergeant Parker's new spirit of cooper-ation. They credited it to military discipline.

Alma knew it was love.

*   *   *

"There will be no more letters from Austin," she answered simply.

Scott looked down at Alma Hammond's face for several seconds, searching for the trace of a smile that would indicate this was part of her plan, just another twist to their private little game. But Alma didn't smile. This was no game.

"Tell me what's happened," he said hoarsely. "What gives? She hasn't been caught, has she? The truth, Alma. In heaven's name, tell me the truth."

Her silence told him he already knew it.

*   *   *

Juanita Martinez had requested a Bible for all the wrong reasons. Guadalupe Bentancourt had denied the request, of course, but one of the prison attendants, a Christian, had overheard the conversation and had slipped a tiny Spanish version of the New Testament under Juanita's door.

She thumbed through the pages with only mild interest. It was the Old Testament, not the New, that she had wanted, and she would have preferred the English translation. Specifically, she wanted to read and reread the book of Ruth, just as she had done for the past several days. Its words made her feel close to Scott.

She knew there would be no more letters from Austin; in fact, Juanita felt sure that by now the small box of correspondence that was tied with a narrow white satin ribbon had been found in her apartment and had been studied by Bentancourt himself. She was uncertain whether Bentancourt would be able to figure out that the letters were from Scott Parker, not her grandmother. Bentancourt was smart, all right, but so was Alma Hammond. Often the cryptic messages were so obscure that even Juanita had struggled with their hidden meanings. She often wondered if her interpretation of the notes came close to resembling Scott's intention. She feared that perhaps she romanticized too much, and that she saw more in the letters than was there.

Because the elderly Mrs. Middleton had always been very active in her church, Scott, writing from the older woman's perspective, sometimes discussed favorite passages from the Scriptures. Such references would send Juanita scurrying to her Bible. Most recently the allusions had been to the book of Ruth. Juanita read the verses several times and fantasized over some double meaning that Scott wanted her to decipher. She studied fervently, not absorbing the Word of God but seeking the message of Scott. She focused on the devotion that Ruth felt for Naomi, and she savored Ruth's pledge of faithfulness: *Whither thou goest, I will go . . . thy people shall be my people*. Yes, that was it; surely that was it. Scott was affirming their bond and saying that in spite of the differences in their backgrounds, they belonged not in their separate cultures, but together.

She felt no guilt at turning to the Bible and using its text as a code. She was not a religious woman, although she had been brought up in two churches. Perhaps that was the problem.

For the first three years of her life she had been exposed to the underground church in Cuba, with its hushed, late-night services that were often cut short by a report that some government official was making his rounds of the compound. Her earliest memories included secret meetings in the homes of her grandparents' friends. There, snuggled in the strong, loving arms of her Grandfather Martinez, she would fall asleep to the soft, rhythmic cadence of the litany as it was recited by a lay leader and responded to by the small circle of neighbors.

Later, in Texas, she would accompany her Grandmother Middleton to a tiny jubilation church within walking distance of their gray-frame bungalow. She would sit erect, wide-eyed, and almost frightened as she watched friends and neighbors slowly assume different personalities, singing, swaying, raising their hands, and chanting emotional responses—*Amen! Yes, Brother! Praise the Lord!*—to the preacher's fiery, mounting, crescendo-like challenges. On Wednesday evenings the ritual would be repeated, though more controlled. It would culminate twice a year, once in June and again in August, when a dank canvas tent, full of rents and patches, would be raised over the adjoining pasture and weeklong revivals would commence. Juanita was entranced by the spectacle of it all and dutifully was rededicated every June and August during the final altar call.

Because the elderly Mrs. Middleton was a fair-minded, God-fearing woman, she felt an obligation to let her young granddaughter choose between the churches of her deceased parents, Rosa and Jim Middleton. Juanita knew that she always was encouraged to skip alongside her Grandmother Middleton down the dusty path to the lively church with the boisterous congregation and the sometimes wailing, always throbbing music. But she also had a standing invitation to accompany a classmate to the more staid, though equally mystifying, services at Santa Maria de Natividad, downtown.

Perhaps because she was allowed to come and go in both churches, she felt at home in neither. She was put off by the frenzy of the one and the formality of the other. In many ways she was like a chameleon, taking on the attributes of the people around her. So successful was she at assuming the characteristics of the group that she drew little attention to herself as she entered or exited the sanctuaries. She knew the right words to say, the prayers to repeat, the lyrics to sing. The only thing she lacked was conviction.

When she graduated from high school and moved 200 miles northwest to attend college in Austin, she took no religious tradition with her. She simply dropped out. After her grandmother relocated to be closer to her, she still made no attempt to find a church home. Tugged between two philosophies, she let herself slip between both.

Her ability to blend into groups, however, was honed to perfection by the church experiences and spilled over into other areas of her life. On a campus that boasted a large Spanish-American population, she could fit in as easily with the international students as with the native Texans. Not only did she speak two languages fluently, but she had the ability to shade her physical appearance in two directions. In jeans and a U-T sweatshirt, with a bookbag slung over one shoulder and hair hanging loose and curly, she looked like all the other American coeds. But with a touch of eye shadow, a sleeker hairstyle, and bright gold hoops through her pierced ears, she had the startling appeal of a Latin beauty.

She became so accomplished at slipping out of one culture and into the other that in later years she could do it without benefit of props. Merely by changing her mannerisms, her demeanor, and of course her language, she melted into a new group, was swallowed up by her surroundings, and became instantly anonymous. It was this ability that had caught the attention of both Alma Hammond and Ambassador Guadalupe Bentancourt. And it was this uncanny talent that had allowed her to successfully fulfill the roles of spy and counterspy without error. At least until now.

"Thy people will be my people," she repeated softly as she clasped the small Spanish Bible in her right hand. Her back was to the door. She didn't see the man in the meticulously tailored gray suit and the soft blue tie standing staring through the barred window of her cell door.

"Book of Ruth, chapter 1, verse 16," said her visitor as he unlocked the door. "How well the dear Sisters did drill us on memory verses. Thank goodness those days—and those women—are gone."

Juanita wheeled around to find Bentancourt poised in the doorway as if awaiting a compliment on his rakish appearance. When none was offered, he shrugged and entered the tiny cell. "My dear Señorita Martinez, I had no idea how religious you were. But then, I'm learning that there are many things I never knew about you." He smiled coolly and waved away the guard. "The accommodations are adequate, I presume?"

"Five-star," she replied curtly.

"We have better lodgings, of course," he continued. "And we have worse. Much depends on your—how shall we call it?—level of cooperation?" He was struggling to speak English, although he had often told Juanita that he hated the uncivilized discordant tongue of the Anglos.

"Why are you doing this?" she asked in Spanish. "Why are you speaking English?"

He brought his face down very close to hers, much as he used to do when he would attempt to kiss her. Only this time nothing but hate emanated from his eyes. "Because you *are* an American," he said harshly.

She pulled away, partly in fear and partly in disdain. At least now she didn't have to hide how she felt about him. No more flirtations, no more coy remarks. Appeals to his ego had succeeded in the past to coax information out of Bentancourt, but now they would be ineffective. Still, she wanted a final favor. This time she would try honesty instead of guile.

"I need a few things," she began. "Personal things. Shampoo, toothpaste, makeup, a change of clothes." His nod of agreement gave her courage to continue. "Perhaps a couple of books," she added. "There is one on my nightstand at my apartment. Jack London. It would help me pass the time." Again he nodded. Bolstered by his apparent willingness to cooperate, she dared to make her last, most important request. "In my desk in the bedroom is a box of letters. They . . . they don't look like much, but they're from my grandmother in Austin. You'll find them in the bottom drawer, tied with . . ."

She paused when she saw his smile. So cold. So full of hate. So triumphant.

" . . . tied with a white satin ribbon," he said.

*   *   *

Alma Hammond was worried about Scott's silence. She could handle anger, could cope with tears, and was an expert in dealing with depression. But his awful silence left her baffled.

Everyone who was gathered around the table shared her feeling of helplessness. Kent pushed his dish away after only two bites of his hot dog. Mom and Pop Mead exchanged concerned glances from their places at the head and the foot of the table. Leo and Thad, the electronic whiz kids who oversaw the technical side of the debriefing sessions, declined dessert and exited, saying they had to pack the cameras for the return trip to Washington.

Alma didn't try to suppress the news of Juanita's capture. The group had grown too close in the last year not to know when one of its members was suffering. Working together for so long in such a remote area of the Allegheny Mountains had caused them to evolve into a support group. They cared about each other and were particularly protective of Scott, the man responsible for their being there. After weeks of hearing him pour out his POW experiences to the penetrating eye of the camera, they had developed deep feelings for this gaunt, often withdrawn man. They admired his strength and marveled at his stamina. They wished him happiness, knowing that for Scott, that meant being with Juanita Martinez.

For once, Mom Mead didn't scold her guests for not eating everything on their plates. Instead, she quietly enlisted the help of her husband and Kent to clear away the dishes and then signaled them to leave Alma and Scott to themselves. Even after the Meads and Kent retreated to the kitchen, Scott and Alma remained silent. It was a standoff, each waiting for the other to give in and speak up. Finally Scott acquiesced.

"What are you going to do, Alma?" he asked abruptly. "How are you going to get Juanita back? You do intend to save Juanita from Bentancourt, don't you? He's ruthless, you know. Smooth, smart, and charming . . . but completely ruthless."

Alma nodded. "We all know about Mr. Bentancourt," she replied. "As far as what we're going to do about Juanita . . . well, I really can't say. The decision hasn't been made yet. It will be on the agenda for tomorrow or Monday's meeting."

"On the agenda? Did I hear you right?" Scott exploded. "Cut the parliamentary procedure bit, okay? This isn't 'old business' and 'new business.' We're talking about life and death!"

Alma refilled her coffee cup and reached for Scott's. He shook his head no. He wouldn't be distracted even for a moment.

"I know how the government works," he continued. "Heaven knows I've witnessed it inch along at a snail's pace these last several months. When I was in 'Nam I was almost choked by all the red tape cranked out in the name of diplomacy. No, thank you, I won't let Juanita's safety be reduced to some item of discussion on a minor official's Monday agenda."

It was Alma's turn to get angry. She liked Scott and she liked Juanita, but business was business. And *her* business was to supervise the overall U. S. intelligence effort in the Caribbean. She had been elevated to the position because of her good judgment and her ability to step back and make sound decisions based on fact, not emotion. She had to be concerned with the big picture and not allow herself to get bogged down in one small operation involving one agent, no matter who that agent might be.

"Your chivalry is very commendable, Sergeant Parker," she began coolly. "But this is the twentieth century, remember? The days of launching a thousand ships to bring back one woman went out with Helen of Troy. Juanita was not duped into taking this assignment. She's a very accomplished agent who knew exactly what she was getting into when she went back to Cuba. She knew the risks, the rewards, and the potential punishments."

"Are you telling me that Juanita is on her own? That the United States government will do nothing to help her?" Scott's voice was reduced almost to a whisper.

"I'm merely telling you that I don't know what our government will do. We'll look at the options, of course; perhaps Cuba will be willing to negotiate. But first we'll have to send a communiqué to Havana expressing our concern for one of our citizens. For obvious reasons we can't identify Juanita as an agent."

As Alma talked, Scott shook his head from side to side. He refused to be placated by her words. His anger wouldn't subside.

"No," he said firmly.

"No?"

"I can't let Juanita go through what I did as a prisoner all those years," he replied. "I'll go there myself if I have to. There are ways to go across from Florida. I'll do anything to get her out."

"Don't be ridiculous, Scott."

His mind was racing. "Surely Bentancourt would be willing to swap if the stakes were high enough. We could make an even trade—Juanita Martinez for Sergeant Scott Parker. What do you think, Alma?"

"I think you're crazy," she answered. "I'd never authorize such a deal."

"I'm not asking you to authorize anything," he said. "Your authorization would take too much time anyway. I'll do this one on my own."

Alma knew Scott wasn't bluffing. What he was proposing was foolish, yes, but it would meet with instant approval from the Cuban Communists. Somehow she had to stop him from pursuing his plan.

"Give me until Monday afternoon," she asked. "By then I will have talked to the Director and explained the urgency of the situation."

"Sorry, Alma, that's not good enough."

She shook her head in resignation. "Give me until tomorrow evening. I'll arrange an emergency meeting with some of the key people in intelligence."

Scott shook his head. "Sorry, Alma."

He was clearly in control, and they both knew it. *No wonder the Communists hadn't been able to break him in 12 years of interrogation*, she thought ruefully. *Talk about stubborn!*

"Okay," she said. "Give me until 4:35 today. That's when our plane lands at National Airport. Pack your things; we're going to Washington."

CHAPTER 3

Phil Compton was old, overweight, and rough around the social edges, but he was also as bighearted and completely honest as a man could be. And he happened to be one of the best judges of human character that Lillian Parker Thompson had ever known.

Lillian liked to hear Phil talk. He never minced words—first, because it was his style, and second, because he was so incredibly rich that he didn't have to worry about other people's opinions.

"My daughter was a spoiled brat and that Yankee boyfriend of hers was a jackal," said Phil.

They were sitting in the cozy lodge that Lillian and her husband, Dave, had purchased from Phil just several months ago, shortly after their wedding. Phil was seated in the same chair he always sat in when he came for a visit and he was drinking coffee from the same oversized mug that Lillian always kept on hand just for him.

Phil had given his name to Compton Gap, Tennessee, their snug little village in the Smoky Mountains. ("Why not?" he had said. "I own it, don't I?") Dave Thompson was a privately employed forest ranger whom Phil had put in charge of his vast tracts of mountain land several years ago. He also was something of a surrogate son to Phil.

"I can forgive my daughter," said Phil. "I raised her to be spoiled. I'd do it again if I had the chance. In fact, I wish I did have the chance. But that old beau of hers had no excuse for being the way he was. If Cat hadn't cared for him so much, I would have strung him up by his thumbs and let him hang

27

until the sun split open that yellow belly of his. Imagine him jilting her after he convinced her to run off to Nashville with him."

Lillian smiled at Phil's backwoods expressions.

"Look on the bright side of things," she admonished as she poured more coffee. "If Roderick hadn't convinced Cat to go to Nashville, she wouldn't have become involved in Drew Sanders' race for the Senate. And if Roderick hadn't jilted Cat and run back to that fancy new lawyer's job in Detroit, Cat probably would have married him instead of Drew. This way you've gotten rid of Roderick and you've gained a son-in-law you can be proud of. Best of all, you know that Cat is happy."

Phil gave a reluctant shrug. "True enough," he conceded, "but it still sticks in my craw that that blasted carpetbagger could come in here and hoodwink my wife and daughter and then run off the way he did."

"I'm not really surprised," replied Lillian. "Country music and Southern hospitality just never seemed to blend with Roderick's image. He's a dyed-in-the-woolsuit corporate lawyer. I should know—I almost married him myself, you'll remember."

"Consider yourself blessed," said Phil. "I never liked Roderick Davis from the start. The pirate! It drove me crazy to think that Cat was setting her cap for him. She was on the rebound, though. She was still lickin' her wounds from losing your Dave. Now *that's* a match I could have gone for. Better for Dave that he got you, though. Cat's a socialite and Dave's like me . . . more akin to nature. It would never have worked."

"You never know," cautioned Lillian. "After all, I was a city girl."

"But your folks—particularly your mama—raised you to appreciate the things the good Lord made for you. Me and Hattie, well, we just kind of let Cat grow up thinkin' about money."

Lillian's eyes narrowed. "My mother? Why, Phil, how on earth would you know anything about my mother? She died years ago."

Phil squirmed a little in his seat. He set his coffee mug on a lamp table.

"Do you trust me, honey?" he asked.

"Trust you? I more than trust you. Dave and I love you. You've been like a father to us. The way you've taken both of us under your wing since we got married has made me not miss Pastor Mead so much. He was always kind of a substitute daddy to me. Now that he and Mom Mead are running the mission in the Alleghenies and Dave and I are here, well, I guess I've learned to lean on you instead."

Phil smiled. "And I've loved every minute of it. Don't you ever think no different, either. But I know, and so does that preacher friend of yours, that there ain't no amount of Dutch uncles that'll ever replace a girl's daddy in her heart. Am I right about that?"

Lillian's hands trembled slightly. It made her cup rattle against the saucer. She hastily set the dishes on the coffee table and then used her hands to smooth imaginary wrinkles out of her skirt.

Phil leaned forward and looked warmly into Lillian's eyes. "Tell me about your father," he asked.

Lillian looked away from Phil and fought to keep her voice light and relaxed.

"Really, Phil, I'm just content to let the past . . ."

"You said you trusted me," injected Phil. "Well, trust me now when I tell you that it's important for me to know about your father."

Lillian folded her hands and gazed down at them. Not only was it painful to remember the details of her father's life . . . and death . . . it was also confusing. How could she tell her father's story without telling her brother's story? Yet Scott's story *must* be kept a secret a few weeks longer.

"Phil . . ." said Lillian, still looking down at her hands, "what I'm about to tell you has to remain a secret between us. I . . . I'm not overstating the situation when I say it's a matter of life and death."

She glanced up and was surprised when she saw that Phil was neither shocked nor confused by her words. It was almost as if he had expected her to say what she did.

"My . . . uh, my father, J. J. Parker II, was a technological genius," Lillian began, "and he also had a lot of horse sense about him. In 1963 he developed the plans for a digital computer that could add, subtract, multiply, and divide and also spell words onto an adding tape. It would seem a crude machine by today's standards, but back then it was an incredible accomplishment, very advanced."

Phil retrieved his coffee mug and took a swallow from it. He did not speak.

"My father sold his plans to a consortium of entrepreneurs in California and he used the money to help develop a new type of computer. It was called the Vid-Mem 766. That stood for 'Video-Memory machine of July 1966.' It had a television screen on it and an internal memory bank . . . way ahead of its time.

"Anyway, the people in California had started to make a mint from the sale of my father's original computer model. So he and my mother felt they should find some financial backers and form their own company to sell his newer computers."

"Michigan Technologies," said Phil.

Lillian nodded. "Right. It began as a limited partnership in 1967 and then went public in 1970. At first my parents insisted on controlling 51 percent of the stock. Later, however, they built a large home, bought a lot of nice furniture . . . you know how it happens. Their stock holdings had dropped to just 37 percent by 1975, when my mother died. But I don't think my father ever regretted cashing in those extra shares. He had given my mother a great life, and that had been very important to him."

"Did your mother take an active role in the company?" asked Phil.

"Not really," admitted Lillian. "My father was chairman of the board and my brother Scott and I worked during summers as typists or switchboard operators or shipping clerks. My mother was a housewife—or as she used to jokingly refer to herself, a 'mansionwife.' She was a good mother to us, too. She was happy and so were we. She and my dad always assumed that Scott would one day follow in my father's shoes. Before any of that could occur, however, he enlisted in the Army. He was declared an MIA in Vietnam in 1971 after his firebase was overrun by the enemy. My mother died thinking that Scott had been killed in the war."

Phil's eyes squinted. "He was alive?"

"He *is* alive," corrected Lillian. "He's living undercover at Pastor and Mom Mead's mission settlement in Barnes Hollow, West Virginia."

"You're kidding!" said Phil, his staid countenance suddenly broken. He had expected certain surprises from Lillian, but nothing like this.

"Last year the CIA traded a captured Russian colonel to the Cubans for my brother Scott, who had been held for 12 years as a POW by the Vietnamese."

"Huh?" said Phil, shaking his head to clear it. "Russians, Americans, Cubans, Vietnamese—who . . . who in blazes had who?"

Lillian had to smile. "I know how you feel," she said. "It confused me too when I first heard it. The Russian colonel had been an advisor to the Cubans. He was kidnapped by Cuban refugees who escaped to the U. S. The refugees offered him as barter for our government's guarantee of asylum. The Cuban government wanted him back, naturally. Our CIA offered to trade the colonel for an American POW in Vietnam. So the Cubans located Scott, helped him escape from Vietnam, and made the trade."

"Darndest thing I ever heard of," said Phil. "Or maybe I should say it's the darndest thing I *never* heard of. How come none of this was ever on TV?"

"It's still a secret," explained Lillian. "The Cubans sent a woman, Juanita Martinez, back with Scott. She claimed she was in love with him. Scott was too ill at the time to say much. The woman was supposed to kill my brother and then return to Cuba. Instead, she sent a false message back that said she'd killed Scott, and then she went back."

"Why'd she do that?"

"Because she was really a CIA agent who had been planted in Cuba several years before," said Lillian. "And because, quite frankly, she really *is* in love with Scott. She had to go back to Cuba for another year, though. The CIA needed her to obtain more information. But she's scheduled to return in just a couple of weeks. Scott wants to marry her."

"So until she's back safe and sound, your brother's gotta play dead, is that it?"

"That's basically it," agreed Lillian. "I go to see him every six weeks or so. He's really looking terrific. He's put on weight and had some dental work done to replace some teeth he lost. And he's so happy helping the Meads. The CIA has been debriefing him all year and they've even provided him with a Spanish teacher."

"Spanish teacher?"

"That's a little surprise that Scott's been preparing for Juanita," explained Lillian.

"Oh, yeah, sure," said Phil. "He sounds like quite a fellow. I'd like to meet him someday."

Lillian grinned. "You already have."

"Say what?"

"My brother was here at my wedding," explained Lillian. "He was the shy, gaunt-looking fellow who was Dave's best man. We just said he was a friend of Dave's. He arrived late and left early and we downplayed his part."

"You mean Dave knows all about this too?"

"He and the Meads are the only ones who do. My brother has a bodyguard named Kent who goes with him everywhere, and there's a CIA section head named Alma Hammond who's supervising the debriefing. Outside of the Director of the CIA, the President, and a few Army personnel involved in Scott's trade for the Russian colonel, it's been kept a secret for nearly a year."

"What do they plan to do with your brother after that little gal of his gets back from Cuba?"

Lillian hunched her shoulders. "Your guess is as good as mine. An announcement, I suppose. Maybe some speeches. They haven't talked to me about any of that. I'm not even sure that Scott knows what they've got in mind. We talk by phone once a month, but we always suspect we're being listened to. When he was here for the wedding we had a few moments alone. He told me then that he has been doing a lot of video-taped interviews—answering questions about his captivity for those 12 years. They'll probably use those tapes for some-thing later."

Phil blew out a long breath of wind. "Well!" he said, "I came here expecting to give you some surprising news, but I guar-antee you, you've sure upstaged me on that account."

"Surprising news? What do you mean?"

"In time, in time," promised Phil. "For the moment, though, you need to finish telling me about your father. Believe me, it's important. Just finish telling about the part where you said he lost controlling interest in the stock of Michigan Technologies in 1975."

Lillian sat back on the couch. "Yes. Well, let's see." She sipped her coffee and gave herself a moment to clear the cobwebs of time. "As I recall, it was about then that computer companies began to spring up all over the place. Competition was ruthless. The board of directors forced my father to hire a lot of outside consultants whom he really didn't want on the payroll. Roderick was hired then. His specialty was patents and new product promotion."

"Was Paul Stattman hired then too?" asked Phil.

"Yes, Paul shared an office with Roderick and they were assigned to . . . hey, wait a minute! How do you know about Paul Stattman?"

Phil raised his hands and waved down the question. "I'll tell you later. Just go on about your father."

Lillian looked perplexed. That was the second time Phil had surprised her this afternoon.

"My father was upset about hiring all these outside consultants," Lillian said, speaking more slowly. "He wanted me to help him keep an eye on things until Scott came home to help him run the company. Crazy as it seemed at the time, my father never doubted that Scott would one day come home. He even set up a trust for him which is now worth more than half a million dollars. He figured that if he died before Scott came back, Scott would still have adequate money in his trust to buy back enough stock to enable him to assume a position on the board."

"In the meantime you hired on, eh?" asked Phil.

"I joined the company in the advertising department in 1978 and was Director of Sales by 1982, when my father died. He was extremely nervous and edgy the last few months before he passed away. He may even have been a little mentally unbalanced, as I look back on it. He kept saying that 'those crooks on the board' were trying to take his company away from him and that one way or another he was going to stop them."

"If it's any consolation to you, I believe your daddy was as sound as a dollar," said Phil with judgmental severity.

"I never knew exactly what he meant by planning to stop the board from taking the company from him," said Lillian, "but after he died, it was discovered that he had embezzled three million dollars from the corporation. I suppose, in his own mind, he thought he was protecting the company. We lost everything in paying it back—the house, cars, furniture . . ."

" . . . and your job, right?" asked Phil.

"Yes, and my job. The corporation exercised a clause which allowed the board to buy up all my personal holdings of stock in the company. Then I was fired. That's when I left Detroit for a long, private vacation here in the mountains. And you know the rest."

"I know a whole hang of a lot more than you can ever imagine, little girl," said Phil, "and I'm about to give you an education."

*   *   *

It was dark inside Dave Thompson's lodge when he arrived at 7 P.M. The fire in the hearth was out and there was no smell of a hot supper waiting for him as usual in the kitchen.

"Lill?" he called as he removed his coat and turned on an entryway light. "Honey? Anybody home?"

"In here," came a soft reply.

Dave moved from the kitchen into the dark living room. He could see his wife seated cross-legged on the sofa. Instinct told him to not turn on a light. He slowly approached her and sat down gently on the couch near her.

"You all right, Lill?"

Lillian raised a lacy handkerchief to her eyes and blotted. She sniffed twice and fought back more tears.

"I've been mourning the dead," she announced flatly.

Dave lovingly reached out and touched her hand. He moved slowly, carefully, not rushing anything. He would be patient.

"Has someone died?" he asked in whispers. "Who? Mom Mead?"

Lillian nodded negatively. "I'm mourning my father's death."

"Your father?" Dave was baffled. "He died a long time ago, sweetheart. He wouldn't want you to still be grieving. I know he wouldn't."

Lillian reached to her side and turned on a table lamp. She left it on the lowest of its three settings.

"You don't understand," said Lillian. She paused a moment to collect herself. "Phil came by for coffee today. He asked me a lot of questions about my father . . . about Daddy's company. He wanted to know all about Michigan Technologies and my father's death and a lot of other things."

"Did he say why?"

"He *showed* me why," said Lillian. "Oh, Dave. It's so awful. Just look." She thrust forward a folder she had been holding.

Dave opened the folder and tried to read the contents in the dim light. "What is it?"

"A report," she explained. "It was compiled during the past several months. When Phil thought his daughter was going to marry Roderick Davis, he hired a detective agency to prepare a complete dossier on Roderick and the company he worked for."

Dave nodded immediate understanding. "Sounds like Phil, all right. He always has been incredibly protective of Cat. But why should this upset *you*?"

"Because of what they discovered," said Lillian. "These investigators didn't leave a stone unturned. They were the best. Completely thorough. So thorough, in fact, that they even placed two people inside the company where they could have access to the computer records."

"And?"

"They found out more than they bargained for. That folder is filled with photostat copies of memos, reports, contracts, and business letters that leave no doubt that my father was squeezed out of his company by greensheeters."

"By what?" asked Dave.

"Corporate raiders," explained Lillian. "Takeover artists. Portfolio sharks. They plotted against my father and stole his company from him. The very consultants that my father's board of directors insisted he hire turned out to be a band of traitors. They drew salary from him all the while they were scheming to get rid of him. And Roderick was one of their chief henchmen. That's why he dumped Cat Compton and went back to Detroit so suddenly. When the company's new board of directors convened, they rewarded their former fellow conspirator with a new position as a chief legal advisor to Michigan Technologies. Roderick is a partner in a law firm that gets paid a big retainer for 'legal consulting.' It's just a way of channeling money to Roderick. He now works for the law firm, but he's just as active in the business of Michigan Technologies as he was when he used to be one of its employees."

"What a snake," Dave said, his hair bristling, "For two cents I'd . . ."

"That's not the worst of it," injected Lillian. "When my father finally discovered what they were doing, he tried a counterploy. As CEO he used his executive privilege to invest all the company's liquid assets into a variety of other companies' stocks. He gave these stocks code numbers so his associates wouldn't know their names. That way it would take them months to figure out how to sell those investments and get access again to the available cash."

"I get it," said Dave. "He was keeping the money working for Michigan Technologies, but he was also keeping it out of the reach of the people on his staff he couldn't trust."

"Exactly. Daddy always was a real thinker. And his plan would have worked, too, if it hadn't have been for . . ."

" . . . the heart attack," finished Dave. "He was trying to buy himself time until he could know who to fire and replace on his staff. But his heart gave out under all the stress before he could do that."

"He'd had a bad heart for years," said Lillian softly. "The loss of Scott, and then Mama's battle with cancer and her death . . . it was really hard on his nerves. He loved them both so much."

Lillian reflected momentarily on childhood memories of family picnics at Belle Isle, trips to the Detroit Zoo, school plays, making popcorn at home—activities they had shared as a foursome. Suddenly her face turned grim.

"They framed Daddy," she said point-blank.

"They what?" asked Dave, not catching the sudden remark.

"They framed my father after he died," Lillian repeated. "Phil's detectives found out about it. After Daddy died, his four closest company officers reported that he had spent three million dollars on secret expenditures. Actually, they knew he had invested it. But the money was gone, there was no doubt about that. And since Daddy had used coded entries on the computer to account for the stock purchases, there was no way to prove that the company still had the money. Even the company's accountants had not been trusted by my father. No one really knew *how* he had spent the funds."

"Except those four officers," noted Dave.

"True," agreed Lillian. "So they announced that my father had taken the money for himself; that he had embezzled three million dollars."

"And since even *you* couldn't prove otherwise, the company attached a lien against your family estate and took everything you owned."

"*Everything*," echoed Lillian. "Our house, our furniture, our bank accounts, our land . . . *everything*. And then they even sent Roderick to fire me."

"At which time he also broke off your engagement, as I recall," said Dave.

"The same time, yes. He was—*is*—the most conniving, coldhearted man I've ever known. I've been sitting here all afternoon thinking about how my poor father's name was ruined and his company and household belongings were stolen by that pack of wolves. How can there *be* people like this in the world?"

"Is there enough proof in here to make a case?" asked Dave, thumbing through the folder.

"I don't know," admitted Lillian. "Phil's not sure either. I told him about Scott. He thinks I should go see him and turn the file over to him."

"You told Phil about Scott?"

"With no regrets," said Lillian. "I can trust Phil. Besides, he gave me a wonderful gift today."

"This folder?"

"He gave me peace of mind. My father was an honest man. Now I know for sure that he was not an embezzler. Phil proved that to me."

"I can appreciate that," said Dave. "But proving it to a judge and jury may be a lot harder."

"That's why I've got to see Scotty," announced Lillian. "Phil has promised to bankroll any court battle we want to make against Michigan Technologies. He still has a personal vendetta against Roderick over the way he treated Cat. But I can't win a court fight without Scott's help. He'll have to come out of seclusion."

"Do you really think you can convince Alma Hammond to let him do that?"

"No," said Lillian, "But Scott could. Maybe."

CHAPTER 4

Guadalupe Bentancourt carefully set the bag of Danish pastries and the container of extra-light coffee on the floor by his feet and began searching his pockets for the key to Juanita Martinez's apartment. He had never used it; in fact, Juanita didn't know he had it. But then there were many things about Guadalupe that Juanita didn't know. He shook his head. *Yes, and there was also much he didn't know about her.* He was learning, however, and that was exactly what brought him to Apartment 3-B.

He inserted the key—it was a tight fit—and felt the welcome release of the lock. Then the key jammed. He stepped to one side and braced himself for the tug between man and door, but only succeeded in crushing the bag of Danish and upsetting the cup of coffee. Lukewarm liquid seeped through the perforated vents of his new Italian shoes.

He hurried inside the apartment and instinctively headed for the modest kitchen in the back. Government housing units were all the same, right down to the placement of the paper towel dispenser over the left countertop. He ripped off several absorbent squares and attempted to salvage his once white but now two-tone leather shoes.

It was then, while sitting at Juanita's dinette set blotting his wingtips, that he noticed the difference. What was it? He lost interest in his shoes and began studying his surroundings. *Nice, very nice,* he thought. But decidedly different.

As functional as the three-room flat was, it had a certain softness to it. He got up and walked slowly back to the living room, squishing slightly with each step. This time he took note of the way the apartment was decorated. Instead of the pre-dictable institutional green, the walls were covered with a chintz-like wallpaper of tiny blue and white flowers. The sofa and overstuffed wing chair had identical coverings and were filled with plump cotton pillows in shades of rose. An ar-rangement of silk flowers, a small Oriental rug, and a cluster of pastel prints from the Impressionist period added warmth and personality.

Personality—yes, that's it, thought Bentancourt. He had known Juanita only a year, but it had been an intensive year during which he had come to appreciate her cool air of detach-ment. They had spent hours together flying across continents, huddled over dossiers, waiting in airports, dawdling at lunch. They had had endless conversations. But about what? He suddenly was aware of how little she had revealed of herself. He had no idea what kind of music she liked, what made her laugh, who her heroes were. Until she had mentioned Jack London, he hadn't known what style of fiction she enjoyed and would have guessed her favorite author to be someone less sensitive and more pragmatic. This apartment didn't fit the Juanita he knew. His Juanita would prefer more simple living quarters with no embellishments beyond a government-approved photograph of President Castro.

But he wasn't here to define Juanita Martinez's personality, he reminded himself. He was here on a mission. He was looking for clues—*anything* that might indicate exactly who Juanita had been working for, how effective she had been at feeding information from Cuba to the U. S., and where Scott Parker was hiding. Especially that.

This afternoon he would accomplish two tasks at once: He would gather the items Juanita had requested—the clothes, the makeup, the books—and he would search her personal possessions for subtle hints of her espionage activity. It was unusual, of course, for someone of his position to conduct such a routine search, but he didn't trust his lieutenants' thoroughness. Hadn't they spent three hours in the apartment and only come up with a box of letters? Not that the letters were unimportant. On a hunch, Bentancourt had called the Stoneycrest Nursing Home in Austin himself and had asked to speak with Mrs. Sadie Middleton. The nurse had been condescending: *Of course Mrs. Middleton couldn't come to the phone*, she had said. *Even if Mrs. Middleton were able to sit up in bed, she couldn't possibly respond to conversation. Didn't Señor Bentancourt understand about Alzheimer's?* the nurse had chided. *So debilitating, and so prevalent these days.*

Establishing that the letters had not come from Juanita's paternal grandmother had been easy. Deciphering the cryptic messages would require more time. One thing was definite, though: The letters had something to do with Scott Parker. In spite of Bentancourt's orders that all correspondence between his Cuban agents and their contacts in the States be screened, Juanita had found a way to maintain a regular dialogue with Parker for almost a year. Realizing that, Bentancourt decided to conduct the search of the apartment himself. He couldn't risk members of his staff discovering other hints of Parker's existence or of his own ineptitude. Bentancourt's masterful plan to have Parker killed in the U. S. had earned him a medal and a promotion. Knowledge that the operation had been bungled and that Bentancourt's personally selected agent, Juanita Martinez, had outsmarted him would surely cost him his job, if not his life. Yes, he would handle this search assignment himself—*gracias*, he had told his superiors. He enjoyed dabbling in field operations from time to time, he had insisted. It kept him humble.

*   *   *

"I feel sort of . . . well . . . *strange* being in your apartment," said Scott Parker as Alma Hammond transferred a stack of *Washington Posts* from the recliner to the floor and indicated that he should sit down.

She looked up at him, her eyes wide with surprise. "Wha . . . why should you feel strange?" she asked, incredulously. "I mean, it's not as if there's anything . . . er . . . person- al . . . ."

He laughed at her loss of composure. Alma *never* stumbled over words, and she certainly never blushed. But right now she was doing both. He understood what she was saying, or at least what she was trying to say. Of course there was nothing personal between them. In fact, the very suggestion of it was so incredible that it made Alma embarrassed, and it gave Scott a good chuckle. That was the point: Scott had never stopped to consider that Alma *had* a personal side. She was always so businesslike. So cool. But even career girls have to go home at night, he realized, and this was where Alma hung her hat. And briefcase.

"It's, uh, very nice," he offered politely.

"It's a mess," she admitted in her usual get-to-the-point manner. "I've got to order some wallpaper, make some new curtains, and do something with the sofa. Trade it for wicker, maybe."

"Then you just moved in?"

"Yeah," she hesitated. "Eight years ago."

They both laughed and relaxed a little. The situation was awkward. Alma obviously wasn't used to having a house- guest, least of all a *male* house guest. But she really had no choice. After she had promised to take Scott to Washington to confer with the CIA Director, she had phoned the airline to confirm her reservation and to arrange for tickets for Kent and Scott. The shuttle flight to National Airport was filled, she had been told. They were welcome to come to the terminal, go on standby status, and hope for the best.

Luck was with them—of sorts. One seat was available if Scott didn't mind the smoking section. He minded, but agreed to settle in next to a real Marlboro Man if it meant that he and Alma would arrive in Washington in time to meet the Director that afternoon. Kent remained on standby for the 8 P.M. flight and, if that didn't work, he was confirmed for the midnight red-eye express. As soon as Kent could make connections and get to Washington he would stop by Alma's apartment, pick up Scott, and take him home with him to Reston, Virginia. In the meantime, like it or not, Scott was Alma's guest. After all, it wasn't as if she could get him a room at the Hilton. Giving Scott his freedom in a city filled with government officials, foreign embassies, ambassadors, and other diplomats would be reckless, to say the least. Uncomfortable as it was, Scott and Alma were going to have to spend a few hours together, if not the entire evening.

"Sorry. The Director doesn't answer his private line, and the receptionist must be gone for the day," apologized Alma, placing the phone down on its receiver. "I knew it was a long shot, but I thought we might catch him before he left the office. It's the traffic. It's already 6:30. By now he's probably on the Outer Belt and halfway home. Dinner at the Director's home is served promptly at seven when he walks in the door. If you think *I'm* regimented, wait until you meet the Director. He and his wife exchange salutes, the kids march in from KP, and they all sit down and give thanks for their daily rations."

Scott laughed. He knew it would do him no good to be impatient with Alma. She had honestly made an effort to contact her supervisor. She had tried to call him from the airport in Appalachia and from National Airport when they arrived in Washington and had gotten busy signals both times. She had tried again as soon as they had entered her apartment. The fact that the Director wasn't available wasn't her fault. Scott wouldn't blame her for what she couldn't control. Besides, she looked tired and hardly in the mood to be scolded. "Speaking of rations . . ." he began.

"Zucchini lasagne or linguini," answered Alma.

"Huh?"

"All I have are zucchini lasagne or linguini—frozen," she explained. "I eat them because they're fast and can't spoil in the freezer. You get first pick as long as I get the linguini. It's my favorite." She moved a pile of *Newsweeks* from the sofa to the coffee table and sat down. Then she propped her feet on top of the coffee table and the *Newsweeks*.

"What I'd really like is a good Chinese dinner," Scott said, recalling a carryout restaurant they had passed during the taxi ride into town. "Mom Mead's cooking is fine, but Oriental delicacies aren't her forte. After a year back in the States, I'm anxious to sample a little rice again. How about splitting a double order of chop suey, a side dish of egg rolls, and some wonton soup?"

Alma brightened. Away from the glare of video equipment, Scott Parker could be downright affable. She kicked off her shoes. "Can we have it delivered?"

Scott gave her the thumbs-up sign and reached for the yellow pages. He smiled. Take her clipboard away from her and Alma Hammond was pretty good company.

"Fortune cookies?" he asked.

*   *   *

Mom Mead swung open the door and welcomed her house-guest with a warm hug. "Come in, come in," she said. "You're just in time for dinner. I hope they didn't feed you on the plane." Before Lillian Thompson could reply, she was ushered into the kitchen, where Pastor Mead was awaiting his favorite stroganoff over rice. With Scott gone, Bea Mead could finally serve rice again. She had quietly deleted it from her menus nearly a year earlier, when Scott Parker came to live with them. She had been afraid it would bring back painful memories of the POW camps, where uncooked rice was often the bill of fare for breakfast, lunch, and dinner.

"My dear, my dear," Pastor Mead said with obvious joy. "Why on earth didn't you tell us you were coming so I could have picked you up at the airport?"

"It's no trouble to rent a car, really," explained Lillian. "Besides, I kind of wanted to surprise Scotty." She looked around. "Where is he, anyway? Is Alma still here? Are they in the chapel? I figured their taping session would be over by now and I could have him to myself for a little while. We really need to talk. Is he out cutting wood with Kent or something?"

Mom Mead busied herself with getting a plate and some serving utensils for Lillian. She hated to share bad news, so she would let her husband handle the task. Pastor Mead leaned over and patted Lillian's hand.

"I'm afraid you missed Scott by a couple of hours," he said. "He and Alma should be in Washington by now. It seems that Alma received a rather disturbing report about Juanita."

Lillian waved aside Mom Mead's attempt to put a dish in front of her. "What happened? She wasn't discovered, was she? She's okay . . . not hurt or anything?"

"We don't have the details," Pastor Mead answered. "You know how tight-lipped Alma Hammond can be. All we know is that Juanita was on some sort of mission for Alma, her last assignment, and she was caught in the act. As far as I know, she wasn't hurt, but Alma didn't say much. Scott filled me in when I helped him pack a few things for the trip."

"What trip? I don't understand. Why is he in Washington? I thought it was so important for him to keep a low profile. It seems as if Washington would be the last place in the world that Alma would want Scotty to visit."

Pastor Mead shrugged his shoulders to indicate he didn't have the answers. "I'm not sure if Scott even knows why he went to Washington. He just felt helpless out here, I guess. Alma said any decision about Juanita would be made at the Pentagon, and from that point onward Scott insisted on making the trip. He's afraid Juanita will be forgotten in all the diplomatic red tape. He remembers what it was like to be a prisoner and to be written off as a POW. He doesn't want Juanita to become another entry in a book of government statistics. He doesn't want her to endure what he endured. You can't blame him for that, Lillian."

Lillian nodded her head in understanding. When she finally spoke, her voice was almost a whisper. "It doesn't make sense, does it? I mean Scotty has been through so much already, and just when everything finally seemed to be going his way, this had to happen. He was counting the days until Juanita would come home. That's all he talked about the last time I was here. Those letters from her were almost worn out from being read over and over again. I think the bits and pieces of notepaper from Cuba, as obscure and unintelligible as they might have been, were all that were holding his life together."

Pastor Mead withdrew his hand from hers and took a deep breath. "You're wrong, Lillian," he said almost sternly.

"What do you mean?" she asked, looking at him in surprise.

"I'll tell you what I mean," he began. "Better yet, I'll *show* you what I mean. Put your coat back on."

The firmness in his voice startled Lillian. Without questioning him, she dutifully put her coat around her shoulders and waited for his instructions. She felt like a child who had said something naughty, but she had no idea what she had uttered that was so offensive to him. She looked to Mom Mead for an explanation. Mom winked and smiled reassuringly. Again, Lillian felt like a child, but this time it was a warm feeling. She remembered all the times as youngsters growing up in Michigan she and Scott had been the beneficiaries of Pastor Mead's important lessons about life. She had the distinct feeling that she was about to receive another. He led her outside and across the yard to the garage.

"It all comes down to patience," Pastor Mead said, after helping her into the passenger side of his old red Buick, slipping in next to her, and turning on the ignition. "Patience and timing. Haven't we ever talked about that?"

If they had, Lillian didn't remember. Not that it mattered much. A refresher course—doled out piecemeal as they drove across the mission's acreage—was on its way. She settled down to enjoy the experience.

"Look over there," said Pastor Mead, nodding to his right. "See that?"

She squinted, waited a few minutes until they were closer, and then answered, "The shed? No, wait a minute, it looks like a cabin, but a very small one. I don't think I ever noticed it before."

"That's because it wasn't there before," explained Pastor Mead. "At least not until about six weeks ago, when your brother convinced four or five of the men from town that the mission needed a retreat . . . or, more importantly, that *they* needed a retreat. He told them they ought to have a place away from home, even away from the church, where they could spend an hour or two on a Thursday night having a fellowship, reading the Bible, and talking about what was going on in their lives. They didn't understand at first . . . didn't see why they couldn't just take turns meeting at each other's houses. But he explained that they needed a place that wasn't full of distractions—even nice distractions like kids, dogs, and wives offering coffee and pie. He told them they needed a place where as soon as they entered they knew exactly why they were there and what they needed to do while they were there. The place alone should jolt them to their purpose. Once they understood his idea, well, it didn't take long for them to dig the basement, pour the foundation, and put the frame up. They've already met twice, and now they're talking about an addition . . . a teen club room. Scott has been working on the plans and has a steering committee made up of dads and sons."

Lillian smiled. Yes, that sounded like Scott. Some people would say he was a dreamer, but he was better than that. He was a doer. He had the imagination and vision to dream, but he had the will and stamina to make reality out of his dreams. But where was the lesson in all of this? Lillian knew her brother well. Pastor Mead wasn't telling her of attributes she hadn't recognized and boasted of many times.

They pulled up to the church and the elderly preacher left the engine running so the car's headlights would illuminate the path leading to the old stone steps. He took her arm and gently guided her toward the building. She had attended church there only once, and he was sensitive to the hidden ruts in the walkway that could cause her to turn an ankle.

"He's ordered bricks," explained Pastor Mead. "He showed me a picture of a wide winding walk made of bricks and bordered with evergreens. He clipped it out of *Southern Living*. Just between us, I'm not so sure it will work in the rough terrain we've got here, but I've learned not to question that brother of yours. If Scott says it will be all right, well, I'm willing to believe somehow it will be all right."

They entered the church and Pastor Mead snapped on the lights in the narthex. "By Christmas we hope to have all the pews refinished and stained to match each other," he explained. "We priced new ones a few months ago but we decided our budget couldn't quite support the expenditure, at least not this year. These old pews, on the other hand, have been supporting folks for a good many years, so we thought we'd dress them up for the holidays. Scott got a crew to work every Saturday afternoon. They sanded down three at a time, stained them, and then coated them with varnish. Every Sunday morning three old ones were gone and three 'new' ones were in their place. As folks started to notice the difference, they took pride in the way the sanctuary was looking. We were able to recruit more helpers. Now Scott has added a Monday night shift. At this rate we should be done ahead of schedule. Thanksgiving, maybe."

Lillian sat down and gently stroked the smooth finish of a refurbished pew. She smiled, knowing that her brother was responsible for its beauty. She looked at Pastor Mead inquisitively. "I get the picture—now help me with the lesson. Tell me about patience and time," she said, patting the seat as a way of inviting him to sit next to her.

"Don't you see?" he began, settling into the graceful slope of the pew and draping his arm over its back. "You said a while ago at the house that Scott has been counting the days until Juanita could come home to him. And that's true. But he hasn't just counted the days, he's used them. Every one of them. While he could have passed the time feeling sorry for himself for all the years lost in the prison camp, he decided to make up for those years and catch up with what he's missed.

"At first, there was some resentment," Pastor Mead continued. "We talked about it, and I couldn't blame him for his feelings. He wondered why 12 years of his life had been taken from him—years when he could have helped your father in the business, years when he could have watched you grow up and go off to college, years when he could have consoled your mother in her illness, and years when he could have started a family of his own and known the joys of being a husband and father. He felt resentment for Juanita's obligation to her job and for Alma's insistence that he go into hiding in this out-of-the-way place. He often asked me why, after waiting so long for happiness, he had to wait one more year. My explanation didn't satisfy him, but before long he found his own answer. And it was better than mine."

Lillian closed her eyes. "Go on," she said.

"It came from the way people reacted to him, Lillian. It was the effect he had on others. As folks learned about what he had been through and about how he had never given up or given in to the enemy, they began to congregate around him. He realized that he had a forum and that he could use that forum to make a difference, whether good or bad. People listened to him because he had credibility in their eyes . . . more credibility than I could ever have."

Lillian started to object to his words, but he shook his head. "You don't understand, Lillian. People who live around here have known more hardship than we can imagine. I can preach about the importance of sacrifice, and about how Jesus can make our burdens lighter, but I'm an overweight old man with gold fillings in my teeth. Sure, I've had my share of grief, but I haven't gone to bed hungry too many nights. And I've never endured pain because I couldn't afford to see a doctor."

Lillian nodded in understanding. "But when my brother talks about sacrifice and about Jesus, he has more . . . more clout. They can relate to him."

"Exactly," said Pastor Mead. "When I speak, they listen politely. When Scott speaks, they believe wholeheartedly. In the end everyone has benefited. Scott has found his ministry and his answer. He knows now why God made him wait. In His infinite wisdom, God had a special place reserved for Scott. When Scott realized where that place was, he seized the opportunity, claimed it as his own, and directed every bit of his energy toward it. What the people of Appalachia don't realize is that just as they have grown stronger in their faith because of Scott, so too has your brother grown stronger in his faith because of them. The miraculous thing is that none of this could have happened if God hadn't asked Scott to wait just one more year."

Lillian smiled. "And what about you?" she asked. "You said that in the end everyone has benefited. How have you benefited?"

"Me?" replied Pastor Mead. "God has a place reserved for me, too. My work is nearly done, Lillian. And now I've found my successor."

"Scotty?"

"Scotty."

CHAPTER 5

The handwriting had fooled him at first—so delicate; even feeble at times. However, his phone call to Austin had quickly determined that Mrs. Sadie Middleton had not written the stash of lavender-scented notes and letters tucked in the bottom drawer of Juanita Martinez's desk.

He had hoped that the search of Juanita's apartment would explain not only the letters, but also the depth of Juanita's involvement with American espionage activities in Cuba. He wanted to find names, addresses, and titles. He wanted answers . . . conclusive evidence about Juanita and her associates in Washington and Havana. He hoped for reassurance that Scott Parker was no threat to him, that Juanita was only a beginner in her service to the U. S. government, that she had been recruited during her recent trip to the States . . . attracted by Scott Parker and coerced by Alma Hammond.

But his exhaustive search—five hours of shuffling through papers, rifling drawers, studying the contents of every purse, pocket, shelf, and wastebasket—had yielded only more questions. In the end, he had left the apartment empty-handed. He had no more than he'd had at the beginning. Only the letters . . . tied with a white satin bow.

Under less threatening circumstances, Guadalupe Bentancourt would have relished the mystery. He was a man of detail, trained to track the tiniest clue and able to pick up on subtleties that other, less careful operatives would have overlooked. But this was no standard investigation. He had too much at stake in its outcome. Still, he knew he had to maintain a detached attitude and proceed with his fact-finding as if he were not personally involved. He couldn't let fear muddle his judgment; he couldn't let his colleagues sense his growing apprehension that he might soon be exposed as an incompetent blunderer. Emotionally, he had to remove himself from the picture and direct the probe as if it were merely another case involving names he didn't recognize and actions he neither condoned nor criticized.

Determined to follow this game plan, he had forced himself to go home after his search of Juanita's apartment. His gut instinct had been to drive back to his office and begin a careful study of the letters. But, no, he would surely meet his coworkers as they were preparing to leave for the day. There would be questions, remarks, speculation. *Mr. Ambassador, sir, is there some kind of emergency? Will you need after-hours secretarial help? Shall we order your dinner to be sent in, sir? Should we alert maintenance that they should not disturb you by cleaning your suite of offices? Sir, the switchboard will want to know just how late you will be working in case there are any calls.* Such patronage had always delighted him. It had made him feel important. But not now. Now it made him nervous . . . more nervous than he had ever been in his life.

Because of this he had driven home and gone through the motions of preparing a light supper. He read the day's editions of both *Granma* and *Trabajadores*, and had stretched out on the couch at 11 P.M. Surprisingly, he had slept.

His advice to himself had been sound. When he awakened the next morning he felt remarkably in control. He timed his arrival at his office precisely to coincide with the arrival of the cabinet minister he reported to. He liked to be seen carrying his bulging briefcase and dressed in his exquisitely cut Palm Beach suit. His smile and his banter, first with the cabinet minister and then with the secretarial pool, came easily and naturally. He accepted a cup of extra-light coffee and a croissant from the receptionist and nodded at her explanation of why the stack of mail was double its normal size. It had accumulated the previous day while he was out of the office conducting the search of Ms. Martinez's apartment, she reminded him. Ah, Ms. Martinez, he replied. Yes, he remembered. In fact, he had some work to do with those letters of hers. The ones tied with the satin ribbon.

"No interruptions, *por favor*," he requested with a toothy smile. He closed the door to his private office and exhaled a deep sigh of relief . . . then another, and a third. He *was* in control. Surely he was in control.

*   *   *

When Scott had confided during their trip to Washington that he disliked flying, Alma Hammond had suggested he try breathing exercises. Not content with merely prescribing the treatment, Alma insisted on overseeing it, counting each inhale ("one, two, three") and each subsequent exhale ("four, five, six").

It wasn't so much the plane that Scott objected to, but rather the close quarters of the cabin. He attributed his discomfort to all those years he had been shoehorned into a solitary cell, or, at best, overcrowded prison barracks and herded shoulder to shoulder with other GIs in tight human convoys that snaked across miles of unfamiliar Vietnamese countryside.

Since business in Washington prevented Alma from accompanying Scott and Kent on their return flight to Appalachia, Alma had secured a small supply of Dramamine for Scott. The over-the-counter drug would calm his queasiness, she had told him, as she deposited the medication in one of his hands and placed a glass of apple juice in the other. Kent was entrusted with an extra dosage and was instructed in the nuances of counting inhalations and exhalations: "one, two, three, four, five, six."

Even so, when the small commuter plane gently touched down on the Bluefield, West Virginia, runway and the stewardess opened the hatch and announced that passengers could deplane, Scott Parker was the first to bolt from his seat, stride down the aisle, and step into the freshness of the afternoon. He didn't need Alma or Kent to monitor the deep gulp of mountain air he hungrily took into his lungs. Although he had been gone fewer than 24 hours, it had been his first trip away from the mission, and he was surprised to realize how much he had missed it. Truly it was becoming his home.

He squinted at the brightness of the sun, then did a double-take as his eyes swept past the terminal. A smile spread across his lean face and he bounded down the metal stairway.

"Lill! What are you doing here?" He lifted his sister off the ground and whirled her around two times. When he finally set her down they were both laughing from dizziness. "This is fantastic!" he said. "What a homecoming! And the timing is perfect. I was going to call you tonight. Have I got news for you!"

"Are you alone?" asked Lillian, scanning the knot of passengers hurrying across the breezy landing strip. "Where's Alma? And Kent . . . where's Kent? Surely he didn't leave you on your own."

"No such luck," replied Scott with a laugh. "Alma decided to stay in Washington to firm up some details of a . . . er, joint project we're working on. Kent will be here in a minute. I was so anxious to get off the plane and stretch that I sort of left him fumbling with the luggage. We didn't have much. Just overnight stuff."

They walked arm in arm toward the parking lot where Lillian had left Pastor Mead's oversized red Buick.

"I've got something wonderful to tell you," Lillian began. "At least I think it's wonderful; that is, it *will* be wonderful if everything works out. Gosh, just listen to me babble! I'm so excited. I was all set to tell you last night, and then you weren't there. Or here, I mean." She laughed at her own confusion. "Anyway, I'm going to need a lot of help. Your help, Scotty."

"Whoa, slow down, Lill," Scott said. "I've got something I'm anxious to tell you, too. But it will have to keep for now. And, from the looks of things, yours has just been put on hold, too. Unless, of course, you can share it with Kent." He nodded toward the terminal exit where Kent was standing, his right hand shielding his eyes as he scanned the parking lot for Scott.

"Tell you what," Lillian proposed quickly. "After dinner tonight we'll ask permission to walk down to the retreat. Kent can sit outside and make sure we don't try to reenact the Great Escape or anything."

Scott shook his head. "Crazy, isn't it? I can't even have a private conversation with my sister without King Kong hovering over me."

"Never mind," said Lillian, punching him teasingly. "Surely it won't be for much longer."

Scott brightened. He draped his arm over Lillian's shoulders. "You don't know how right you are, Lill. It's a matter of time now. And you know what? All the credit goes to Alma. She's turned into a real friend." He smiled at the mysteriousness of his words. He didn't mean to play games with her. "I'll tell you all about it later. At the retreat."

He watched as Kent spotted the Buick and started walking toward it. Lillian's eyes also followed Kent's trek across the parking lot, but her mind was elsewhere. She could think only of Alma.

"I hope you're right about Alma, Scotty, because I'm really counting on her cooperation."

*   *   *

When it came to giving credit where credit was due, Guadalupe Bentancourt was generous, even magnanimous. In the case of the Austin letters, he had to admit that Alma Hammond had performed brilliantly.

First was the stationery itself. Not only was it monogrammed, but the monogram was engraved: Mrs. Sadie Middleton. The watermark, seen only when he held the heavy sheet of beige bond to the light, was that of Neiman-Marcus. *Nice touch*, Bentancourt acknowledged. Not everyone would think to order the stationery from the most famous and most posh department store in Texas. But Alma Hammond would.

As far as the handwriting was concerned, he decided not to attempt to trace it. An expert within Bentancourt's division had confirmed that the letters had been written by an elderly woman, left-handed, with some arthritis in the index finger and thumb. Since Bentancourt was convinced that Alma had supervised the execution of the letters, the actual writing could have been jobbed out to any older woman willing to sign a pledge of secrecy. No, Bentancourt was more interested in who composed the messages rather than who put pen to paper. Was it Alma or Scott Parker? The author would reveal himself—or herself—through the messages. And Guadalupe Bentancourt would identify the author by studying the clues. He was, after all, a man of detail.

He reached for the tidy stack of correspondence and chose the letter on top. He would start with the most recent.

> August 3
> My dear little Nita,
>
> My room is much brighter today with the addition of the picture you sent in your last note. It sits on top of the dresser and is admired by everyone who comes to call. You said it was taken in Nassau, but you must tell me more because I have never been there. The hat you are wearing—did one of the islanders make it? I have always read that people in the Bahamas are very fine craftsmen . . . .

Bentancourt felt the blood rush to his face. She had made a fool of him! The letters were from Parker, of course. Why else would she send a photograph of herself? Alma Hammond would have no use for a picture. But a long-distance lover

. . . that was quite a different story. How he would value such a sentimental remembrance! And to think Bentancourt had facilitated the gift! Not only had his lieutenants allowed the photo to pass through the routine screening procedure, but he—Bentancourt himself—had taken the picture during their last trip to Nassau. It had been a business trip, of course, but Juanita had allowed him to buy her a red straw hat on the condition that he would take a snapshot of her wearing it. It was for her scrapbook, she had said. She wanted something to remind her of the special day they had spent together. Fool! He had played right into her hands.

> I have been planning a small gift for you, my dear. I have no need for the ring that your grandfather gave me on our wedding day so many years ago. I would like you to have it to wear on your right hand. Later, when you meet someone very special, someone you want to marry, the ring can be taken off the right hand and placed on the left during the wedding ceremony. May I send it to you?

Frankly, Bentancourt was surprised that Alma Hammond had allowed that paragraph to be included in the letter. It was so obvious. Parker was in love, and like so many American men, he thought a relationship wasn't binding until a ring was involved. *Americans are so materialistic*, he sputtered. Juanita probably hadn't had time to respond because her arrest at the Russian embassy had occurred so soon after the letter from Parker had arrived. However, Bentancourt made a mental note to look for the ring on her right hand when he next visited her in prison. Just to make sure.

> I must go. It is nearly 8 P.M., *60 Minutes* is over, and it is time to watch *Murder, She Wrote*. We enjoy trying to solve the mystery before Jessica (Do you remember the actress Angela Lansbury?) does. How I wish you were here to share the simple

pleasures of a quiet Sunday night with us. I look
forward to hearing from you soon, especially about
your grandfather's ring.

We enjoy trying to solve the mystery? Bentancourt wondered who, in addition to Scott Parker, comprised the "we."
Parker was in hiding, but apparently he wasn't alone. Yet
where was he? And who was with him?

Something about this particular letter bothered Bentancourt. He reread it several times before finally putting it aside
and reaching for another. Whatever it was that was wrong
with the letter would come to him sooner or later. After all, he
was a man of detail.

* * *

"Okay, let's have it," said Scott. "I want all the details."

He was sitting in a folding chair opposite his sister in the
mission's new retreat. The furnishings were sparse, second-
hand, and not particularly comfortable. The chairs were
arranged in a large circle, ready for the Thursday night men's
Bible study.

"We'll be able to buy carpeting and maybe install a small
kitchen," said Lillian, almost to herself. "Wouldn't Mom Mead
love that? At dinner she was telling me about her plan to have
a Christmas arts-and-crafts bazaar. Well, this is the *perfect*
place. With kitchen facilities the women of the church could
serve lunch or maybe just have a buffet of light refreshments.
Either way, it would be a great fund-raiser and . . ."

"Lill, any minute now Kent is going to get suspicious and
start knocking on the door," interrupted Scott. "Mom Mead's
bazaar sounds wonderful, but I doubt that you flew all the
way from Tennessee to discuss *that*. What gives?"

Lillian smiled. "Sorry. I get carried away sometimes. But if
we're successful with our lawsuit, my daydreams may become realities soon."

She reached into her purse and pulled out photocopies of various documents and business letters. She spread them out on the chair between them and then looked up at her brother.

"I hardly know where to begin," she said. "I'm here about Daddy."

"Dad!" said Scott. "What in the world . . . ?"

"I've got to tell it in order or else it won't make sense," insisted Lillian. She tapped the stack of papers. "I have proof here, Scotty, that Daddy did *not* embezzle funds from Michigan Technologies. In fact, he was doing his best to save the company from a group of men who were working on the inside to wring M-T dry of all its assets. Daddy's plan might have worked, too, if he hadn't gotten sick. Poor thing. He must have been under tremendous pressure. If only he had told me what was going on."

Scott looked bewildered. "Wait a minute. Slow down, okay? Who told you all this?"

"Dave's boss, Phil Compton. You remember him. He gave me away at my wedding."

Scott rubbed his forehead with his hand. Lillian's wedding was little more than a blur. Alma Hammond had not wanted him to attend, but she had agreed to allow it only after he had promised to stay very close to Kent, to speak only when spoken to, and to leave as quickly after the ceremony as possible.

It had been difficult to watch his younger sister get married before he'd even had a chance to get to know her again. He would have been honored to give the bride away in the absence of their deceased father, but his relationship to Lillian needed to remain a secret; as such, he had taken a lesser role.

Then there had been the issue of Juanita. At the time of Lillian's wedding, he had not yet reconciled himself to the disappointing fact that he would have to wait a year before he could contemplate marriage for himself. The topic of weddings in general was still painful for him.

"I don't get it. How could that old guy know anything about Michigan Technologies? Is he a stockholder? A speculator?"

"No, nothing like that. It was personal, strictly personal. Phil's daughter, Cat, had intended to marry Roderick Davis after he and I broke off our engagement. Phil didn't trust Roderick, however. He hired some detectives to find out all they could about Roderick. To find out about Roderick, the detectives had to find out about the places where he had worked and the people he'd been associated with."

"And among his former employers was Michigan Technologies," surmised Scott.

"Exactly. I've got copies here of all the M-T reports and records and documents the detective agency turned over to Phil. Those people were good at their digging, Scotty. Phil told them to spare no expense and, believe me, they didn't. Besides using surveillance equipment, they even managed to get two of their people hired as inside workers."

"Sounds to me like this Davis character may have met his match in old Phil Compton."

"They *all* have," said Lillian. "Phil's got the goods on enough of the key people to shake out half the management. After he heard about you, though, he decided to wait until we talked."

"You told him about *me*?"

"Yes—I know that won't please Alma. But believe me, Phil's trustworthy. He's as angry over what happened to Daddy as we are. You and I lost a company, but Phil nearly lost a daughter to one of those cutthroats in Detroit. He's on our side, Scotty, you can believe that."

Scott waved off his sister's insistence.

"Your judgment of Phil is good enough for me. Let me have a look at those papers."

Scott slowly read the documents, pausing frequently to review earlier paragraphs and compare one page of evidence with another. Midway through his study he got up, stretched, and paced the length of the room, all the while carefully studying a sheaf of letters in his right hand. When he was done with the last page, he rubbed his eyes with both index fingers, frowned, and sat back down. Lillian had been watching his every move.

"Well, what do you think?" she asked.

Scott looked at her earnestly. "I think our father would still be alive today if it hadn't been for Davis and the others like him. They eased their way into the organization and steadily sapped the company of its resources . . . and Dad of his strength.

"Can you imagine what Dad must have gone through, Lillian? He didn't know which person to trust and which to fight. He couldn't confide in anyone. He was overruled in the board room, outvoted at the stockholders' meetings, even ostracized by his own employees. But he never gave up. That's what's so incredible. He *never* quit."

Lillian smiled, although tears threatened to spill down her cheeks. "He was tough, all right. Roderick, Paul Stattman, and the others weren't satisfied with just stealing the company from Daddy—they wanted him to grovel and plead for mercy. But he never did. Not once. I'm so proud of Daddy; and that's why you owe it to him to finish his fight. You're the man of our family now. Daddy was still battling when he drew his last breath. Now it's up to you to continue that battle until you clear his name. You can do it, Scott. I know you can."

Scott looked at her a long time before answering. He crossed his arms and pushed back solidly against his chair.

"I'm sorry, Lill. This can't be for me," he said. "I know what you're saying is right, but I just can't take on this fight. Not now at least."

"Why? Because of Alma? Surely you can convince her of the importance of this. She told you that you had to stay hidden for a year; so, okay, the year is almost up. Don't you think . . ."

Scott sighed heavily and shook his head. "It's not Alma," he said.

"What then?"

"Pop Mead told you about what happened to Juanita, right?"

Lillian nodded. "A little. He said she'd been taken into custody."

"Custody?" said Scott, his mouth twisting. "They've *arrested* her. She's in prison, Lillian."

"That's terrible," said Lillian softly, still not comprehending the real weight of Scott's words. "I'm really sorry, Scotty. It'll probably take a couple of months of negotiations before she can come home, right? What a pain."

Scott was amazed at Lillian's naiveté. "A pain? Lillian, this isn't a minor inconvenience we're talking about here. Those people are planning to kill Juanita. And they will, too, unless we get to her first."

"Kill her? Surely not. Oh, Scott you must be sick with worry."

"I was until I went to Washington," admitted Scott. "Alma was wonderful in Washington, Lill. She managed to get me in to talk to the CIA Director himself. Can you believe that? Then she backed me up every time I asked if I could be part of a rescue effort to free Juanita. I think the poor Director got tired of the two of us badgering him. Even so, I don't think he would have agreed if Alma hadn't reminded him of all my military training. She seems to know my background better than I do."

Lillian seemed perplexed. First surprise, then fear, spread across her face as she grasped what her brother was explaining.

"What are you saying? No, Scotty, you can't be thinking about going to Cuba," she began haltingly. "Surely Alma wouldn't let you put your life in danger, not even for Juanita. Scott, you can't. Tell me you won't."

"It's already settled," he confirmed. "As soon as the schedules are worked out, we'll be gone. I have no choice, Lill. I love Juanita. I couldn't live with myself if I turned my back on her now. It's something I have to do. Even Alma seems to understand that. I'm afraid you'll have to go to Detroit and clear Dad's name on your own. I'll try to join you if and when I can, but I can't promise anything."

Lillian took a wad of blue tissues from her purse and blotted her eyes. Scott got up and walked behind her chair.

Gently he put his hands on her shoulders and began massaging the tension from her muscles. She sighed, giving in to the warmth and strength of his kneading fingers.

"For 12 years we lived with the pain of believing you were dead," she whispered. "Then you came back to us; please don't make us endure that hurt again. Please . . ."

He was silent for a while, rhythmically applying pressure to her taut neck muscles, then lightly circling her temples.

"You said something about daydreams, Lill. It reminded me of when we were kids. Remember how Dad used to scold me for spending so much time looking out the window and daydreaming? He always said I was going to dream my life away if I wasn't careful."

Lillian laughed softly and nodded.

"But when I was in Vietnam for all those years and there wasn't anything for me to do *except* dream, I stopped," Scott said. "I had plenty of time, but that's all I had. I had no hope for the future and no reason to believe that any of my dreams would ever come true. So I protected myself from disappointment by not allowing myself to fantasize."

Lillian's eyes were closed and her head was bent slightly forward. Scott continued to apply pressure at the base of her neck. Gradually she relaxed.

"My love for Juanita and my work here at the mission gave me some reasons to dream again. I sat on that hill outside the window for days thinking about what this retreat might look like. I sketched it in the dirt with a stick; I drew up plans on the back of napkins. But it really took shape in my mind when I started thinking about how it could be used. I could see the retreat as the perfect setting for a young couples' Bible study group. I envisioned Juanita as part of the circle, growing in her faith as she helped others to grow in theirs. I purposely decided not to do too much as far as decorating the walls and picking out furniture . . . I thought that might be something Juanita and Mom Mead could do together. It might draw them closer if they could work on a joint project. I want them to be good friends."

Lillian turned to face Scott. She smiled as she saw how happy he looked when he spoke of the future.

"Your dreams center on Juanita, don't they?"

"Most of them, yeah. I'm trying to be realistic, though. I know Juanita and I have a lot of differences to work out. Her life has been pretty exciting up until now. A little *too* exciting, if you ask me. I worry sometimes that the place might seem awfully dull to her. And I wonder about her commitment to Christ. My faith has become so much stronger since I've been working here with Pastor Mead. I worry that maybe Juanita won't share my beliefs, at least not with the same intensity I feel.

"But before we can resolve any of those questions, we have to spend time together. A lot of time. Quiet time—not intense moments like we shared in the hospital when I was weak and we knew she was going to be called away any minute. Those were romantic hours, but not typical of life over the long haul. Juanita needs to see me when I'm working in the garden and I'm hot and tired and even grouchy. She needs to spend Sunday evenings with nothing more to do than watch *60 Minutes*, read a book, or play a game of Scrabble. We need some normal time together. Does that make any sense, Lill?"

Lillian offered an accommodating grin.

"Of course it does," she said, "And it works both ways. You need to see Juanita when her hair isn't perfect and she isn't wearing makeup. You need to talk about *her* daydreams. Does she want a family? Children? Would she rather work?"

Scott shrugged as if to admit he didn't know.

"First I've got to get her home," he said simply. "And that may not be easy. Like I said, Alma's in Washington working on the plan and timetables now. She and the Director gave me their word that I would be part of whatever they decided on. I've spent nearly a year hidden away up here. I've done everything they've asked me to do. Now I want to stop being a bystander and get involved. I want to help bring Juanita home."

Lillian sighed. She understood, although she didn't approve of the idea.

"Do you really think I should go to Detroit? I mean, without you?"

"Yes," answered Scott. "And as soon as you get there, hire the best lawyer you can find. If all goes well in Cuba, I promise I'll join you in Detroit. Will Dave be able to go with you? I'd feel a lot better if I knew you wouldn't be alone. Maybe you can look up some of your friends from school, or maybe the office. Were you close to anyone at Michigan Technologies?"

Lillian thought for a moment. "I'm not sure I should contact the girls from the sales department. Who knows where their allegiances might be these days? But you're right—I'll need a good friend *and* a good lawyer." She nodded slowly as an idea came to her. "And I think I know just who that person might be."

"Friend or lawyer?" asked Scott.

"Both," she replied.

*   *   *

It was nearly 7 P.M. by the time Guadalupe Bentancourt called the switchboard and announced he was leaving for the day. The stack of phone messages would have to wait until Monday morning. He was hungry.

His growling stomach had alerted him that the afternoon was gone and that he had eaten nothing since he had nibbled the croissant nearly 12 hours earlier. Still, the time had been well spent. He had uncovered three important bits of information since he had begun his scrutiny of the Austin letters.

First, the correspondence was undoubtedly from Scott Parker. That fact not only confirmed Parker's existence but also erased any question about his relationship with Juanita Martinez.

Secondly, Bentancourt had been able to determine the general location of Scott's hiding place. The first letter he had read provided the clue, although it took several readings before Bentancourt recognized it. In the letter, Scott Parker, writing from the perspective of Mrs. Sadie Middleton, had mentioned that it was 8 P.M., and that *60 Minutes* was over and *Murder, She Wrote* was the next program on television. Bentancourt remembered all too well the confusion he had experienced once when traveling in America on vacation. It had taken him a long time to understand the concept of time zone changes, especially during the summer months, when certain parts of the country followed something called "daylight saving time."

A quick phone call revealed that *60 Minutes* was aired from 6 to 7 P.M. in Texas during August. However, it was televised from 7 to 8 P.M. on the East Coast. Bentancourt could assume that Scott Parker was somewhere in the East, probably not in a large city where he might be noticed, but surely close enough to Washington D.C. to enable CIA experts to conduct frequent debriefing sessions with him. Good, the net was closing.

Finally, Bentancourt gleaned from the letters that the feelings shared by Sergeant Parker and Juanita Martinez were much deeper than he had first guessed. This, more than anything, worried him. He knew firsthand of Parker's stubbornness. In 12 years as a POW, the American had never given in to his captors. Such resoluteness might cause him to act foolishly now. If the American government didn't retaliate for Juanita's arrest quickly enough to suit him, Parker might attempt a rescue mission of his own. He had the nerve for it, of that Bentancourt was sure.

"But first he'll have to find her," vowed Bentancourt quietly. "Perhaps it is time for Señorita Martinez to see a darker, more obscure part of her native country."

CHAPTER 6

It was the nine-month anniversary of the marriage of Miss Catherine "Cat" Compton to the Honorable Drew Sanders, U.S. Senator from the State of Tennessee. That would have called for a little celebration *anyway*. After all, what was the sense of being newlyweds if you couldn't be a little sentimental about it, Cat always said? Drew usually agreed . . . at least when they were in private and he wasn't too self-conscious about the way his beautiful young wife lavished attention on him. (Ear-nibbling was *not* for public places, he continually reminded her.)

Cat checked herself in the mirror as she sashayed into the dining room of their Washington apartment. Yes, vanity aside, she had to admit she looked terrific. The dress wasn't new, but that was on purpose. She was wearing the long, slinky black evening gown with the high side-slit that she'd worn the first time she had ever "dressed up" for Drew. It was his favorite outfit on her. She had decided to wear it again tonight, while she still could.

She lit the two candles on the dining room table and inserted Linda Ronstadt's new compact disc into the CD player. Drew had promised to come home directly after the meeting of the Senate Subcommittee on Population Control. Cat giggled to herself about the irony of that. Wait until he heard what she had to announce later tonight.

Cat debated on when and how to actually share the big news with Drew. Should she offhandedly mention during dinner, "Oh, by the way, I saw the doctor today. It wasn't the flu after all?" Perhaps after dinner she should say, "I didn't have time to go out and buy you something, dear, but if you'll give me about nine months, I'll give you a gift you'll never forget." Or maybe she should wait until after they were alone in bed, wrapped in each other's arms, and then whisper, "I thought you had already made me as happy as I could ever be, darling, but now I know even greater joys are ahead for us."

She decided, finally, to let the evening unfold as it would. Whenever it seemed like just the right moment, she would share the news.

She couldn't wait to see Drew's face. He would be delighted . . . uncharacteristically silly with joy. It took quite some doing for Cat to get her ever-businesslike hubby to unleash the boyish personality that lay just below the surface of his serious outer demeanor. Once it was loose, however, no one could be more fun than Drew Sanders. And Cat loved those times.

They had talked a lot about children. Drew was now 45 and Cat was not quite 28. Drew had wondered if he might be getting too old to start a second family, especially when he considered that his son Todd was now almost 25. After his first wife, Marie, had been killed in an automobile accident, Drew had raised Todd alone. It hadn't been easy. But then again, it had been worth it. Drew never showed any restraint when opportunities arose to brag about his son. He couldn't imagine what his life would have been like if Todd had not been there, giving him a reason to go on. No . . . no doubt about it, kids *were* worth all the effort it took to raise them.

After talking and praying together about the matter, Drew and Cat had decided just to "see what might happen."

Well . . . now something had happened. And Cat Sanders was hardly able to contain her excitement. Four times that afternoon she had picked up the phone to call her parents in Compton Gap. They would have been thrilled. Each time, however, she had not completed the call. It was only right that Drew, the daddy, should hear the news first. Besides, she wanted Drew to listen in on the extension when she told her folks about their future status as grandparents.

Cat nervously looked at her watch. It was after 6 P.M. Drew would be putting the key in the door at any minute now. It was going to be an absolutely perfect evening. Nothing, she assured herself, would spoil the wonderful night that lay ahead for them. Nothing.

At that moment the phone started ringing.

*   *   *

It was nearly 6:30 P.M. when Drew stepped off the elevator and quickly made his way to the door of the spacious apartment that he and Cat now called home. He smiled to himself. He knew what to expect. It was another "anniversary" night. She would have soft music playing, a nice dinner would be prepared (steak and salad, the only things she'd mastered in nine months of marriage), and she would be dressed to the nines. At first he had thought she was overdoing things but now he looked forward to these events. And especially to the time that came after dinner.

"Sorry I'm a bit late, dear," he started to apologize as he hurried inside. "The Chairman added two last-minute items to our agenda and . . . and . . ."

Drew looked around. Was he in the right apartment?

"Welcome home, sweetheart," said Cat, crossing the room to help him with his hat and coat. She was dressed in a cute but very casual print dress. No plunging neckline. No earrings. There was no mood music playing in the background, no wafting scent of perfume was in the air, not even dimmed lights and candles.

"You were saying . . . ?" prompted Cat.

Drew closed his mouth. He looked at her and put on a small smile.

"Uh, the agenda," he repeated. "Two extra items."

Cat stood on tiptoes and kissed him. "No problem. Come on in the kitchen. I was just setting the table anyway."

Drew dropped his briefcase on a living room chair and followed Cat toward the kitchen. As he passed through the dining room his quick eyes noticed two things. A small piece of candlewax, a dripping, was on the polished table, and the drawer to the linen buffet had the corner of a hot pad showing out of it. Cat, a perfectionist, would never have missed such things . . . unless for some reason she had set the dinner in the dining room and then had hastily transferred everything back to the kitchen.

But why? He was only a few minutes late. Besides, she certainly didn't seem upset with him. Could she have already become tired of the monthly private anniversary parties? He hoped not. Not yet, anyway. Surely they weren't "settled into a rut" so soon.

"Catherine?"

"Yes?"

"Is everything okay? You . . . well, you aren't mad at me or anything, are you?"

Cat looked up from the salad she was tossing. "Mad? Of course not." She came over to him and placed her arms around him and gave him a bear hug.

Drew wrapped her in his arms and squeezed her even closer to him. He smiled. "I'm paranoid," he confessed. "I'm so crazy in love with you, I get worried if anything seems out of the ordinary. It's the nineteenth of the month. I expected this to be another party night."

Cat loosened herself from his arms. "Now see there," she said, "I just *knew* I was becoming too predictable. Good. I've fooled you. But beware—you never know what new things I may be plotting even now. Sit down. You've got to be hungry."

Drew found his place. "Actually, I was kind of looking forward to . . ."

"Would you say grace, honey?" Cat cut in. "The steaks are getting cold."

* * *

Across town in another part of Washington, the lights were on in the office of the Director of the CIA. The Director was pacing his office, awaiting a phone call from Appalachia. The Juanita Martinez incident had gotten to be a sticky affair. The Director was more than a little annoyed at how it was demanding so much of his time. First the woman had bungled her final assignment and had been caught. That was bad enough, but then Parker had insisted on being part of a liberation force to free her. What swashbuckling dribble! Small matter, though, since Parker had already told his story on videotape. Better to have him alive to tell it again, but not crucial. And if there was a chance that Parker would help rescue the Martinez woman, so much the better. The information in her head . . . yes, that would be a delight to know. Surely worth a go at springing her. Even worth risking Parker's neck.

The Director had put every paid informant he had in Cuba to work on watching the prison where Juanita was being held. *Follow the schedules, note the weaknesses, carry on with standard surveillance procedures.* They'd find a chink in the armor and report it. Then Parker and the boys from the Navy's Sea-Air-Land "SEAL" squad could make the raid. In a week it would all be over.

Or it should have been.

Blast it all, the Director growled to himself. *Bentancourt can read my mind. He's staying a jump ahead.*

A coded message had come an hour ago. Juanita Martinez had been seen being put into a car. She'd been taken from the prison. No one knew yet to what new location she had been transferred.

The news would be upsetting to young Parker, there could be no doubt of that. But it would do no good to have him leave his cover and start chatting with the press corps. It might ruin his credibility. Even worse, it would deny the President the glory of taking the credit for Parker's rescue.

A dashing and daring Parker being killed during the rescue of his sweetheart would make his videotapes even more appealing to the American public; but a ranting, raving lunatic who was roaming the nation proclaiming himself an escaped POW, well that would never do.

Parker had to be given the news of Juanita's "disappearance" in such a way that he would take it calmly, rationally, reasonably.

That's why the Director had sent Alma Hammond to break the news to Parker.

*　*　*

Drew pushed his chair away from the kitchen table and dropped his napkin beside his plate. He loosened his tie and unbuttoned his collar.

"You want to tell me about it now or wait awhile yet?"

Cat stood up and began to clear away the dishes.

"Tell you what?" she asked. Her eyes avoided his.

"Whatever it is you want to break to me gently," he said. "We've spent the last hour talking about TV programs, the political situation in Argentina, our vacation next summer, and the last novel you read. You're working so hard at trying to make this a *routine* evening, you obviously want to try to slip something into our conversation in hopes that I won't give it the weight of consideration it deserves. Now out with it. What gives?"

Cat shook her head. Either the man was clairvoyant or she was wearing her emotions on her sleeve.

"Oh, Drew. Was I that bad? Really that obvious?"

"The makeup was the immediate giveaway," he explained with a smile. "You had time to change out of whatever dress you had been wearing, but that 'come-hither' makeup was still on your face. I've never seen you use three perfectly descending shades of blue on your eyes just to match a simple housedress." He kissed her lightly and added, "Besides, I didn't spend 20 years negotiating contracts without learning how to read people pretty well. So, can we cut the charades and get down to some real talking?"

Cat poured them each a cup of coffee. "Let's go into the living room, okay?"

They entered the large room and Drew eased down onto the puffy velvet-covered couch. Cat pulled a wingback chair near the coffee table and sat opposite her husband.

"I got a call from Lillian Thompson just before you came home. She needs my help, Drew."

"Something serious?"

Cat nodded. "She's going to sue Michigan Technologies for theft, slander, and fraud, and she wants me to be a consulting attorney on the case."

"*You*, Catherine? But why? Your courtroom experience was limited to Legal Aid volunteer work when you were in law school. You're not ready to square off against veteran attorneys. I admire your loyalty to Lillian, sweetheart, and I'm not knocking your intelligence, but for a case like this you need lots of experience."

Cat was not offended. One thing she appreciated about Drew was that he never patronized her. He gave her his opinions straight from the shoulder, but he also gave fair consideration to any differing viewpoints she might have. It made not only for a good marriage, but also a good friendship.

"You're not saying anything I haven't already said to Lillian," agreed Cat. "But she needs me there anyway, Drew. She's scared, and she needs someone she can trust to be at her side through all this. Besides . . . there's another matter."

Drew lifted both eyebrows. "Which is?"

"Some unfinished personal business for Lillian and me. Lillian told me that Roderick Davis is now a partner with the Detroit law firm of Copas, Schweickart and Sherrill. Since Roderick used to work for Michigan Technologies, his law firm assigned him to serve as its legal advisor to the company.

Apparently that law firm has had the Michigan Technologies account ever since Lillian's father started the company."

"So that means that if you agree to represent Lillian in this case, you'll be facing off against Roderick Davis in court, is that it? I thought you told me everything between you and him was over."

"It was . . . is. . . ."

"Then why this?" asked Drew.

"Because he's a horrid man, that's why," said Cat, raising her voice. "I know that if I take this case it'll seem like I'll be out for revenge because Roderick broke off our engagement and left me alone in Nashville a year ago. But that's not it, Drew. Honest, it's not. My Christian faith has helped me get past the hateful thoughts I used to have for Roderick. You, of all people, know how I've changed since I accepted Christ in my life. I don't want to hurt anyone . . . not even Roderick."

She left her chair and sat on the couch next to her husband.

"But Roderick's a cold man, Drew. He wouldn't think twice about doing anything necessary to Lillian in order to win this case. He hurt her so much before. He fired her and then broke off their engagement and gave me her ring. I can't let him hurt her like that again. She's the closest thing I've ever had to a sister. I really care about her."

Drew was silent for a moment. At last he said, "The case could drag on for weeks, maybe even months. It would be an exhausting ordeal. And we'd be apart most of that time. I'm not at all sure I could handle that."

Cat nodded.

"Well . . . uh . . . that's something else I have to tell you."

"What do you mean?"

Cat reached over and laced her slim, soft fingers amidst Drew's large, strong hands. "I wanted it to be more romantic than this, really I did. I had planned to do a lot of special things and to look pretty and to play music . . . and to fix some . . ."

"Catherine . . . ?"

"I'm pregnant, Drew. We're going to have a baby. I saw the doctor this morning."

Drew didn't flinch at the announcement. Instead, a slow wide grin spread across his face. Gently he pulled Cat into his arms and started to stroke her hair with one hand.

"I . . . I didn't want to get my hopes up," he said in a low voice. "When you weren't feeling well the past few mornings, I began to wonder if it just might be this. I so desperately hoped it was. I went through this once before, you know . . . back when Marie found out about Todd. The years haven't changed the excitement. Catherine, this is marvelous." He shook his head almost in amazement. "You have no idea how wonderful I feel at this moment. I didn't think I could love you any more, but right now . . . at this minute. . . ."

Cat began to cry softly. "I love you too, Drew. I'm so glad you're happy about the baby."

"It's the greatest anniversary present you've given me so far," he teased.

Cat had to laugh at that, amidst her tears of happiness. Then a related thought came into her mind. She turned her head and whispered, "It *is* still our anniversary. Care to maintain a tradition?"

Drew lifted her into his arms and carried her from the living room.

*　　*　　*

Scott Parker's eyes revealed the pent-up rage within him. His fixed stare was riveting. Alma felt mesmerized by the look of judgment that Scott was casting on her.

"You *lost* Juanita?" he said in measured tones. "*Lost* her?"

"She was moved," Alma countered. "Our people weren't able to follow the car. We'll find her again. Believe me. We're making inquiries already. We're checking every possible lead."

"Making inquiries?" repeated Scott. "You make it sound as if you're calling all the local hotels and checking their registry books. Knowing Bentancourt, he could have Juanita in an asylum or a work camp or even off in another country by now. Wherever she is, she's in misery. I've been in Communist prisons, Alma. I know what they do to their inmates there. It's hideous. I want Juanita found and *now*!"

"So do we, so do we." Alma assured him. "I feel a personal responsibility for Juanita. I recruited her, remember? She's not just some name on a roster of agents to me. She's a person. I know her. We've worked together for years. I want to get her out of there as much as you do. You'll just have to believe me when I tell you that I'm doing everything possible to find her."

Scott considered that. He had never cared for Alma's by-the-book way of doing things. It always seemed too calculated, so systematic, as if every human crisis that arose could be resolved by following an established procedure. Nevertheless, Alma had never lied to him and she had always done her best to help him or Juanita in any way she could. Scott realized that he and Alma would never see eye to eye on *how* things should be done, but in fairness he had to admit that Alma truly was on his side. And Juanita's.

"I'm sorry, Alma. It's all this inactivity, this infernal waiting. It makes me tense. I hate it."

"It's okay. I understand."

Scott checked his watch. "You're spending the night here?" he asked.

"Yes, but I have to put through a call to my Director. He's waiting to hear how you took the news."

"Hold off a bit on that, will you? I need a few minutes alone to think about all this. I'm going over to the chapel. I'll be back in half an hour."

Alma rose from her chair. "I'll tell Kent to stay here. But don't be gone too long. My Director hates to wait as much as you do."

Alma made a high sign for Scott's bodyguard not to follow him.

When Scott walked out, Alma bit a fingernail. *If he makes a run for it, we're all doomed*, she thought. She was banking on Scott's honor. Her Director would not approve. But then, there was a lot about her Director that Alma didn't approve of. It all averaged out. This was a judgment call, and Alma felt she was better able to judge Scott Parker than her Director was.

She noted the time. She would wait 30 minutes, no more.

*   *   *

Lillian Thompson checked the wall clock. She smiled. Everything was all right. Cat had told her that if she didn't call back by 9 P.M. then her answer would be yes, she would meet Lillian in Detroit and take the case.

It was 9:01 P.M. and Lillian was breathing easier.

"Thank You, Lord," she prayed. "Now please be with us."

*   *   *

Scott didn't turn on the lights when he entered the small chapel. The moonlight through the uncurtained windows helped him find his way to the front pew. He sat, head bowed and silent, for several minutes.

"Lord . . . Lord," he whispered hoarsely, "why can't *anything* in life be simple? I thought that when I got back to the States everything would be normal again. I just wanted a job, a wife, and a chance to be near the people I love. Now Lillian's facing a big lawsuit and Juanita's in prison and here I am, still a man with no identity.

"Why, Lord? Why? I've done everything I could to serve You here at the mission settlement. I've asked nothing in return except that You protect my sister and my fianceé. I trusted You. I depended on You. How could You turn from me like this?

Please, God, help me understand Your ways. Help me know what I'm supposed to do."

Scott fell forward on his knees. "Hear me, Lord. Don't hide from me. Show me what I must do. Please, Lord, show me . . . show me."

*   *   *

Cat lay awake listening to the steady, rhythmic breathing of her husband. She felt the gentleness of his breath on her bare shoulder. She could smell the mild fragrance of his after-shave lotion. She felt secure, protected, sheltered. This was ideal. Why would she ever want to leave the care of the man she loved, especially to enter an angry arena to battle a man whose very name disgusted her? Why, indeed?

She knew the answer. She wasn't going to Detroit to face Roderick, but rather herself. She had told Drew that she didn't hate Roderick, and with all her heart she wanted to believe that. But she wouldn't know for sure if she had really buried that spite and vengeance unless she faced Roderick and found out for sure.

If she could stick to the facts of the case and not be swayed by old love or new anger, she would then be convinced that she had successfully put Roderick out of her system. She had prayed about the matter for a long time and had turned the anger she felt for Roderick over to God, as Drew had said she should do. Drew had even forgiven Nick Ingresano for all he had done to try and ruin Drew's career back in Nashville. That kind of grace had been almost too much for a new Christian like herself to comprehend, but it had given her something to strive for in conquering her bitter memories about Roderick.

Still, she carried doubts. And in her times of private prayer she had asked God to help her remove the skepticism, to show her a way in which she could put Roderick behind her. She had wondered how and even *if* God would answer her prayer. And that's when the call had come from Lillian.

Cat had known she would agree to go to Detroit. She had known it as soon as Lillian started explaining her plans. It was her destiny. There was no way she could avoid it.

*   *   *

Alma was right at the point of sending Kent to search for Scott when he suddenly appeared in the doorway of the settlement dining hall.

"Give me a minute, Kent," said Scott. The bodyguard flashed a questioning glance at Alma, who nodded approval. Kent walked outside.

Scott walked over to where Alma was seated. He remained standing.

"I thought maybe you had lost your way," said Alma.

Scott shook his head. "I had to make a call."

"Call? But you aren't allowed to call anyone except me. You gave your word."

"I did call you," explained Scott. "Your office, that is. Then I asked to be transferred to the Director. They put me through when I said it was in regard to Operation Homing Pigeon. Isn't that what I'm still known as back in D.C.?"

"Why on earth would you try to contact the Director without going through me? That's not procedure. Besides, you knew I planned to call him tonight anyway."

"But you wouldn't have relayed my message. And it was important. I had to discuss a deal with the Director."

"A deal? How dare you go over my head! What kind of a deal?"

"Something you never would have agreed to," continued Scott. "The Director is more pragmatic, however. He's going to offer Bentancourt a trade. Me for Juanita."

Alma sprang to her feet.

"You can't! They'll kill you!"

Scott slowly turned his back on Alma and stepped a few paces away. Without turning around he said, "They might, yes. But then again, I might get lucky a second time around and find myself swapped back for somebody else Bentancourt wants."

Alma eased herself down into her chair. "It'll never happen," she said dogmatically. "The only reason Bentancourt traded you the first time was because he had assigned Juanita to kill you before you could tell your story. As long as you're alive, he'll never feel safe. He'll have you shot ten minutes after he takes you into custody."

Scott turned around, a smile spreading across his thin face. "And many happy returns to you, too, Alma. Wow, what a depressing cheerleader you are."

Alma looked pleadingly at Scott. "Call it off," she begged. "Juanita would be haunted by the guilt of it for the rest of her life. If you really love her, you won't do this. Scott, please. Let us try other ways. There's absolutely no way you can come out of this alive."

"Without Juanita I'm already dead," he argued. "It's been decided. I'm supposed to tell you to return to Washington by noon tomorrow. It's out of your hands now, Alma. Whatever happens, you're blameless. I've brought this on myself."

"And receiving your personal absolution is supposed to make me lose all concern for you and Juanita, is that it? Well, I'm human too, mister. I told you before, people are more to me than just names on a roster or stickers on a file folder."

Scott hung his head. "Forgive me, Alma. I'm a desperate man. I can't bear the thought of Juanita sitting in some stone cell while we're all here, free. I'm sorry I went over your head on this. I couldn't think of any other option."

"And the Director agreed? So easily?"

"It's simply a matter of priorities," said Scott. "My information is all transferred to videotapes. Juanita's is still in her head. I'm disposable. She's vital. I knew the Director would see it that way."

"What? As long as you can rationalize a trip to the grave, then suicide is acceptable? Is that it? You've really gone off the deep end this time, Scott. Okay, if you want me out of your life so badly, you've got it. Go get yourself killed. See if I care. But keep in mind, *you* turned on *me*. I would have never done this to you."

She slammed the door on her way out.

Scott, as he had been so many other times in his life, was left standing alone with his troubles.

*   *   *

At dawn the next day, Roderick Davis was up early to spend an hour hitting volleys against the backboard of an indoor tennis court before having breakfast. On Saturday he followed a more relaxed, half-day schedule. He arrived at the law firm at 8:55 A.M., still revved up from his early-morning workout. His secretary, Jennifer Wilkinson, followed him into his personal office.

"Have you heard?" she asked anxiously.

Roderick started to open the day's edition of the *New York Times* on his desk. "Heard what?" he said with little interest. "Get me some coffee, will you, Jen?"

"Mr. Mason from Michigan Technologies has been trying to reach you since seven this morning," Jennifer continued, ignoring the request for coffee. "He's already called three of the other partners at home. He's really upset."

Roderick set the paper down. "Upset? About what?"

"*Her!*" said Jennifer. "She's suing the company. The papers were delivered by overnight courier. She's hired a law firm here in Detroit to represent her and she's bringing in a special legal counsel from Washington, D.C.—the wife of a U.S. Senator, no less."

Roderick raised both hands.

"What in the world are you jabbering about?" he demanded. "Who is being sued *by whom?*"

"The founder's daughter," explained Jennifer. "Lillian Parker—her married name is Thompson—is suing Michigan

Technologies. She claims her family stock was stolen from her. She's seeking three million dollars in reclaimed assets, plus another million compensation for defamation of character, libel, slander, fraud . . ."

"That'll do," interrupted Roderick. "Get Mr. Mason on the phone for me. I'll hear all this firsthand, if you don't mind. Oh, and while I'm talking to Mr. Mason, hook your modem into M-T's computer and get me a printout of everything they have on file on J. J. Parker II and Lillian Parker."

"Yes, sir," said Jennifer, somewhat deflated over having been cut off before being able to finish her gossip. "I'll bring your coffee when I come back with the printouts, Mr. Davis."

"Oh, one other thing," said Roderick. "This special counsel from Washington. Would the name be Mrs. Catherine Sanders?"

Jennifer looked surprised. "Then you did know about it?"

"No, not really," admitted Roderick, "but you don't need to be Sherlock Holmes to figure out what's going on here. Ha! This will be fun. I'll chew them to ribbons once we get in that courtroom. The scorned woman times two, is it? Good enough then."

Roderick rubbed his hands together in anticipation of the pending face-off. He would have all the advantages. He would be magnificent. Once again he would be the company's grand defender. And the press coverage in the business periodicals? Incredible! He could already visualize the headlines the editors would come up with to relay how the embezzler's money-grubbing daughter was outmaneuvered by the suave and clever corporate attorney: QUEEN OF TARTS UNDONE BY KING OF TORTS. Ha! Delightful! The only difficulty this case would present would be in trying to keep it going long enough to milk enough publicity from it. With nothing to base a case on, Cat and Lillian might be tossed out of court in a day or two. He'd have to hold back a bit at first. It would only serve to make his eventual triumph all the more stunning.

Jennifer cleared her throat. The sound broke Roderick from his daydreams. He swiveled his chair in her direction.

"Oh, my coffee. Thank you, Jen. Just set it here. Did you reach Irving Mason?"

"His wife told me he's already on his way over here," she answered.

"All the better," mused Roderick. "And the printouts?"

Jennifer shrugged her shoulders. "I tapped into the computer and called for a scan-and-search, but nothing came up under the two names you gave me. So I called M-T's data processing center on the off-chance that Ruth Burns might be working some extra hours. She was and she did a manual check for me. You're not going to believe this."

Roderick looked concerned. "Try me."

"Ruth said that everything related to J. J. and Lillian Parker—in fact, the whole Parker family—had been purged from the computer."

"Purged!"

"Not only that," continued Jennifer, "but the backup hard-copy files are gone too. Ruth looked for them herself. She said it was as if someone on the inside had purposely tried to get a corner on all the company's information about the Parkers. Ever hear of anything so odd?"

Roderick suddenly seemed distracted, lost in new thoughts. His eyes narrowed.

"Have you, sir?" repeated Jennifer. "I mean, ever heard of such an odd thing?"

Roderick ignored the question. "Go find me some aspirin," was all he said.

CHAPTER 7

Scott had slept fitfully all night.

Alma had apparently changed her mind about spending the night at the mission settlement. After their argument she had simply vanished; Scott presumed she had returned to Washington. More surprising than that, however, was the fact that Kent had gone with her. Kent hadn't left Scott's side since the day he had arrived at Scott's hospital room nearly a year ago. Now he was gone.

Alma obviously hadn't been kidding. She really didn't care about Scott anymore. *Go get yourself killed. See if I care*, she had said.

Bizarre dreams kept Scott rolling in his bed all night. He was on the bottom of the ocean in a diving bell, trapped, with no one to pull him up. He was in an endless tunnel, feeling his hands along the wet, cold walls, inching his way forward, yet never coming to an opening. He was sloshing his way through an algae-covered swamp, battling swarms of mosquitoes and trying to elude pursuing alligators and pythons.

He awoke with a start. His heart was racing and he couldn't seem to catch his breath. He eased himself into a sitting position and fought to get control of himself. Ever so slowly, he began to regain his composure. Nights had often been this terrifying during his imprisonment in Vietnam, but since getting home he had steadily learned to relax and return to normal sleeping habits.

Scott looked at this hands. They were shaking. Why this sudden return of the night terrors? He knew the reason. In a few days he would either be back inside a Communist prison camp or standing against a firing squad wall. Both thoughts sent fearful chills over him. He really wasn't sure he would have the strength to face imprisonment again.

He needed to find Mom and Pop Mead and talk with them.

Scott dressed hurriedly and headed toward the garden patch which the Meads kept near their small parsonage. The mid-August sun was already up, but the early mountain air was still cool. Scott could see Pastor Mead using his pocket handkerchief to clean off the blade of his garden hoe.

"Whatsoever a man soweth, that shall he also reap," announced Pop Mead as Scott approached. "That is, if he has the patience to wait long enough. It takes two summers for strawberries to yield their fruit. Did you know that, Scotty? I set these slips out during a visit here last May, a few months before we came back to live here permanently. I knew I wouldn't get anything from them last season. This year, though, I had fresh berries for my cereal. Speaking of which . . . you're just in time for breakfast. Come in."

Scott looked away. "Actually, I don't have any appetite. I was hoping we could talk."

"I figured you'd be over early," said Pop. "I told Bea to set a plate for you. Food's ready. Let's talk and eat at the same time. Bea's taken the pickup to town for some sewing supplies. She won't be back until lunch."

"You knew I was coming? This early?"

"Had a hunch," said Pop, leading the way into the cabin parsonage.

"But how?"

Pop pumped some water and washed his hands at the sink. He then began to move the breakfast food from the wood stove to the table.

"Your friend Miss Hammond came by here before she pulled out last night. We talked for more than an hour. She told me about your plan to get Juanita out of Cuba. I kind of figured you'd come by early to tell me your version of it."

Scott showed some surprise. "Alma's definitely gone, then? Back to Washington?"

"Left around midnight. Took Kent with her. I sure hated to see that boy go. He really was a good one for pitching in and helping. As long as he could keep you in sight, he'd do any-thing. I always wondered if he grew up on a farm. He could handle an axe, a shovel, a hammer, even a plow. Just didn't talk much."

"He didn't talk because he was trained to listen," explained Scott. "He probably learned how to handle tools in survival training in the Green Berets or whatever other unit he was assigned to before joining the CIA. Kent was the Great Stone Face. He never talked about himself. You're right, though, about him being a good worker. He's that all right."

"So is Miss Hammond. Are you sure you did the right thing in getting her removed from overseeing Juanita's rescue?"

"No. But I had to do something."

Pastor Mead bowed his head and said a blessing for the food. After he lifted his eyes, he spent a minute buttering two biscuits and salting his scrambled eggs. Scott only toyed with his food.

"How much did Alma tell you?" asked Scott.

"All of it," said Pop. "Juanita was moved, and it made you panic. You called Alma's Director and talked him into trying to swap you for Juanita. Alma's convinced you'll be dead before the ink is dry on the exchange documents if that deal goes through."

Pop finished some sausage and took a deep drink of black coffee. Scott stared at him.

"My pending death doesn't seem to have spoiled your appe-tite," said Scott.

Pop poured gravy over his remaining eggs. "A man's gotta do what a man's gotta do. Pass the pepper, will ya?"

Scott flinched noticeably.

"That's it? That's your only comment?"

Pop halted his fork midway to his open mouth. He peered over the top of his bifocals at Scott. "Uh, well, *vaya con dios*, and all that. We sure do wish you well, boy."

Scott's eyes widened. "You wish me well? You *wish me well!* I'm going to Cuba to get my head blown off and all you can think to say is that you wish me well? I can't believe you, Pop. Haven't you been paying attention? I may never see you again. Doesn't that bother you? Don't you even care?"

Both men eyed each other intensely. Finally both looked away.

Slowly Pop pushed his chair back and rose from the table. He left his half-eaten breakfast. He strode over to the cabin's door. He looked out over the settlement. For several minutes his eyes surveyed the scene before him. The fields of corn were Kelly green; russet and yellow husks were swollen and pointed skyward from every angle. The little chapel nearby was sporting a new coat of tan paint, a newly mortared foundation, and new shutters for the windows. The flagpost was painted and a new flag was atop the mast. The paths between the buildings were outlined by large rocks buried halfway underground with their top halves painted white. A new chicken coop and toolshed had been built since spring. Everywhere people were moving about, working and helping. The children were playing tag or frolicking with pets.

Pop Mead felt a tear come into one eye. Angrily he denied himself this sentimentality and instead thought heavily of how the idyllic scene before him might now be threatened. He cleared his throat roughly.

"You're a fine one to ask if I care about you," he said, turning to face Scott. "How dare you question *my* feelings after what you did last night?"

"Me?" gasped Scott. "But . . . but what?"

"Week after week, month after month, we've cared for you as if you were our own son," admonished Pop. "Like the strawberries, we figured you needed a year of care before you'd bear any fruit. We gave you that time and care, Scotty. When you needed a nurse after you arrived here, didn't Bea sit all night by your bed putting cold compresses on your forehead and holding your hand? When you needed someone to talk to you, didn't I always go for a walk or go fishing or pray with you? Didn't we feed you and give you some useful responsibilities around here and love you like real parents?"

". . . but I've loved you too, Pop. . . ."

"Then last night you decided all on your own to pull off this crazy scheme of yours. You didn't talk to us about it or come to us afterward—you just made a brazen announcement to Alma Hammond and then went back to your cabin. Now, today, you've come over here to have me hear of your noble deed so that I can pat you on the head and tell you how proud I am of you. Well, you'd better look elsewhere for your praise. Bea spent the whole night crying while I paced the floor trying to decide whether or not I should go over and shake you until your teeth rattled."

Scott was awestruck by Pastor Mead's response. The man had always been a rock, the very example of calmness and logic. His behavior now was completely out of the norm. It was so . . . so . . . *unguarded*.

"Hasn't a year with me taught you anything, Scott? Haven't I always told you to think and pray and meditate and even seek the advice of other brothers and sisters of like faith? Haven't I always stressed that you need to see the full scope of things?"

"Really, Pop, I meant no harm or insult," Scott insisted. "This was a private matter between Juanita and me."

"Private matter? You can't be serious. You've got a sister who has spent the last year trying to get used to the fact that her dead brother is alive again. Now you want to take that joy away from her. It would devastate her, believe me. And you've got a good friend in Alma Hammond, but you've seriously damaged her career and you've violated the trust she had in you. That was completely uncalled for. And, what's more, you've got Bea and me. In our quiet moments we've prayed that when we got too old to carry on the work here, you might step in as supervisor . . . maybe even as pastor, too."

"Pastor! Me?"

"Why not? You love the Word. And you've done a tremendous job of leading the men's Bible study on Thursday nights.

The people here trust you. You've been able to speak their language. They're poor, but the 12 years you spent in POW camps makes this place seem like paradise. You've helped them see what they have, not what they don't have. God has prepared you for a very special ministry, Scott. That's another reason why it so grieves me to think you might follow through with this plan of yours to go to Cuba."

Scott's limbs suddenly felt very heavy. He lowered his head and raked his fingers through his hair. "I didn't mean for it to seem this way. I just didn't want anybody else to be burdened by my problems."

"Bea is crushed," said Pastor Mead. "She really didn't need those sewing supplies. She just couldn't be here to look you in the face this morning. She loves you and Lillian. You're the son and daughter we always wanted, but never were blessed with."

Scott slowly stood to his feet and crossed the room.

"Pop, you've got to understand, I'm not trying to act like a hero. Really. The truth is, I'm so afraid of going back to prison my stomach is twisted in 20 different knots. I went to the chapel and tried to pray last night. When I hit upon this idea of trading myself for Juanita—something I had warned Alma I would do if she couldn't get Juanita home—I acted on it right away.

"It wasn't that I didn't value your advice or input, it was just that I was worried that I might not go through with it if I didn't act immediately. So I did. I made the call and committed myself. I'm sorry if I've worried or hurt you or Mom or Alma, but I just couldn't live from moment to moment until I knew that Juanita would be freed. I love her more than my very life, Pop. Surely you, a minister, should be able to comprehend such a depth of love. Please, Pop, give me your support in this. I need your approval. Please!"

Pastor Mead reached out hesitantly and gently touched Scott's hair.

"It's too hard, son, it's too hard. You're my whole life. We're all so happy here. I can't bear the thought of sending you off, so far away, knowing in advance that you'll suffer so desperately and then be killed. It's so unfair. You've done nothing wrong."

"But I'm the only one who can be sent," said Scott. "That's the realization that came to me again last night in the chapel. There's no other way. I'm terrified about it, but my love will provide the strength I'll need. I have to go. I have to."

Pop Mead put his short, calloused hands on both sides of Scott's face and caressed him. He pulled Scott toward him and the men embraced in a bond of mutual devotion.

"Do what you must, son. You know I'll be proud of you."

*   *   *

Guadalupe Bentancourt had "contacts" in every realm of the Cuban government. He made it a point to provide favors for these special friends in advance of needing any return favors on his part. In this way, useful people were always available.

One such contact was Captain Juan Reyes, an officer in the Cuban Army responsible for security at the hospital where "political surgeries" were performed. A separate wing of Ché Guevara Memorial Hospital had been set aside for "mental readjustment procedures." Individuals who caused the state too much trouble were arrested and brought here for brain surgery. When they left, they not only could not remember their anti-Cuban slogans, they couldn't even remember their names.

Captain Reyes controlled the paperwork which arranged for prisoners to be transferred to the special wing of Guevara Memorial. Bentancourt had no intention of letting Juanita come to trial as a spy. Though the trial would be good propaganda against the U.S.A., it might also be too revealing for Bentancourt. So he arranged for Juanita to be released into his personal custody. He then filed a medical request with Captain Reyes, asking that Reyes and his troops escort Juanita later that week to the hospital for a general checkup. In private conversation Bentancourt convinced Reyes to have Juanita's paperwork become mixed up with a woman scheduled for "readjustment" surgery. Reyes was to make it look like an administrative slipup had occurred and the wrong woman had been operated on. Reyes promised Bentancourt he could handle it.

Captain Reyes was on good terms with most of the hospital personnel. One woman, however, had never warmed to him. Head Nurse Rosa Garcia was a stickler for procedure; additionally, she would not tolerate any rough treatment of her patients, even those who were prisoners. This had been the source of frustration on more than one occasion for Captain Reyes. He now wished to use the Juanita Martinez "mix-up" as a way of putting a black mark on the career of nurse Garcia.

On the afternoon after Reyes and Bentancourt had had their secret talk, Reyes came to the hospital at 5:00 P.M. Rosa Garcia's shift had ended at 4:00 P.M., so Reyes now felt safe in invading the hospital's paperwork. The general information forms on Juanita Martinez had been delivered earlier that morning. So had the papers for a female prisoner named Carmen Rodriguez, a political activist. Knowing the efficiency of the hospital staff, both forms would no doubt already be in the file cabinet.

It was Reyes who always came to the hospital to deliver the "treatment procedure" requests of the government whenever prisoners were brought for medical attention. His plan now was simple. He would attach an order for a general checkup to the information form of Carmen Rodriguez and attach an order for a "mental readjustment procedure" to the information form of Juanita Martinez. In a few days, when both treatments were completed, it would be discovered—much to everyone's great surprise—that the wrong prisoner had been operated on. Juanita Martinez would be mentally unfit for trial . . . or anything else. An investigation would ensue and Rosa Garcia would be found to have been negligent in her duties.

As Reyes flipped through the file folders and did his work, he smiled. Not only would this put him in well with Ambassador Bentancourt, it would also provide him an avenue of revenge for the iron-willed Rosa Garcia. He felt that nothing could foil his plan.

What Reyes was unaware of was the fact that at that very moment, in a modest apartment some miles from the hospital, Rosa Garcia was studying a copy of the information file that her nursing department had received that morning on the prisoner Juanita Martinez.

"Isn't this just wishful thinking on your part, my dear?" Ricardo Garcia asked his wife. "After all, Martinez is a very common name. So is Juanita, for that matter."

Rosa nodded her agreement. "I know, I know. But all the other information makes it too much of a coincidence. It says here she is exactly the same age my daughter would be now. And this photo of her—it's a story in itself. Look at how her eyes and lips and hair are identical to mine. And the shape of her face and the form of her nose are exactly like Jim's. Besides, it says here that her eyes are blue. How many blue-eyed Cubans have you ever met? It's *got* to be her."

"But if this is so, how can she be here in Cuba? Your cousin told you that your father had sent your baby to America."

Rosa tapped the papers before her. "This woman was arrested last week as an American agent. That's why she's in prison. If she *is* my daughter, it's possible she could have made it to the States and later came back as a spy or something like that."

"But what can you do?" asked Ricardo. "How can you find out if she is your daughter or not? And even if you do, there's nothing you can do to help her in there."

"She's just been moved from Havana and is under house arrest at a government-owned retreat center 16 miles east of here," answered Rosa. "Two of the nurses under my supervision will be rotating shifts out there watching over her. I could trade duties one night with one of them and go see this woman for myself."

Ricardo's face revealed concerns. "It sounds very dangerous to me. Why risk your life, darling, if there's nothing you can do anyway? It can only lead to misery for you. I thought you were happy with me and that you had forgotten the past. Haven't I been good to you these past ten years?"

"I love you, Ricardo," Rosa assured her husband. "But I can never forget the past. You are my present life and my future. I'm yours forever. But I've carried love in my heart for my daughter for years. I've imagined what it would be like to see her one day, if only for a moment."

"But this woman in prison," interrupted Ricardo. "What could you say to her?"

"I have no idea," said Rosa. "Maybe nothing. Maybe everything. That isn't important. All I need to do is see her. If she is my daughter, I'll know it. I have to go to her, Ricardo. And I will. Somehow, I will get to this woman named Juanita Martinez."

*   *   *

Cat Sanders was not one to pack lightly. When she entered the opulent foyer of the Westin Hotel in Detroit's Renaissance Center, the afternoon shift of bellhops snapped to attention and then gaped at the assortment of taupe luggage piled atop endless racks weaving through the doors on wobbly casters.

Her arrival time had been projected by the concierge to be 4:45 P.M., and all employees knew that the wife of Tennessee's junior senator was to be accorded the full VIP treatment. The staff was prepared with flowers, the customary fruit basket, and a complimentary setup of Perrier's, lemon slices, and ice. The manager had done his homework well and knew the beverage preference of his special guest.

What no one was prepared for was the special guest's extensive collection of luggage. As one suitcase after another was passed from the taxi driver to the doorman to the carts, word went forth to stock Room 807 with extra hangers and to add a temporary wardrobe rack and a small chest of drawers.

"Maybe we should vacate the west wing and turn it into a closet," suggested the bell captain under his breath.

Cat had been so anxious to join Lillian in Detroit that she had given her travel agent carte blanche in making arrangements. She had forgotten to specify that she didn't want to arrive when traffic was at its peak, and she certainly didn't want to be driven across town when the late August heat was at its most intense. However, the travel agent had put expediency before comfort and had booked her on an after-lunch shuttle from Dulles Airport to Chicago and then on a "puddle-jumper" to Detroit's Metro.

Not only did Cat feel wilted when she entered the hotel, but her stomach was also protesting the bumpy trip. She knew, of course, that this was all part of what Drew called her "delectable condition," but the knowledge didn't quiet the symptoms. Waiting at the reservation desk to check in, she savored the thought of taking a hot bath and stretching out for a nap before calling Lillian. But a note, left with the clerk before lunch, urged her to phone her friend by 5 P.M. That left barely enough time for a sip of Pepto-Bismol.

*   *   *

"Want to drive through the tunnel and have dinner in Windsor?" asked Lillian. "When I worked in Detroit we always used to go to Canada for fish and chips on weekends. Who knows, I might even bump into some of the old office gang."

The Pepto-Bismol hadn't calmed Cat's queasiness, and the mention of fish and chips caused new waves of nausea to wash over her.

She was looking forward to sharing the news of her pregnancy with Lillian, but didn't want to do it in the negative terms of morning sickness. She wanted to talk about the joy

that surfaced every time she thought of the tiny being growing within her. She somehow wanted to communicate the
incredible love she felt for the man who had changed her life
in so many ways. But at the moment she could hardly talk
about anything, least of all food. The doctor had warned her
there would be discomforts. He had even offered remedies.
What was it that he had suggested? Carbonated drinks and
soda crackers . . . yes, that was it.

"I think I'll pass on dinner," Cat said with a smile. "We had a
snack on the plane. Why don't we just order from room
service and I'll have some ginger ale and a few crackers and
cheese."

Lillian agreed, dialed the kitchen, and ordered a patty melt
with extra onions, a basket of fried mushrooms and a wedge
of pecan pie large enough to split with a friend, please.

"Do you feel okay, Cat? You look sort of pale."

"Just a little airsickness," she replied. "The flight was sort
of bumpy."

Lillian looked at the mounds of taupe luggage that en-
croached on the sitting area and limited its occupants to one
path to the powder room and another to the bedroom.

"I know court cases can drag on," she joked, "but I had
hoped we'd be home for the holidays."

"Labor Day or Christmas?" teased Cat.

She loosened the top button of her skirt, kicked off her
shoes, and propped her feet on the bed. The air conditioner
finally had rid the suite of its stuffiness, and the temperature
was holding at a comfortable 75 degrees. Cat rested her head
on the back of the chair and breathed deeply. She decided if
she could just stay in the chair without moving and without
being subjected to the taste or scent of food, she might survive
after all.

"Business before pleasure, as the tired cliché goes," she
said. "Can you work on an empty stomach?"

Lillian nodded and passed a thick file folder to Cat.

"Here's your homework," Lillian explained. "I've already given a copy to the law firm downtown, so we'll all be working with the same information when we meet Monday morning."

"Monday?"

"Nine-thirty sharp."

Cat put on her tortoise-shell glasses and began a careful study of the documents. At one point she lifted her pen to underline a phrase.

"May I?" she asked.

"Of course. They're yours," said Lillian.

Cat looked at her thoughtfully over the top of her glasses. Her friend seemed so earnest about the togetherness of their mission, but Cat still wasn't certain what role she was to play in it. After all, Lillian had retained the city's top law partnership to represent her. If they couldn't prove J. J. Parker's innocence, no one could. Least of all her.

"Why am I *really* here, Lill?"

Lillian started to say something trite about moral support, friends to the end, or sticking together through thick and thin. But she decided to be honest instead.

"Because I'm scared, Cat. More scared than I've ever been in my whole life."

Cat nodded slowly, encouraging Lillian to go on.

"I feel like I'm the one who's on trial here," explained Lillian. "I know *what* I'm doing is right, but I'm not sure *why* I'm doing it is right." Lillian smiled at Cat's puzzled expression. "Look, my father was wrongfully accused of stealing from his own company. A lot of people who believed in him were deeply hurt by the news of the missing funds. Even if they didn't lose any money, they lost respect for my father. They had believed in him . . . trusted him . . . and suddenly they felt tricked."

Cat shrugged, still not following Lillian's logic. "So now you have a chance to prove that your father was innocent," she said. "People who believed in him will have their faith restored. His name will be cleared. I understand all that; what I don't understand is why you're afraid. Sure, every lawsuit carries some risk, but from the looks of this file, you're going to win this hands down."

"I'm not sure I can explain my fear," admitted Lillian. "It has something to do with pride, revenge, jealousy, and a lot of other negative traits that Christians aren't supposed to have."

Cat turned her head to one side as if she were beginning to understand. "And Roderick?" she said. "It has something to do with him, too, doesn't it?"

Lillian nodded. "A part of me wants to get even with him for the hurt he caused me. So many memories came back yesterday when I drove downtown, Cat. It was the first time I had been near Michigan Technologies since that awful day when Roderick told me the board of directors had fired me— *dismissed* was the word he used—and had taken my stock. I'll never forget that afternoon. Never! He said he was the only one who defended me to the board. I remember feeling so shaken and alone. I wanted him to hold me, but he was cold. Incredibly cold. Then he said he wanted to postpone our wedding plans. . . ."

Cat shivered.

"I'm afraid that my motive for being here isn't as noble as it seems," continued Lillian. "Suddenly I have evidence that can salvage my father's name and destroy Roderick Davis' reputation. By doing one, I accomplish the other. But my father is dead and can't possibly benefit from any of this; Roderick is alive and can be ruined by it. So why am I *really* doing it?"

Cat got up and adjusted the thermostat on the air conditioner. She had felt a chill and didn't know whether to attribute it to the temperature or to the conversation.

"I had some of the same thoughts when you called me in Washington and asked me to help you," said Cat. "I knew I'd make the trip as soon as you explained the circumstances. But I wondered about my motives. Sure, I wanted to help you, but I knew that by helping you I'd be hurting Roderick. And remember, Lill, Roderick caused me as much pain and embarrassment as he caused you. I'll never forget the party my parents had the night before Roderick and I left for Nashville to open our law practice. The whole town turned out to wish us well. A few days later Roderick had reclaimed his 'friendship' ring and had left me in a strange city without a partner, a friend, or a nickel in my jeans."

Their room service order arrived, and Cat was relieved that the smell of Lillian's dinner was almost inviting to her. She gingerly nibbled on a fried mushroom cap, carefully washing the bites down with sips of ginger ale.

"Maybe we should forget all this courtroom nonsense and go home and start families," joked Lillian.

Cat looked up, startled. Had Lillian guessed? "You make it sound like an either/or situation," she replied. "*Either* you fight Michigan Technologies *or* you have a family."

"Well, you certainly wouldn't do both!" said Lillian. "Can you imagine anything worse than being separated from your husband when you were expecting his baby? Some people do things like that, I guess, but it seems selfish to me. It's like denying a man the joy of sharing the pregnancy. After all, it's *his* baby too."

Cat's face flushed and her queasiness returned. Lillian's words stung. Was Cat denying her husband joy? Was she being selfish? She shook her head in confusion. Her concerns about the lawsuit and the trip to Detroit surfaced again. She would sort out her feelings later. But for now, she decided, she would tell Lillian nothing about her pregnancy. She hated deception, but the news would only complicate the situation. Lillian would insist that Cat return to Washington, and Cat would feel guilty about leaving Lillian alone in Detroit.

"If only you had some family to help you bear the burden," said Cat kindly. "Isn't there anyone?"

Lillian looked away from Cat's steady gaze. She knew the tiniest hint of emotion would lead to questions about her family. Now, more than ever before, Lillian had to deny Scott's existence. Juanita's life depended on the success of Scott's proposed rescue mission. And Scott's life was at stake, too.

"No one," Lillian answered simply.

Cat yawned and Lillian quickly suggested that they both needed to rest from their long trip. Cat offered little argument since she wanted to review the trial folder before she went to bed.

"We're going to win this case," promised Cat. "Honesty will prevail."

They hugged each other good night, grateful that their eyes didn't meet and reveal their lies.

"Honesty will prevail," repeated Lillian.

*   *   *

Juanita Martinez felt groggy. The effects of the drug were still controlling her. She could hear voices, but they seemed distant. They came to her through echoes. She lay still and strained to make sense of what was being said.

"The sedation should wear off in an hour or two," a gruff male voice was saying in Spanish. "When she comes around, give her something to eat if she's hungry but keep her in this room. She is to talk to no one except you."

"Yes, Captain," the voice of a young woman answered.

"She will be transferred to the hospital in six days."

"Hospital?"

"The Ambassador-at-Large has arranged for her to have an operation. It seems this poor woman has difficulties with her memory. It works too well. Our surgeons say they can cure that." The man snickered at his own grim humor.

"But wouldn't a bullet or an injection be much easier?" asked the woman.

"Not this time," said Captain Reyes. "She can be damaged, but not dead. Not even the Americans are stupid enough to make a trade for a dead agent. Take good care of her. All she needs to know is that she has been transferred to this private hacienda until the day of her trial. Say nothing else. You and another nurse will rotate shifts until it's time for the surgery."

"I understand, Captain."

"Good. Now let me explain a few other procedural things to you. . . ."

The voices started to get fainter and fainter as once again a veil of blackness seemed to close over Juanita's consciousness. She struggled to stay alert, but the drug was still too potent in her system. She started to drift again.

Help me, Scott . . . help me . . . help . . . me. . . .

CHAPTER 8

Technically speaking, Alma Hammond was no longer in charge of the Juanita Martinez recovery operation. The Director was negotiating directly with Guadalupe Bentancourt for the trade of Juanita for Scott Parker. Scott had insisted on this arrangement when he had called the Director. He wanted Alma to be blameless for the consequences of the trade, whatever they turned out to be. Not surprisingly, Bentancourt had made the same demand. After receiving the trade offer from the CIA, Bentancourt had sent word that he could agree to it, but only if the personnel involved were kept to a minimum and only if he could negotiate directly with the head of the CIA. There were to be no intermediaries.

"So you are not to be involved in this operation anymore," the Director explained to Alma when they met on Monday afternoon following her return to Washington. "Officially, you are off the case." The Director poured them each a cup of coffee. "Unofficially," he continued, "you will remain in charge of the operation. I have no one, including myself, who understands Cuba *and* Señor Bentancourt better than you. I'm not about to ignore the advice of my most qualified expert in this matter."

"Thank you, sir. I appreciate your confidence. I won't disappoint you."

"I'm glad to hear that," said the Director. "I know that you are fond of this Parker fellow. Can't blame you there. From what I've read of his record, he's first-rate. A bit impatient perhaps, but that's understandable considering the years he was kept penned like an animal. But hear me on this, Alma, and let's have no misunderstanding about it: If we can bring

Juanita Martinez home without having to trade Parker, we'll do it; *but*, if trading Parker winds up being our only option, I'll do it without hesitation. The information Juanita can give us will provide security for our entire country. And that's our whole reason for being here."

Alma nodded. "I understand, sir. If it comes to that, you'll have my full support. No arguments. You have my word."

The Director sipped his coffee. "Good. I was sure I could count on you. Now, I'd like your thoughts on where we stand in regard to our agreement with Ambassador Bentancourt. Am I safe in assuming that your opinion of his honesty is as low as it has previously been?"

"He'd take the fillings out of your teeth if he could get away with it."

"Just so. In that case, what about our agreement?"

Alma wrapped both hands around her coffee mug and leaned forward in her chair, her eyes narrowed in thought. "We've backed Bentancourt into a corner. Whatever choice he makes, he'll gain something and he'll lose something. If he keeps Juanita in Cuba, she'll never give us the information she has. However, when Parker tells his story in America, the Communists will know how Bentancourt double-crossed them. On the other hand, if Parker is traded for Juanita, Bentancourt can have him killed and his body cremated. Then, if we show videotapes of Parker's debriefing, Bentancourt can mock them and demand that Parker be brought forward to verify his story. It would certainly lessen the impact of our claims if we were unable to produce Parker."

"But with that plan, Bentancourt would have to release Juanita to us," said the Director. "He doesn't want that. First of all, she knows so much about his base of operations and about him personally that she could help us set his plans back ten years. If that didn't get him shot, he'd at least be removed from office." The Director finished his coffee. "And second, he's a vain and sadistic man. Juanita has not only outwitted him, she has rebuffed his advances. That's too much for an ego like his to endure. He'll need to hurt her, really hurt her in as cruel and vicious a manner as possible. In that way he'll again see himself as her superior, her master."

"He certainly has a psychopathic lust for power, all right," said Alma. "I agree with what you're saying. Juanita and Parker are equal threats to Bentancourt. As a matter of personal survival, he needs to silence both of them. But we haven't given him that option."

"I'm rather surprised he hasn't approached us with some alternate offer."

Alma shrugged her shoulders. "What could he propose? He could suggest they both live in Cuba, but nobody would fall for that. He could demand that Juanita not be allowed to talk about all she knows. We'd agree to that in order to get her back, but we'd never stick to such a foolish promise. He knows that."

"Are there any other possibilities?" asked the Director.

"Not really," said Alma. "If he could send a hit squad to the States to find and kill Parker . . . but he'd need authorization for that, and it would make these secret negotiations more publicized than he could afford down there. Besides, no one knows where we've hidden Parker."

"And he's still being protected?"

"Yes, sir. Only he doesn't know it. Kent is still there. He's keeping a careful eye on Parker from a distance. I also had a long chat with Charles and Bea Mead, the preacher and his wife who supervise the church mission. I told them about Parker's sudden independence. I really believe they may side with me in trying to convince Parker to see reason. That may serve to alienate Parker even more."

"Shock of isolation?"

"Exactly," concurred Alma. "If Parker feels that I've dropped him and that Kent is no longer there to protect him and that the Meads can't agree with his decision, he'll soon begin to recognize how powerless and vulnerable he really is. At that point I believe he will be a team player again. And that's when we can make our move."

"Our move? We have one?"

Alma smiled. "Pending your approval, of course. My plan is unorthodox, but necessary. Like yourself, I'm convinced Bentancourt plans to harm Juanita. We need to act quickly. His ego is so inflated that there would be no limits to what he'd do to wreak his vengeance on her. I dozed off on the plane coming here from West Virginia and had a horrible nightmare about Bentancourt. In my dream he ordered Juanita to be given a blood transfusion which infected her with a deadly virus. I could hear his ridiculous laugh as he relished her slow death."

The Director scowled. "Dreams? What nonsense! I want facts, not fantasies. I hope your plan for helping Juanita is equal to the melodrama of these silly nightmares of yours. Stick to reality."

Alma looked slightly embarrassed. "I'm sorry. It's just that I've dealt with Bentancourt before. I know how he thinks. And that's enough to give anyone nightmares. He's got ice water in his veins."

"Very well then, let's hear your plan. I have a feeling you're not going to have too much trouble getting me to approve it."

*   *   *

Juanita Martinez finished eating the bowl of soup.

"More?" asked the young woman in the dark green nurse's uniform.

Juanita shook her head. "Where am I? What is this place?"

"A country villa used as a retreat by military officers. You'll be kept here, right in this room, until your trial. You'll be fed twice each day and you'll never be left alone."

"Why was I moved here?"

"I have no idea. It's not my concern."

Juanita's mind was still confused. She couldn't remember what was real and what was a drug-induced hallucination. The conversation about the operation . . . had she really heard that or had she only dreamed it? Perhaps she could trick the nurse into telling her.

"My operation is still scheduled for Friday, right?"

The nurse was caught off-guard. "But how did you know?" Immediately she stopped herself. "I don't know what you're talking about."

"Of course not," said Juanita. "I bet they promised to let you be part of the scrub team if you did a good job of guarding me, right?"

"I'm not your guard," responded the woman. "This place is surrounded by officers of the Soviet Union and a crack platoon of Cuban militia. I don't need to worry about guarding you. You're not going anywhere."

"We'll see," said Juanita. "We'll see."

*   *   *

Time might prove Roderick Davis to be a better trial attorney than Cat Compton Sanders, but when it came to staging media events Cat was in a class by herself. She figured it would be better to play her strengths rather than her weaknesses. So she announced a press conference and scheduled it for the Renoir Room of the Renaissance Center.

Cat wasn't content merely to draw the business writers. She needed *massive* coverage. If she hoped to win her case in the media before it ever went to court, she would need the help of society page editors, gossip columnists, and even the fashion critics. She had made personal calls and had extended personal invitations to everyone in Detroit who could type or carry a camera. Her only failure was in not being able to think of some angle for the sports reporters to become interested in what she was doing. Oh well, she'd make do with what was available.

By 2:00 P.M. noon the Renoir Room was packed with members of the press corps. TV cameras and radio microphones were being placed in predetermined spots. Caterers were distributing appetizers, fruit wedges, cake slices, and cups of punch. Cat was moving through the crowd introducing Lillian to various people whom she herself had met only hours earlier. Cat was dressed in a smartly tailored linen jacket and shirt. Her white silk blouse was modestly embellished with a narrow blue ribbon at the collar. Lillian had on a short-sleeve navy dress, narrow at the waist and pleated in the skirt. It was accented by a silver necklace with matching earrings and bracelets.

Lillian smiled, answered questions (many totally unrelated to the pending court case), and stayed close to Cat. She knew that some of the people in the room were genuinely interested in covering the Michigan Technologies case for its effects on the local economy, but most of the reporters were here to see and meet Cat. The press corps loved her in D. C., so why should Detroit be any different?

And yet, Lillian could sense that things *were* different here. Back in Washington, Cat stayed in the news for the same reasons Jackie Kennedy used to—the dazzling clothes she wore, the witty things she said, the extremely photogenic expression of her face. Cat went along with it all because it was good for Drew's career and because it was fun for her.

But now, in Detroit, Cat was looking like and acting like and working like an attorney. The splash with the press corps was staged to win public support for Lillian's case. She knew that. Perhaps some journalist had come to ask Cat about her husband's interest in a bid for the White House . . . or about Cat's autumn wardrobe . . . or about Cat's feeling about Washington society. If so, they would be disappointed, for what they would hear would be about Lillian's case against Michigan Technologies.

Lillian felt Cat touch her elbow and motion her toward a raised platform with microphones. As they made their way across the room, several journalism students from nearby Wayne State University appeared at the double doors leading to the hallway. They were carrying armloads of white folders containing press releases and photos. They mingled among the reporters and distributed the press kits.

The room lights were flickered twice to signal for silence.

"Good afternoon, ladies and gentlemen, and thank you for coming. I'm Catherine Sanders. I am representing Mrs. Lillian Parker Thompson in a suit against the stockholders and current directors of Michigan Technologies, a company which Mrs. Thompson's father founded and with which she was formerly employed. Because I expect this case to be one which will be of great importance to the business community of Detroit, I thought it would be wise to explain to you members of the press corps just what the suit is seeking."

Cat motioned for Lillian to step near the microphone. "In order to save time, Mrs. Thompson would like to read a brief statement to you. Afterward, I will field any questions you may have. Lillian?"

Lillian unfolded a piece of typing paper, cleared her throat gently, and began to read.

"My name is Lillian Parker Thompson. I am the daughter of J. J. Parker II, the man who founded Michigan Technologies in 1967 and served as its chief executive officer until his death in 1983. After his death, my father was accused of having withdrawn three million dollars of the corporation's money for stock investments. No trace of this money or the stocks was found, so it was termed an embezzlement. Our family estate was subsequently liquidated to repay this money. My mother had died in 1975. She and my brother Scott, an MIA in Vietnam, lost their stock as part of the debt recovery. I was forced to sell my personal stock holdings because they were co-owned by my father and, under a technicality, were vulnerable to a buyout by the other board members after my father's death. I received 30,000 dollars for the stock; today its value is more than 200,000 dollars. I was also fired from my position as Director of Sales.

"Recently, evidence has come into my hands which has led me to believe that consultants and inside employees of my father's company were conspiring to remove my father as CEO of Michigan Technologies and were planning to sell the company to a group of outside investors. Furthermore, I believe that the three million dollars of corporate money which my father was accused of stealing was actually invested by him on behalf of the corporation. The corporate officers of Michigan Technologies recovered the missing three million but did not report it to the stockholders or to the government. They also kept my family's money.

"I am seeking to be repaid three million dollars of personal money, plus 270,000 dollars in lost interest earnings, plus one million dollars in punitive damages, another million for loss of reputation, and 500,000 dollars for mental suffering. Although I have no intention of staying with the company, I also want to be reinstated immediately in my former job and be awarded 147,000 dollars in lost income as verification that I was dismissed improperly. Furthermore, I want to be reissued my personal holdings of 3000 shares of stock in Michigan Technologies and be awarded payment of 50,000 dollars for lost dividend earnings.

"We've requested an immediate court date. I will be represented by the Detroit law firm of Smith and McKeand, with Mrs. Catherine Sanders serving as a consulting attorney. Thank you."

The room was immediately abuzz with side comments and whispered remarks. Hands were raised everywhere. Cat moved herself between Lillian and the crowd and began to field questions.

"Why are *you* involved in this case, Mrs. Sanders?" a woman near the front asked.

Cat had expected this to be the first question. She was ready for it.

"Before I was married, I had planned to set up a private practice in Nashville. Lillian and her husband, Dave, promised to be my first clients," said Cat. "I was maid of honor at Lillian's wedding. Dave works with my father. We're old friends. When this case came up, Lillian hired a very experienced local firm of attorneys to represent her, but she asked me to be involved, too. Naturally, I wanted to do all I could to help, so I agreed to come to Detroit."

An older man standing to the side raised his pen in the air. When called on, he identified himself as a columnist for *Metro Business Quarterly*. "Wasn't Lillian Parker, er, Mrs. Thompson, once engaged to Roderick Davis, the consulting director of legal affairs for Michigan Technologies?"

Cat had also expected this question to come up sooner or later.

"Lillian and Mr. Davis called off their engagement more than a year ago. It was something they mutually agreed on. It has no bearing on this suit against Michigan Technologies. But while we are on that topic, I will share openly with you that I too was acquainted with Mr. Davis last year and that we even discussed the possibility of setting up a law practice together in Nashville. It never transpired. Mr. Davis accepted his current position in Detroit and I . . . well, I became involved in politics."

Everyone laughed at this simple understatement. This is what they had come for, the witty one-liners Cat was known for in Washington.

"A reference was made to some evidence of a conspiracy," said a young woman in tight slacks with a wide imitation leather belt around her waist. "What is this evidence and how did it find its way to you?"

Cat knew her kind—a 19-year-old journalism major at a local junior college who wrote a freelance "Around Town" or "In Our Neighborhood" column for a once-a-week shopper tabloid. She saw herself as Brenda Starr or Lois Lane incarnate, even though she probably earned ten bucks per byline.

"Copies of some of the documents are in your press kits," said Cat. "Others will be shared after they've been presented to the judge as evidence. As to their procurement, they were discovered indirectly by a private detective agency during the course of a separate investigation. I'm not at liberty to say more about that right now."

A handsome man in a gray business suit motioned for a Minicam operator to move in for a close-up of him asking a question of Cat.

"Mrs. Sanders, how does your husband feel about your private ambitions to make it on your own as a trial lawyer?"

Hairs rose on the back of Cat's neck, but she steadied herself. *No scenes, no scenes*, she admonished herself. She smiled coyly.

"I've been making it on my own since I entered finishing school at age 13. And, personally, I think they finished me rather well, don't you?" Cat shot a wink at the cameraman and the audience roared its approval. Even the newsman had to chuckle.

"And Drew's only comment about this case was, 'I expect you to win, honey, because you're the biggest contributor to my campaign funds.' "

Again the laughter swelled. Cat, remembering the oldest adage in show business, saw this as a good chance to end the question-and-answer session. She waved to the crowd, called out her thanks, and then nodded to a security guard to help escort Lillian and herself out the side door. As they exited, four waiters entered with fresh trays of appetizers. Perfect timing. The waiters blocked the reporters from trailing Cat and Lillian, and the fresh supply of food made everyone not worry about it.

"That was impressive, Cat," said Lillian, as they entered a waiting elevator. "The whole thing came off exactly as you said it would. You're terrific!"

"I have my moments," agreed Cat, buffing her fingernails against her jacket in mock self-assurance. "I have my moments."

*   *   *

Washington, D. C. has a reputation for being the *smallest* big city in the world. That is to say, because it is filled with opposing political parties, lobbyists, reporters, press agents, foreign dignitaries, researchers, analysts, investigators, authors, and protestors, it is a place where it is the business of everyone to know the business of everyone else. And for this reason privacy is hard to come by.

Alma Hammond was only too aware of this problem. That's why she had asked Gregor Kotusov to meet her at her apartment in Virginia. Two men in her flat in the same week, she mused to herself. A record.

Kotusov was a cunning combatant on the battlefield of the Cold War. He had served the USSR nobly, during his 14 years of assignment to Washington as an attaché to the Russian consulate. He loved his country, but in an ironic way he also had an appreciation for America. After so long a time as a citizen of one country and yet a resident of the other, he had developed a desire for mutually satisfying coexistence. He still considered democracy to be an illogical way to govern—why should one give the uneducated and the poor the right to vote just because they had been alive 18 years?—but he was no advocate of nuclear holocausts or germ warfare or starvation as ways of changing things. (As he once wittingly told Alma, "I'm against the Bomb, the Bug, and the Bloat. Everything else is fair play.")

The doorbell to Alma's apartment rang. Alma opened the door to find Kotusov standing with flowers and a wrapped package.

"Punctual as always," said Alma.

Kotusov was wearing soft leather loafers, tailored dark slacks, a pale green open-necked dress shirt with a stylishly half-knotted narrow tie slung low on his chest, and a beige tweed sport coat. He had dark eyes and dark hair. His appearance was Western rather than European—certainly nothing resembling Russian.

He entered and handed the flowers to Alma. "The motivation to be on time was what made the difference. It's good to see you, Alma."

"You, too. It's been awhile, hasn't it? Go in and sit down. I'll just put these in some water. They're beautiful. Thanks."

Kotusov winked. "You know what they say: 'Beware of Russians bearing gifts.' "

"That's Greeks," Alma corrected, calling back over her shoulder, "but I'll keep it in mind anyway. I've fixed some cheese and fruit in the living room. Help yourself. By the way, what book did you bring me this time?"

"Come in here and open it and see for yourself," called Kotusov as he entered the living room.

"Yours is on the table," said Alma. "It's new, but not gift-wrapped. Sorry."

This was an ongoing routine whenever Kotusov and Alma got together. Because they knew it was usually months before "business" would require them to get together again, they always gave each other a book to read. It was often a large book, and always by an author native to their respective countries. Kotusov had given Alma copies of Tolstoy's *War and Peace*, Dostoyevski's *Crime and Punishment*, and Turgenev's *Fathers and Sons*. Alma had given Kotusov copies of *Life on the Mississippi* by Mark Twain, *In Our Time* by Ernest Hemingway, and *U. S. A.* by John Dos Passos.

Alma entered the room. She placed the vase of flowers on the window seat. She stood back and surveyed their appearance. "Perfect," she decided.

Kotusov said, "Yes . . . you are."

"Huh?" said Alma, turning.

"I was saying how nice you look," he repeated. "I very rarely get a chance to see you like this, dressed in a pretty sweater and skirt. You're always in uniform—horn-rimmed glasses, pulled-back hair, dark blue jacket, pure white blouse. Why do you hide your femininity, Alma? I don't think I ever knew before how long your hair really was. And you have some contact lenses, eh? I must tell you, you're very pretty. Indeed, very pretty."

Alma reached for her hair the way all women do instinctively whenever anyone says anything about their appearance.

Suddenly she felt self-conscious. Was Gregor teasing . . . or flirting? Why should she care about his remarks? She knew the answer: She was self-conscious because she had "spruced up" tonight on purpose. She had tried to tell herself earlier that she wasn't actually primping, just trying to create a more relaxed appearance in order to make Gregor feel at ease. But she knew better.

Ever since Scott Parker had come to her apartment earlier in the week, she had started to wonder how men perceived her. There had been that one awkward moment with Scott when they had realized that, despite the fact that they were working together, they were nevertheless a man and a woman of about the same age, both unmarried, suddenly put together in a completely private setting. They knew the "possibilities," and it had made them see each other in a new way. Had Scott not already been totally committed to Juanita, the awkwardness between Scott and Alma might have led to some "icebreakers." Instead, they had quickly reined in their emotions and had retreated to their previous roles as friends and working cohorts.

Still . . . the incident had made Alma begin to think about her womanly desires unrelated to career success. Had she purposely avoided relationships or had she just been too busy? Did she fear that she might not be attractive to men? Something in her needed to know the answers to these questions. So, consciously or subconsciously, she had decided to reveal a different Alma Hammond to Gregor Kotusov tonight. And, lo and behold, he'd noticed.

"Thank . . . you," said Alma. "I just . . . well, I just thought I'd put on something more casual. We, uh, don't always have to be so stuffy, right?"

Gregor stabbed a piece of white cheese with a toothpick. He took a bite. "I couldn't agree more."

"Well, let me open my book," said Alma, hoping to divert the subject. She took the package from Kotusov and pulled off the wrapping. "Dostoyevski again, eh? *The Possessed*. What's this about, demonology?"

"Literally, no," said Kotusov, with a small smile, "but figuratively, yes. It's about two men dedicated to creating mayhem. It will scare you. The two characters are so like your President and our Premier that it's unnerving. Thank goodness there are still people like you and me who believe in cheese, fruit, flowers, and books."

"I'll read it carefully," promised Alma with a grin. "I can always use the perspective."

"And what is *Safekeeping* by Jonellen Heckler about?" asked Gregor, leafing through his gift from Alma.

"Something very contemporary. It's about an MIA in Vietnam and how his family back in America tries to live from day to day not knowing whether he's dead or alive. It's poignant and tough. It's the best book I've read in years. You may not appreciate its viewpoint . . . but then, you can always use the perspective, too."

Kotusov grimaced. "We're bobbing and weaving, Alma. This is all obviously leading someplace. Where?"

"Cuba," answered Alma bluntly.

"Ah, Cuba. Yes, I had anticipated that. You sent one of your agents to bug our embassy there recently and she was caught, wasn't she? So, what now? Do you wish to apologize?"

Alma laughed.

"No?" said Kotusov in mock surprise. "You really should, you know. That wasn't nice, Alma. Why don't you people mind your own business?"

"Spying *is* my business. It's yours, too, my friend. Don't get self-righteous with me. Now, listen. I need your help."

"In Cuba? Out of the question," protested Kotusov. "Surely you haven't forgotten that barely a year ago I asked you for some help regarding a matter in Cuba. But you refused me. I'll tell you, I haven't forgotten that, Alma."

"The only reason I refused you was because I knew that you were already going to have your problem solved for you," Alma countered. "I just couldn't tell you about it back then. You wanted Colonel Bupchev of your Russian army returned to

Cuba where he had been serving as an advisor. I knew that Bupchev was already scheduled to go back to Cuba. I arranged it myself."

"You! *You* arranged it? What are you talking about?"

"It's a long story. Sit back and start taking mental notes."

*   *   *

It took Alma nearly an hour to brief Kotusov on how the Scott Parker trade had been arranged by Bentancourt. The most disturbing parts of the story for Kotusov were the many times Bentancourt had used the Soviet Union for his own advantage. Alma sensed this sore point and used it to win Kotusov to her side.

"So, that's it," Alma summarized. "Bentancourt snatched Parker from Vietnam without ever telling your people or the Chinese. He then made it look as though he personally had wrangled the return of Colonel Bupchev. That helped get him named Ambassador-at-Large."

"We even gave him a medal," said Kotusov bitterly. "Such a deceiver."

"Bentancourt is not looking out for Cuba, Russia, or anything except his own personal advancement," underscored Alma. "When Juanita Martinez was caught, he offered to have her severely punished, didn't he? That was so your people at the embassy would return Juanita to him. He wants her dead. She'll never stand trial, you can count on that. If she told all she knows about the Scott Parker deal, she'd ruin Bentancourt. He'd never let her talk."

"Then why isn't she dead already?"

"Bentancourt has another problem equally as threatening."

Kotusov nodded. "Sergeant Parker. He knows as much as the woman."

"Precisely," said Alma. "My Director has contacted Bentancourt and offered to trade Parker for Juanita. It was Parker's idea. He's a noble man."

"He acts like a knight but thinks like a jester. It's an idiotic plan. Bentancourt will inject the woman with a time-delayed poison, trade her back, and then kill Parker."

"Our doctors could handle the poison."

Kotusov considered that. "Yes, that's true. He must know that too. Otherwise he would have done that to Parker a year ago when you traded. I'm afraid that means an even worse fate is in store for your agent."

"What do you mean?"

"A lobotomy or some sort of laser surgery to destroy memory cells or induce disorientation," said Kotusov. "Castro's officers have used it to control dissident students, protest leaders, even political opponents. It's ghastly, but 100 percent effective."

Alma looked away. She said something under her breath.

"I'm sorry," said Kotusov, "but it's a reality of life in Cuba."

"No, no, it's all right, I understand," said Alma. "It just makes me more determined to go ahead with what I had already planned to do."

"And, I suppose, that's where I come in?" questioned Kotusov. "I hope you don't intend to ask me to help you get your agent safely out of Cuba. I can't. What she knows about Russian operations in Cuba is too valuable to be turned over to the CIA. I appreciate the friendship we have, Alma, but I'm no traitor to my country."

"I'm through dealing with Bentancourt," said Alma. "I want Juanita back and you are my only chance at arranging that. I'm not asking you to turn against your country. I'm asking you to help me arrange a deal."

"Ah! Bartering! Yes, that's what you and I do best, isn't it? All right, let's hear it." He stroked his chin as if in rapt attention.

"Your part of the bargain would be this," said Alma. "You would use your connections in Cuba to locate where Bentancourt has moved Juanita. Once you've found it, you would arrange for all Russian personnel to withdraw from that place at a designated time. We then would send a rescue team to recover Juanita, and you could deal with Bentancourt as you see fit. We'll even give you one of Parker's videotapes as evidence."

"I told you, I don't want that agent of yours to get back in American hands any more than Bentancourt does."

"We know that. But we're prepared to offset any disadvantages that Juanita's return may cause you."

"How?"

"Several ways," promised Alma. "First, we will return two of your agents whom we've been holding for the past four years in our prisons. One is Alexi Sokonikov and the other is Boris Gentur."

"Keep them," said Kotusov, feigning boredom. "No one back in Moscow even knows they're missing."

"Second, you'll be able to expose Bentancourt for the turn-coat he has been to the Communist movement worldwide," continued Alma.

"That's not something we would publicize. Besides, my superiors would have an easier way to handle Bentancourt. Someone in Havana would be told to put two sticks of dynamite in his car. Instant solution."

"And third," said Alma, "we will loan you two of our finest nuclear physicists for six months to help your people design and install a new power system for the one that melted down in Kiev."

Kotusov made no joke this time. He sat quite still, thinking intently. Alma had definitely caught his attention.

"You have clearance for this? It's official? To assist at Chernobyl?"

"Straight from the President," Alma assured him. "We'll deliver the Parker video along with Sokonikov and Gentur to you tonight if you like. As soon as the mission in Cuba is completed, we'll arrange for the, uh . . . cross-cultural scientific exchange. Surely you can dig up two Soviet professors to plant at one of our universities while our two scientists are 'lecturing' in Kiev."

"Yes," said Kotusov, with a wry expression. "I think that could be arranged. In fact, I think the whole thing could be arranged. The priorities of the Soviet Union are to care for at-home matters before worrying about long-distance concerns."

"How wise," said Alma, nodding approval. "I like you when you're so decisive, Gregor."

Alma smiled. "And when you bring me books."

*   *   *

The evening editions of the Detroit newspapers gave the Lillian Parker Thompson lawsuit a front-page splash. This was yet another headache for Roderick Davis to contend with. His phone had maintained a constant ring all afternoon. Brokers were starting to receive sell orders from shareholders of Michigan Technologies stock anticipating a sudden loss of corporate liquid assets. Reporters wanted to know what Roderick's response was to the claims laid against the corporation he represented. Executives at Michigan Technologies were outraged that Roderick had not squelched this suit before it had gone public. Everyone was after Roderick for answers. But, as yet, he had none.

At 4:00 P.M. Roderick told Jennifer he was leaving for the day. He took the elevator to the basement parking ramp and drove out a side exit. Fearing that reporters would be waiting for him at his place, he drove instead to Paul Stattman's apartment. He had to wait half an hour in the hallway until Stattman arrived to unlock the door.

"You took long enough," said Roderick by way of greeting.

"Hey! Cut me some slack. It's clear across town. I got here as soon as I could."

"Just hurry up."

They entered the apartment. Roderick immediately reached for the wall thermostat and turned up the air conditioning. He was warm, excited, and nervous- -he needed air.

"You made the news on 1590-FM," said Paul. "I heard it in the car. You seem to be on the side of the bad guys."

"You think that's funny?" charged Roderick. "You'll be laughing out of the other side of your mouth if this whole thing blows up. You're knee-deep in this as much as anyone else. You didn't get named Director of Overseas Marketing because you have a winning smile, Stattman. Some of J. J. Parker's blood is on your hands too. You'd better remember that and stop with the jokes."

Stattman set his briefcase on an antique rolltop desk in his living room. He went into the kitchen and came back carrying two cans.

"Have something cold to drink," he said. "You're getting all bent out of shape over nothing. What's with you?"

Roderick dropped into a leather armchair. His shoulders were drooped.

"They've got us by the throat. I saw one of those press packets they gave away this morning. I couldn't believe it. They've got the minutes from the board meeting when we discussed firing J. J. and then usurping his stock. They've got copies of six contracts with outside consultants we hired and channeled funds to without J. J.'s approval. They've even got a memo from the accounting department notifying the chairman of the board that 'extra stock purchases' had been reported and were traceable to the dates when J. J. was supposed to have embezzled the money. I'm telling you, man, we're going to fry. They've got us dead to rights."

Paul finished his drink and went to the kitchen for another. "And I'm telling you we've got nothing to worry about."

Roderick followed him. "I'm worried plenty. Plenty! It was supposed to be a simple takeover. J. J.'s four board members felt he wasn't running the company the way it should be. Okay, so they went out and hired you, me and three other guys as consultants—with J. J.'s approval—and it was our job to mess up the company just enough to get J. J. out but not so much that we couldn't turn things around again once our four bosses took over."

"And we came through, didn't we?" mused Stattman, leaning over the refrigerator door and surveying the contents. "The company sure went into a tailspin after we started running things. Of course you, cautious ol' Rod, covered all bases after you heard J. J. was starting to look into matters. You quickly got yourself engaged to J. J.'s daughter just to hedge your bet. If J. J. discovered what all was going on and started firing the consultants, you planned to marry Lillian and stay with the boss. But if J. J. didn't catch on and wound up out on his ear, you planned to drop his daughter and accept a promotion from the four new honchos you were helping to take over the company."

"But none of that was illegal," protested Roderick. "Sure, it was all premeditated and not very ethical, but you can't hang a guy for managing a company poorly or for getting engaged to the boss's daughter."

Paul, still calm, removed some cold cuts from the refrigerator and proceeded to make himself a sandwich. "But it didn't stop there, did it, Rod?"

"And whose fault was that? J. J. must have been off his nut to yank three million from liquid funds and plunge it all into the market."

Paul bit into his sandwich. With a mouthful of food he mumbled, "He wasn't crazy and we both know it. It was a brilliant counterploy. He tied up our cash flow yet kept the company solvent at the same time. If he'd lived, he'd have hung us all out to dry. Lucky for us his ticker gave out just when it did. Say, you want a sandwich?"

Roderick began to pace the small kitchen. "Those four guys were crazy for not admitting they later found the missing three million in stock investments. They could have paid Lillian back and still had control of the company."

"Whoa! Hold on there a minute. Let's not forget that none of this has ever bothered you until this week, my friend. And let's also not forget that while the three million was slowly absorbed into the company, it was sponged out again to increase your retainer fee as chief counsel to the corporation."

"And to pay you a bigger salary and fatter bonuses and to remodel your office and . . ."

"Okay! So, okay!" injected Paul. "Who's denying it? We've all made out like . . . well . . . like bandits. Why not? After all, that's what we are. You included, counselor. You're an officer of the court, but you never reported the crime. You're as guilty as Denay, Brown, or any of us. But don't worry. We're all going to go on enjoying the good life. Only seven or eight of us know anything about any of this. J. J. is dead and we got rid of Lillian and anyone else who might have remotely had access to any information related to this."

"Yeah? Well, why didn't you get rid of the information itself while you were at it? How could you be so careless, so utterly stupid?"

"I thought it *had* been destroyed, or at least some of it," said Paul. "We started transferring or firing everyone out of the records section who had been hired by J. J. That was our first priority. We didn't want anyone around who might be able to fit any pieces together. We had planned to purge the records later."

"Brilliant strategy!" barked Roderick. "In the meantime you hired someone who was working for Lillian or Cat—or J. J.'s ghost—and that person came in and systematically copied all the information needed to condemn the lot of us. What's more, that person left us with no copies of the records. We don't even have a way of building a defense."

Paul flashed a Cheshire cat grin at Roderick. "But that's the very key to our freedom, Rod, ol' man. That *is* our defense. And the big boys at M-T want that known as soon as possible. Their message to you is to push for an early trial date. The sooner the better."

* * *

It was dark when Scott Parker knelt beside his bunk. The cicadas, katydids, and crickets were in chorus outside his screen window. The orange moon was casting oblong shadows on all the walls. The whiff of a distant campfire was in the night breeze. Simple pleasures, yet priceless to Scott. This setting was home.

He could have made plans to leave. Financially, he was a wealthy man. He had no thoughts about pretentious wealth, though. He had signed over all his accumulated back pay to his sister. He had never even made a withdrawal from the trust fund that his father had left to him.

Wealth? Scott was already wealthy, and he knew it. He had good friends and a loving sister. He had regained his health and he had found a useful purpose for his life. He relished his work at the mission settlement.

Maybe Pop Mead was right. Maybe God could use his 12 years in POW camps as preparation for him to be a minister to these poor mountain people. Him? Scott Parker, a preacher? Well, why not? Christ had focused His ministry on the poor and needy, the outcasts, and the forgotten. It certainly would be honorable service. But how could it ever be possible for him?

"Oh, God, I'm confused and terrified," said Scott softly. "You seem so far away now that I need You most. I've prayed for strength but I'm still so weak. I can't sleep . . . I hear Juanita calling me . . . I hear myself promise to take her place . . . then I see the walls and bars and I start to choke and suffocate. How can I go back in, Lord? I'll go insane. The walls . . . the tight confinements. How can I do it, Lord? You know I love her. She's depending on me. How, Lord? How can I endure it?"

Scott's mind flashed an image of gray slabs closing in on him from all sides. He put his hands to the sides of his head and squeezed his eyes shut. He felt the dreaded sense of suffocation coming over him again. He could hear himself begin to gasp. His chest became tight, his breathing shallow.

Then suddenly he thought of Juanita's face. He imagined her reaching for him with outstretched arms. He *had* to make it to her somehow.

With a forced effort he began to suck in air.
One . . . two . . . three. . . .
He slowly began to breathe out again.
Four . . . five . . . six. . . .

* * *

The muffled squish of Rosa Garcia's gum-soled shoes against the terrazzo floor caused Juanita Martinez to murmur softly in her sleep. Rosa stopped, remaining motionless until Juanita's deep breathing resumed. Only then did she cautiously approach the bed and study the patient's face.

At 11 P.M. the lights in the hacienda were dim. Still, there was no doubt. Rosa put her hand to her mouth to keep a cry from escaping. After so many years she was not only looking at her daughter, but also at her husband. The girl's features, in profile, were delicate versions of Jim Middleton's. Without thinking, Rosa reached down and brushed aside a long, damp strand of dark hair from her daughter's forehead. Blue eyes fluttered open.

"Wh . . . wh . . . why are you looking at me that way?" whispered Juanita, trying to shake off her sleepiness. She was quickly on guard, her eyes searching the darkened room for signs of a military escort. Surely it wasn't time for the trip to the hospital. Days were blending into each other, and she had lost her sense of time, but intuition told her she had two, maybe three, days remaining before her scheduled surgery.

"Who *are* you?" she asked.

Rosa struggled for words, but each new gesture and expression by Juanita startled her. The eyes, particularly the eyes, were so reminiscent of her husband.

"My name is Rosa Garcia," she began haltingly in English.

The switch in language took Juanita by surprise. "You speak English?"

Rosa nodded. "Yes, my husband . . . my late husband . . . was an American. From Texas." Her voice quivered. "Galveston."

Juanita smiled. The familiarity of the city's name—Galveston—sounded so comforting in the alien surroundings of the hacienda. "Galveston? I grew up there," she said, almost to herself.

"I know."

Juanita looked puzzled.

"I know that you grew up in Galveston," repeated Rosa, carefully watching Juanita's reaction to each of her words. She didn't want to shock her daughter or to touch off any physical reaction that would harm her. She was a nurse, after all, and she was aware that drugs had strange side effects. She had no way of knowing what kind of sedatives Juanita had been given since her arrest.

"How could you possibly know anything about me?" demanded Juanita. "Oh, I get it. Bentancourt, right? You're one of *his* people. Well, you can just tell Senõr Bent . . ."

Rosa lifted her right index finger to her lips in a motion of silence. Juanita stopped speaking and both women listened as the soft footsteps of the guard passed outside the window.

"I'll get you something to make you sleep," Rosa said too loudly. Juanita began to protest, but then understood that the nurse's words were meant more for the passing guard than for her.

"I'm cold," said Juanita. "Please close the window." Rosa smiled and did as she was asked. This assured their privacy.

"Who are you *really*?" asked Juanita as Rosa smoothed the bed linens and filled the glass on the nightstand.

"I'm going to turn off the night-light now," replied Rosa, avoiding the question. I don't want to take a chance that the guard will see us talking. If you don't mind sitting in the dark and speaking very softly, we can visit for a few more minutes. Of course if you're too tired. . . ."

"Who *are* you?" Juanita persisted.

The older woman bowed her head, uncertain of what to say. "I've already told you. My name is Rosa Garcia," she repeated.

"Garcia?" echoed Juanita. "That doesn't sound like an American name to me. Didn't you say you were married to an American? Someone from Galveston?"

Rosa was grateful for the darkness. She dabbed at one of her eyes to prevent a tear from spilling over onto her cheek. "Yes, but that was a long time ago. Before Castro. My husband—my first husband—was killed in a raid at San Pedro. You probably have never heard of San Pedro, but it's located . . ."

"I know where it is," answered Juanita. "My father died there. In a raid."

They were becoming adjusted to the darkness now. Still, each avoided looking at the other. Rosa, her head down, struggled with renewed doubt. Maybe her husband, Ricardo, had been right after all. They had a good life together. Couldn't she just leave it at that? Tears filled her eyes again, but this time her tightened fist could not brush them aside. She got up from the chair, mumbling an excuse that she had paperwork to complete. Charts. Medical records. She was nearly to the door when the words she had both anticipated and dreaded called her back.

"Tell me about him," Juanita pleaded, her voice choked. "Tell me about my father."

CHAPTER 9

Pop Mead left the dinner table, dropped into his leather easy chair in the corner of the living room, and picked up the newspaper. He opened it double-wide and sat looking at his wife through a huge cutout hole in the front page.

"Bea!" he barked. "How many times have I told you not to cut up my Detroit paper until I'm finished reading it?"

Mom Mead turned slowly from the kitchen sink. Her arms were covered elbow-deep with soapsuds.

"I'm sorry, Charles. I thought you had read it at the breakfast table this morning."

"That was the paper from two days ago. Today is Wednesday. *This* is yesterday's paper."

Bea Mead shook her head. "How am I supposed to keep track? Your copies always arrive a day late . . . except for Sunday's paper, and that doesn't get here till Tuesday . . . unless Monday is a holiday, which puts both weekend papers three days late. . . ."

"Never mind, never mind," interrupted Pop Mead. "Just go fetch whatever you've hacked out of here and bring it back. Just because we don't live in Detroit anymore doesn't mean I still don't like to keep track of local events. My congregation was huge. Hardly a day goes by that I don't pick out a name in this paper of someone I used to preach to."

Bea dried her arms and walked toward their bedroom. "Your congregation was modest. And you seldom, if ever, see a name you recognize in that paper. I think you only subscribe to it because you're so amazed that Detroit can get along without you now that we've moved away."

"Well, if this paper annoys you so much, why are you forever ripping out recipes and engagement announcements and—"

"Hush, Charles," admonished his wife, coming back from the bedroom lugging a large scrapbook. "Don't be such an old fuddy-duddy. The world won't come to an end just because someone clips an occasional article or two from your precious paper. Can't you hear how cranky you are? You've been out of sorts ever since Scott left."

"I have not!" said Pop Mead, crumpling the paper onto his lap. Then just as quickly, "Oh, yes, I have. I hate this, not knowing anything. It's exasperating, Bea. Why can't someone write to us or give us a call?"

"I know it's hard," said Bea. "Look, Charles: The old scrapbook I kept with clippings about all the folks from our congregation. That's why I cut up your paper. I've been adding the new articles about Lillian's court case to the old clippings I kept about all the Parkers."

Pop Mead tossed his paper aside and began to thumb through the scrapbook. "Look at this . . . my, my, my, I'd forgotten how thorough you were. This is amazing, Bea. Look, here's the obituary for Sarah. Listen: *Sarah Christina Parker, wife of industrialist J. J. Parker, mother of Scott Parker, killed in Vietnam in 1971, and Lillian Parker.* This clipping is dated April 14, 1975 . . . can you get over how things have changed since then? I haven't gone through this scrapbook of yours in ages."

"I've got everything ever printed about the Parkers in that section," said Mom Mead. "Look, Charles, even articles about Scott's memorial service—imagine that. And articles about J. J.'s embezzlement, his heart attack and death, the new management takeover at Michigan Technologies, and even the auctioning off of the Parker estate."

Pop Mead let out a sigh. He looked directly at his wife. "I can remember those times so vividly, can't you, Bea? Sarah was such a saint all during the roughest months of her cancer. And

J. J., though no saint, was always open for a cup of coffee and a good chat."

"They were fine people," agreed Bea. "I'm going to leave this scrapbook to Lillian when I die. It'll mean something to her."

Pop Mead's eyes flashed.

"Why make her wait another 50 years, Bea? Every time I think of Lillian having to go through that legal battle without any family, I feel guilty. Maybe this is the excuse we need. Let's go give it to her now. I say we set out for Detroit tonight. If we stay here we'll just be sitting on pins and needles. If we're up there, at least we can lend moral support during the trial. How about it? How long will it take you to pack?"

"Me?" said Mom. "I'm ready now. I've been packed for two days. I just haven't known how to break the news to you that I planned to go north to help Lillian."

Pop grinned. "Ha! Still one jump ahead of me, eh, ol' gal?"

Mom bent over to kiss her husband's forehead. "And don't you ever forget it," she said.

*   *   *

The photo was old and yellowed and had a jagged white crease across the lower left corner. Juanita handled it carefully, gently stroking the out-of-focus image of her parents taken with a box Brownie camera nearly 30 years ago on their wedding day. Jim Middleton had joked that the camera, purchased at the PX, was part of his dowry, offered to Joe Martinez in return for Rosa's hand.

"Another cookie?" offered Rosa. "Look, chocolate chip. Your favorite."

"How do you know what my favorite kind of cookie is?" asked Juanita with a laugh.

Rosa put her finger to her lips as a signal that they needed to keep their voices to a whisper.

"I used to play games," she admitted softly. "After I found out that your Grandfather Martinez had taken you to the Red Cross and had arranged for you to go to Texas I tried to imagine you there. It helped me feel close to you. I'd picture you coming home from school and walking into a beautiful kitchen filled with the smells of baking. You would sit down with a big tumbler of milk and with chocolate chip cookies in both fists, and you would tell your grandmother about your day in school. You'll never know how much I wanted to be there to listen."

Juanita instinctively reached out to her mother, then quickly withdrew her hand. Both were aware that they were under the sporadic surveillance of a guard circling the hacienda every ten minutes. Rosa had taken a risk by shuffling schedules to be on duty four nights in a row; there could be no hint of camaraderie . . . no audible conversation, no physical contact.

Still, in the four evenings they had spent together they had managed to establish a firm bond. They had traded memories as each had prodded the other to share every aspect of their years apart. Rosa had needed assurance that Juanita had been well taken care of, loved, and guided under Mrs. Middleton's watchful eye in Texas. Juanita had wanted to know about Rosa's injury at San Pedro—the fractured shoulder and concussion that had resulted in several weeks of hospitalization. The head injury had left Rosa disoriented and had caused her to lose precious time in tracking down her family and her daughter. She had searched for months to no avail. Finally she volunteered to work in a field hospital in the hope she might locate other refugees or transients who could give her news about her parents, husband, or infant child. When no immediate news was available, she asked to stay at the hospital to study nursing. During the next 18 years she studied, worked, and continued to ask questions about her missing family. At last she gave up. A late-in-life chance for marriage arose, and she accepted it. Ricardo had been a good husband these past ten years.

"I never thought it would take so long," said Rosa with a smile. "I used to pray that one day I would be asked to care for a little girl, and when I would go to her bed I would look down and there you would be. It's a miracle, Juanita, because that's exactly how it happened. Only the little girl is a grown woman."

Rosa's eyes filled with tears. "I should have known that God always answers our prayers. Some answers just take a little more time than others."

Juanita nodded slowly. "Pray for me now, Mama. I've tried not to think about it, but I know my time is running out. What day is it? Wednesday? Thursday? Isn't the surgery scheduled for Friday? I'm sure that's what I heard the nurse say. But you can check that . . . you can look at the chart."

She knew by her mother's expression that Rosa was well aware of the chart's contents. Yes, today was Wednesday, and yes, the surgery was set for Friday.

"There's still a chance, you know," said Juanita, trying to project confidence. "You made the contact?"

Rosa nodded. "I went to the Village of Two Trees yesterday morning. At noon I went to the barbershop of Pedro Vargas and said I was looking for someone to shear sheep. All the men laughed, so I left and went around to the back. In a moment Pedro Vargas came out the back door and confirmed the code. He said, 'To shear sheep, one seeks a wolf,' and I replied, 'To shear a wolf, one seeks an eagle.' He then asked for the message and I told him the location of where you are being held."

"Perfect!" said Juanita. "Thank you, Mama. If the message followed proper channels and made its way from Cuba to Washington, Alma will already be making plans for my release. And Scott will help her. I know he will. Have I told you how wonderful he is, Mama?"

In spite of the circumstances, Rosa had to smile. Her daughter obviously was in love, and every conversation eventually returned to the topic of Sergeant Scott Parker.

"I'm sure one of them, Scott or Alma, has worked out a solution," continued Juanita. "Just wait until you meet Alma.

She always has an answer for everything. She'll figure out something; I know she will. I only hope her plan includes room for an extra passenger. It will be fun to show you the States, Mama. We'll visit Galveston and Washington, and of course we'll spend lots of time at the Mission with Scott."

Scott again. Rosa smiled.

They heard the footsteps of the guard outside and suspended their conversation. When the muffled sound faded, Rosa pulled her chair close to Juanita's bed. She knew she had only ten minutes before she must again keep her distance.

"I had another favorite dream about you during all those years we were separated," she whispered to her daughter. "I used to fantasize how each night before I would tuck you in we would say our prayers together. We would kneel by your bed and. . . ."

Before Rosa could finish, Juanita slipped out from between the covers. She put her arm around her mother's shoulders and led her to the side of the bed.

"Shall we ask for a miracle?" asked Rosa.

"I think we've already had one," replied Juanita.

Rosa nodded in agreement, and they both knelt and silently prayed, without consultation, for the same blessing.

*   *   *

Kotusov's phone continued to ring. He opened an eye and looked at the luminous face of the clock. 2:43 A.M. This had better be good, he vowed.

"What!" he groaned.

"We know where she is," said Alma.

"Who in the world is . . . ?"

Alma persisted. "Wake up, Gregor. This is Alma. We know where they're holding Juanita Martinez."

"The Rancho de Palmas Retreat Center," replied Kotusov sleepily.

A long silence prevailed.

"You . . . you know? You've known . . . and you haven't told me?"

"That's right," said Kotusov. "I was going to wait until you leveled with me."

"Leveled with you? But I've told you everything."

Gregor rolled over and switched the telephone receiver to his other ear. He still refused to turn on a light.

Wearily he stated, "Scott Parker and a squad of U. S. Navy SEALs were put aboard a nuclear-powered submarine at midnight. The submarine is on a direct course from North Carolina to Cuba."

"How do you know about that?" asked Alma, genuinely surprised.

"I know about the course the sub is taking because three Russian trawlers have been monitoring it all night," explained Kotusov. "You could have figured that out for yourself. How I know about Parker and the SEALs being on board is my secret. You should have kept me informed, Alma. You aren't doing much to bolster my confidence in you."

"I *planned* to tell you everything," insisted Alma. "We received an unexpected communiqué from Cuba this evening. It was about Juanita. Everyone was scrambling trying to confirm it, trace its source, decide how to act upon it. . . ."

Kotusov didn't understand the meaning of the English word *scramble* in the context Alma used. Decode? He assumed from the conversation it had something to do with either chaos or excitement. He would look it up in the morning. Meanwhile, he needed to silence Alma and get back to sleep.

". . . and so the Director gave Scott the green light to set off to Cuba," she was saying rapidly, "and he and the SEAL unit reported to—"

"Alma! Alma! Please!" injected Kotusov. "Lower your voice. And stop rattling like a machine gun."

The line went silent.

After a moment, with restrained impatience, Alma said,

"Gregor, I have not held back information from you. I can prove it."

"How? By telling me what I already know?"

"By telling you what you *don't* know. Listen: You only know half the plan. Parker and the SEALs are going to transfer from the submarine to a Canadian freighter later today. The sub will then go to the open sea and wait, but the freighter will pretend to head toward Havana with a cargo of aluminum products. After dark Parker and the SEALs will jump ship, go inland, stage a raid on the retreat center, rescue Juanita, and then leave on the Canadian freighter. Once at sea again, the freighter will rendezvous with the sub and transfer our people, then return to make its official port of call in Havana."

"The Canadians, eh?" mused Kotusov through a yawn. "Interesting. They can bad-mouth you in the press about acid rain and free trade, but when the chips are down they're still your faithful cousins, is that it?"

"Gregor, you must order your people to evacuate that retreat center until Juanita is rescued. The United States Navy does not want its personnel to engage in a confrontation with the soldiers of the Soviet Union. Please, Gregor, help me on this. I haven't double-crossed you. I swear it. Everything else we agreed on has been carried out, hasn't it? I gave you the goods on Bentancourt. We returned your two imprisoned couriers to you, didn't we? And our two nuclear physicists are all set to go to Russia as consultants. There's no sense in this arrangement of ours falling apart."

"It won't."

"What? You mean you'll arrange for your troops to be withdrawn from the retreat center for a day?" asked Alma.

Gregor made Alma wait through another yawn. "I've already arranged it," he said at last.

"What? . . . When? Are you serious?"

"We only have six men assigned there," said Kotusov, "and they have been assigned to three days of weapons training at a base 27 kilometers from the retreat center. Parker and his men will be resisted only by the Cuban militia on guard duty there. They're useless, by the way. Castro refuses to waste bullets on target practice. His men are play soldiers. The SEALs will make micemeat of them."

Alma laughed. "That's *mincemeat*." She changed her voice. "Gregor . . . why? Why did you arrange all this? I mean, especially after you thought I wasn't being completely honest with you?"

There was a pause.

"Don't you know?" he said.

"No. I really don't," she admitted. "It was such a gracious thing to do. And don't tell me you just wanted to make sure our two scientists would still help at Chernobyl. What you've done marks an all-time high for diplomatic relations between us."

"*Diplomatic* relations?" questioned Kotusov. "How nice. Good night, Alma."

He hung up on her.

*   *   *

Guadalupe Bentancourt had gone to bed at 11 P.M. on Wednesday night, but double elements of excitement were keeping him awake even now at nearly 3 A.M. One of his joys came from knowing that in just 30 hours Captain Reyes would take Juanita Martinez from the retreat center and deliver her to the hospital for her "memory cure" operation. His revenge against that woman would be complete.

The other cause for excitement was his recollection of an important phone call he had received just after lunch on Wednesday.

He had been in his office when the call from the Soviet ambassador had come through. His secretary had buzzed the intercom and made the announcement, and Bentancourt had snatched up the receiver instantly.

"Good afternoon, Excellency," he had said. "This is a wonderful surprise."

"Comrade Bentancourt," began the Ambassador, "it has come to my attention that you have been interrogating the female spy who tried to place a listening device in our embassy last week. What is your progress?"

"Nothing new, really," he had bluffed. "I've known for several months that the woman was an American agent. We've been feeding her false information so as to turn the tables on her."

"Yes, so your report stated," the Ambassador had mused. "You also stated that you knew about the listening device."

"True," Bentancourt had continued. "My plan was to let her plant it in your embassy and then to arrest her when she returned here. We knew she took the device with her when she left our office that morning. My secretary was shadowing her when she left here. That was how I was . . . well . . . able to be so 'prompt' in my arrival at your embassy. My secretary was to watch and then alert your security people after the device was planted. Of course, when Juanita . . . that is, the spy . . . dropped the device, plans were changed."

"Humph. So, that's the story, is it?"

"Yes, Excellency," Bentancourt had assured him.

"In that case, I think you had better come by our offices here Friday morning, Comrade Bentancourt. And wear your Order of Lenin."

"Friday? Your offices, Excellency?"

"Yes. About 10 o'clock, if that will be convenient."

Bentancourt remembered rising from his chair instinctively, despite the fact that no one could see him. "Yes, Excellency . . . er, Comrade Ambassador . . . yes, 10 o'clock."

After he hung up he slowly sank back into his leather chair. A grin spread across his entire face. It gave way to a smile and then to a loud laugh. *These Russians*, he had thought. *They'll believe anything. What simpletons! My assistant is caught spying on them and they wind up deciding I need another medal for capturing her. Ha! I can convince those buffoons of anything.*

"Carmelita," he had said, snapping on his intercom. "Clear my calendar of all appointments for Friday morning. And call my tailor and tell him to hurry my order for my new blue pinstriped suit."

"Something important?" the secretary had asked.

"Oh . . . more or less," he had responded, feigning nonchalance. "Another medal or some such thing. All part of the job. Yes, all part of the job."

Thinking back on this now at 3 A.M., Bentancourt smiled. Life was so good.

*   *   *

Cat arose early on Thursday morning to debate about what to wear to court. She inhaled, heaving her rib cage upward as she quickly notched the belt in its most generous position. Ouch! It was useless. What was the phrase . . . pleasingly plump? Matronly? Six months ago she would have panicked at a sudden weight gain, but today she was amused. Even proud. No, she wasn't pleasingly plump, just definitely pregnant, and it was a condition hardly in harmony with high fashion.

She surveyed her bulging closet again, pulled out the black watch plaid jumper with the wonderfully loose empire waist, and wondered if she dared to wear it one more time. Tales of her expansive luggage collection were still being whispered among hotel employees; certainly the waiters, concierge, and bellhops wondered why the senator's young wife, with her limitless wardrobe, insisted on wearing a shapeless plaid tent.

She debated between comfort and style. Style won. Today was too important to risk a negative impression. Surely she could endure the snugness of her pin-striped "power" suit if it subtly underscored the seriousness of Lillian's case.

She took a deep breath and tugged the zipper on her skirt to within an inch of the waistband. Good enough. The jacket would cover the gaping "V." If all went well in court she would be home within a day or two, and then she and Drew could drive to their favorite cluster of shops outside of Alexandria, Virginia, eat oysters on the half-shell, and later shop leisurely for maternity clothes. Anticipation of such an outing caused her nerves to calm, her stomach to quiet, and her confidence to build in spite of the fear that she might pop a button at any minute.

She selected a conservative burgundy scarf, tied it in a floppy bow, and arranged it in place under her crisp white collar. She stepped back to scrutinize the image in the mirror. Very preppy, very proper, and—she smiled—very *pregnant*. She loosened the skirt zipper one more tooth and reached for her briefcase.

*   *   *

Scott Parker had forgotten about military discipline. No, he reconsidered, it wasn't that he had forgotten about it, but that he had never really experienced it as intensely as he was now experiencing it with the SEALs. These guys were strack, a real heads-up group of fighters. They made no mistakes.

Lieutenant Stan Yake was the squad leader, a flint-eyed, square-jawed man whose thick, closely trimmed golden beard made him look more like a matinee idol than a commando. He had made it plain that he hadn't wanted Parker along on this mission. But he had obeyed orders, and Parker had been given a position on the strike force. Lieutenant Yake expected Parker to maintain the pace. No cream puffs.

For the two hours that Scott and the SEALs had been below decks in the cargo hold of the Canadian freighter *Winds of Windsor*, they had reviewed the plan, cleaned their weapons, reviewed the plan, checked their gear, reviewed the plan, and . . . well . . . started it all over again. Scott determined that these 15 men needed neither food nor rest—least of all Lieutenant Yake. There was one consolation, however: At least they were on Scott's side. He was glad of that.

A deckhand appeared below and requested the Lieutenant's presence in the pilot house. Lieutenant Yake returned in ten minutes.

"Good news, men," he announced. "I've just received a coded message. The Ruskies won't be on duty when we hit the compound. Better still, there will be a woman named Rosa Garcia waiting for us at the edge of the clearing. She's an inside plant. She'll tell us which room the Martinez woman is being held in. That will cut our search time in half."

The men nodded recognition and approval. Except Parker.

"Who's Rosa Garcia?" he challenged.

Lieutenant Yake glared at Parker. "Don't ask questions, Parker. She's probably some sort of agent. Just do as you're told."

"Okay, okay," said Scott.

Yake and his men turned as one, staring sternly at Scott. Scott understood instantly.

"I mean, yes, sir," he quickly corrected himself.

*   *   *

"Your honor, if it pleases the court, we are ready to call our first witness."

Cat was lying, of course. She wasn't at all certain she was ready to call anyone other than her husband to come and get her and take her home to Washington.

She had questioned the strategy at first, but had been soundly defeated in her argument by two of the sharpest legal minds in Detroit—Smith and McKeand, the law partners retained by Lillian to handle the Thompson portion of the Thompson vs. Michigan Technologies case. Smith and McKeand's verdict was irreversible, they had said; no appeal would be heard. Cat, not they, would represent Lillian Thompson in Judge Barbara Slater's courtroom. That was final: case closed.

They had based their decision on the stir that Cat had created in the media since she had arrived in Detroit. The public obviously loved her panache, her high-spirited style, and the way she dominated a situation merely by being part of it. If she could dazzle local newspaper readers and television viewers when she was exposed to them in brief sequences, surely she could work her charm on a jury that would watch her perform over a period of days or even weeks. Charisma, they called it. She had it and they needed it. Or at least Lillian needed it.

At first she had bristled at the idea of being used. When the attorneys mistook her hesitation for insecurity, they had countered with assurances that they would do all the necessary legal research and would plan the case down to the smallest detail. They would prepare the package for her to deliver. They would even offer pointers on voice modulation, subtle theatrics, and the image she should project to the male-dominated jury. For instance, the little plaid tent dress was cute, but. . . .

She had agreed to the plan only for Lillian's sake. Cat's courtroom experience was limited, but she had studied law long enough to realize that while evidence was the most important factor in winning any suit, effective presentation was also vital. Lillian's attorneys had powerful ammunition, but they were convinced that Cat was best able to take a shot at the jury.

*   *   *

"State your name for the court, please."

"Walter Hadley."

"And your occupation, Mr. Hadley?" Cat smiled as she worked her way through the routine portion of the examination.

"Computers. Data processing."

"Employer?"

"Currently unemployed."

Cat walked the length of the jury box, paused near the foreman, and then turned her attention to the witness.

"Your last employer, Mr. Hadley?"

"Michigan Technologies. I left earlier this year. The middle of January. The eighteenth, I think."

"I see." Cat was taking her time, building up to what her legal team called the big punches. "Exacty what was it that you did at Michigan Technologies?"

"Systems manager. I was in charge of the systems analysis and design group of our data processing department."

The strategy was working well. Cat noted that the jury members resembled spectators at a tennis match. Their heads turned first to the witness and then to her. Back and forth, back and forth, as she and Hadley rhythmically volleyed dialogue. She asked, he answered, she asked, he answered.

"As a *systems manager*, Mr. Hadley"—she purposely tripped over the alien term to show a shallow knowledge of technology—"did you have access to most of the corporate files?"

"Yes, ma'am. I knew most of the passwords. Of course, some files were closed for security purposes."

Cat nodded. "But someone with your training could surely access these closed files without too much trouble?"

It was Hadley's turn to nod.

"Do you recognize this portfolio, Mr. Hadley?"

While all eyes in the courtroom had been focused on the witness as he explained his duties at Michigan Technologies, Cat had walked to the desk assigned to Lillian and her counsel and had retrieved a large bundle of papers. Hadley examined the folder before answering.

"Yes, ma'am. This portfolio contains hard copies of documents I found in several of the closed files at Michigan Technologies."

Cat folded her arms and thoughtfully stroked her chin with the thumb and index finger of one hand.

"The file that you discovered, Mr. Hadley. Do you know to whom it belonged?"

"Yes, ma'am. Originally it was Mr. J. J. Parker's file. I could tell that by the date of origination and the code name. Of course it had been copied and transferred three or four times since it was created."

"Did you say 'J. J. Parker'?" asked Cat.

"Right. He was the senior officer at Michigan Technologies up until 1983 when he died. I never knew him personally, but people in the department still talked about him when I worked there. Most of the old-timers liked him a lot. They said he was a technological genius. Ran a clean business, too. He always gave his people a fair shake if they were willing to work as hard as he did."

Cat set the heavy file on the table adjoining the court stenographer's desk.

"You said that the 'old-timers' liked J. J. Parker a lot," repeated Cat. "Why the differentiation? Hadn't the young employees liked the boss?"

"There had been a scandal," answered Hadley. "The scuttle-butt was that Parker had lived beyond his means. You know, big house, fancy cars, country club membership, the whole bit. To generate some extra cash he had embezzled three million dollars of the company's funds. The younger employees seemed to believe it. The older folks just wouldn't buy it. There was a lot of tension. People took sides."

Cat sensed some confusion among the jury members. They were looking to her to clarify the witness's testimony. They didn't understand his technical terms and, since she had purposely indicated a lack of knowledge of computerese, they felt a common bond with her.

"This portfolio," she probed. "Where does it fit in?"

Hadley shrugged his shoulders. "I came across it one night when I was working late. I had logged onto the system to download a new program that one of the guys had written. I came across the Parker file by accident. The name caught my eye because I had heard all the stories. I was curious, so I got a printout."

"And this portfolio," she said, nodding to the file near the stenographer. "Is it the printout you're talking about?"

"Yes, ma'am."

Cat was beginning to enjoy herself. The jitters she had felt at the outset of the examination were gone. Her witness, speaking fluent jargon, was building credibility and her case as he doled out morsel after morsel of information. Now it was time to unravel the full mystery.

"In your best opinion, Mr. Hadley," she began, "what was the content of the file that you discovered?"

Hadley turned away from Cat and engaged the eyes of the jury.

"The file contained a list of stock holdings," he said. "Extensive holdings of blue chip stocks . . . worth two or three million dollars, I'd say. Every entry had a code number. At first I didn't understand. After all, Michigan Technologies is a public company and all of its holdings are public record. So I started asking a lot of questions. The old-timers in particular seemed to want to talk about it."

Cat studied the jury members. They were fascinated by the story that was unfolding. She didn't want to break their concentration, so she merely indicated to Hadley that he should continue.

"I found out that Mr. Parker and his board of directors were at odds with each other," said Hadley. "Parker thought there was a plan to oust him from his own company . . . not that he could do anything to stop it, since he didn't own controlling interest anymore."

Cat remembered the directive she had been given by Lillian's attorneys: When important testimony is about to be given, stop the action and rephrase what has been said. In that way, everyone will have full appreciation and understanding of the climactic information when it is offered.

"Let me see if I am following you, Mr. Hadley," she said. "Are you telling me that there was a conspiracy under way to remove Mr. Parker from his position as chief executive officer of Michigan Technologies?" She didn't wait for his confirmation. "And are you further telling me that Mr. Parker was powerless to stop the conspiracy because he no longer owned the majority of Michigan Technologies' stock?"

Hadley shook his head in agreement. "Yes, ma'am. But he did have one option, and that's where this portfolio comes in. According to company policy, the chief executive officer has the right to invest corporate assets—liquid cash—any way he sees fit. And that's exactly what J. J. Parker did. The file I discovered was documentation of where three million dollars in funds were. The money he was later accused of stealing actually was invested in blue chip stocks to build a war chest to save the company from an unfriendly takeover."

Cat flashed a quick glance at the jury to see if the impact of her witness's testimony had been felt. Their faces and the subtle looks of approval by both Smith and McKeand told her that she had succeeded in her interrogation.

"Your honor, I object," interrupted Roderick. He was on his feet, standing very erect, his eyes flashing righteous indignation. "I object to this line of questioning and I challenge the admissibility of this evidence. In fact, I am appalled that counsel would even suggest that we should accept the testimony of an informant planted in Michigan Technologies on assignment to conduct a covert investigation."

The eyes of Judge Slater and members of the jury quickly turned to Roderick, who basked in the rapt attention.

"Please approach the bench, Mr. Davis and Mrs. Sanders," ordered the judge.

Cat's confidence diminished as she looked hurriedly to Smith and McKeand for direction. One shook his head, the other shrugged. This hadn't been part of the game plan. She was clearly on her own until they could ask for a recess, regroup, and discuss the developments. In the meantime she had no choice but to join Roderick, already up front, in a conference with the judge.

"Judge Slater, it is not my intention to publicly attack the character of the witness," assured Roderick. "However, he is known in corporate circles to be a highly skilled practitioner of industrial espionage, a man who will stop at nothing to provide a client with whatever information the client wants. Ethically, Mr. Hadley is bound not to reveal the name of the person who hired him to spy on Michigan Technologies. Of course, if the court insists on knowing this information and Hadley refuses to give it, the court could cite him for contempt."

Judge Slater's eyes narrowed, her own contempt showing by now. "Mr. Davis, I am well aware of the options available to the court."

Cat stood to one side, saying nothing, but silently hoping the judge would not press her witness for the name of his employer. She wasn't sure she could explain that the man who hired Walter Hadley to delve into Michigan Technologies' records was none other than her father, Phil Compton. How could she possibly convince the jury that her father's motive had been nothing more than to run a security check on Roderick Davis, his prospective son-in-law? Cat knew that she and Drew would be embarrassed by the public revelation; she would appear fickle in her relationships with men—engaged to one man and married to another within a year.

She looked at Roderick. Could it be that he too would prefer that the information remain secret? After all, it had been his questionable character that had caused Phil Compton to underwrite the investigation in the first place.

"My client, Michigan Technologies, has no desire to ruin Mr. Hadley's reputation," said Roderick. "At the same time, we cannot accept evidence that we believe has been manufactured to support a case that does not exist."

Judge Slater looked simultaneously confused and exasperated. "Would counsel *please* get to the point," she prodded.

"Sorry, Your Honor," replied Roderick. "Our point is this: We challenge any qualified computer expert to thoroughly explore the data bases at Michigan Technologies and to locate any secret file such as the one Mr. Hadley has described. We launched our own search when we began preparations for this case. Needless to say, we found nothing."

Judge Slater turned to the witness. "Mr. Hadley, could you reenter the Michigan Technologies' data base and call up Mr. Parker's file in order to verify its existence?"

Hadley shook his head. "No, ma'am, I can't. The file was purged from the system after I got the printout."

Roderick smiled smugly. "So, you see, Your Honor, this so-called 'file' could have been created yesterday as evidence. Even if it did exist, there's no way of telling how it has been rewritten, modified, and altered. To rest the validity of the entire case on this piece of fictional evidence would be a grave injustice to my clients."

Cat felt trapped. Her legal coaches had prepared her for nothing like this. With resentment she assessed her position and realized that her role was little more than that of a puppet. She had been placed in the courtroom, given a script, and told to look pretty while reciting her lines. Why had she agreed to such a strategy? Was it ego? Was it the opportunity to play the part of serious attorney without doing any of the real work? She suddenly felt nervous and cornered. The experience surely would teach her a lesson, but it might also cost Lillian her case.

"Under the circumstances, Mrs. Sanders, I see no alternative but to rule this evidence inadmissible," said Judge Slater. "You may call your next witness."

*   *   *

Mom Mead shook her head in disbelief.

"It must have been awful, child," she said sympathetically. "Whatever did you do? Ask for a recess? Surely the judge must have known that you needed time to plan your next move."

Cat continued to sip slowly from her glass of iced Perrier. At Mom Mead's insistence she was sitting on the sofa in Lillian's hotel room with her feet elevated on the coffee table in front of her. Her ankles were swollen from the heat and from the seemingly endless day of pacing the courtroom as she attempted to salvage Lillian's case. The swelling, Cat knew, was just another symptom of her pregnancy; she only hoped no one else made the connection. Lillian and the Meads were being so kind—too kind—and Cat wasn't sure if their kindness stemmed from pity for her poor performance as an attorney or from empathy for her obvious discomfort.

"Cat was wonderful," replied Lillian, looking up briefly from the scrapbook the Meads had brought her. "She couldn't ask for a recess because she didn't want the jury to be left with the impression that Walter Hadley was some kind of high-tech spy. She had to try and erase that image, so she called me to testify. It's all my fault that things didn't work out."

Lillian was stretching out on the bed with pillows propped between her shoulders and the headboard. She closed her eyes and sighed at the recollection of the day in court.

"I was awful," she said simply. "Cat tried to establish that I had been squeezed out of the company, and that Daddy's enemies had stripped me of my title and my stock. The jury was listening, and I think we were making some headway until Roderick began his cross-examination. I just wasn't prepared for his questions."

Mom Mead was impatient. "Well? What did he ask?"

"It wasn't so much *what* he asked but rather *how* he asked it," replied Lillian. "He made me describe my last day on the job at Michigan Technologies. He took advantage of all the personal information I had shared with him when we were engaged. He asked me if I had always wanted to work at Michigan Technologies or if Daddy had insisted that I go into the family business. He made it look as if I hated my job and that I welcomed the chance to get out of it. He asked if I hadn't gladly accepted severance pay; then he made me tell how I had used the money to take a long vacation in Tennessee and that while I was gone I had never even called the office to request a meeting with Daddy's replacement. Of course it was all true, but he twisted it, and I came off looking like the spoiled boss's daughter who's now trying to regain the family fortune."

Lillian shook her head in dismay and directed her attention back to the scrapbook. She turned the pages slowly, immersing herself in the past in order to forget the present. The Meads' timing had been perfect. The yellowed newspaper clippings and family photos caused her to smile as long-forgotten memories came rushing back to her.

"Look at this, Cat," she said with a chuckle. "Here's how I like to remember my dad . . . so much fun and full of life." She carried the album over to the sofa and laid it in Cat's lap. "That was the *real* J. J. Parker," she said, pointing proudly to a picture in the *Detroit News*. "He wasn't at all like the defeated, desperate man you've been hearing about in court. Everyone in the industry liked him. Or at least *almost* everyone did: Reporters were always calling him when they needed a comment from a computer expert. He was one of the industry's founding fathers, all right, but he never tossed around a lot of scientific jargon. He was 'quotable,' the reporters used to say. Sometimes *too* quotable. He'd tell you exactly what was on his mind!"

Pop Mead laughed at Lillian's assessment and sat down next to Cat to share the memory. He looked at the clipping and nodded knowledgeably. He scanned the article that accompanied the animated photograph of J. J. Parker.

"I'll never forget the day this story ran in the paper," he said. "That morning your dad had received a check in the mail from the U. S. Government for Scott's death benefit. He was furious. Absolutely beside himself! He didn't believe his son was dead and he wouldn't tolerate anyone saying so, least of all the United States Government."

Lillian and Cat huddled over the scrapbook to read the words of the page-one article.

"J. J. was so angry," continued Pop Mead, "that he called the newspaper and ordered the editor to send a writer out to his house immediately. He wanted the whole world to know that his son was alive and well, thank you, no matter what Washington, D. C. had to say about the matter."

Lillian laughed at the thought of her father fighting the system. It bolstered her determination to take on Michigan Technologies. Maybe she wasn't jousting with windmills after all. Maybe she was just following a Parker family tradition and standing up for what she believed.

"Did anyone pay any attention to Daddy?" she asked.

"They surely did," replied Pop Mead. "The story caught everyone's fancy. Your father became sort of a hero for a while. Patriotism wasn't exactly in vogue after Vietnam, and people loved to read about the devoted Detroit father who wouldn't accept the death of his soldier son even though the government was offering money in order to close the case."

Lillian began to turn the page, but Cat stopped her. She had said nothing as the story had been recalled, but her interest had increased with every detail. Now she wanted to hear more.

"The government check," she began. "What happened to it?"

"J. J. refused to accept it, so it was sent back," replied Pop Mead. "Actually, it was hand-delivered with great pomp and flourish. Our congressman back then was a fellow named Anthony Williams, and he was one of those politicians who was always trying to grab the spotlight. When he read about J. J.'s crusade against the government he decided he could benefit by jumping into the battle. So he announced that since he was located in Washington, he would personally carry Scott's death benefit check back to the Pentagon."

Once again Lillian attempted to turn the page, but Cat shook her head, not wanting to move on. She sat silently, biting her lower lip, obviously deep in thought.

"That's it," Cat finally said. "Yes . . . yes. I think that's it."

Lillian and Pop Mead exchanged glances, then looked to Mom Mead, who shrugged her shoulders. They waited, not wanting to interrupt Cat's thoughts.

"Don't you see?" asked Cat. "Don't you see? That's it!" She began to smile, new fire igniting her eyes. In spite of her swollen ankles she jumped to her feet, walked to the phone, and began dialing Drew's office in Washington. Midway through the numbers she noticed her audience—Lillian plus Mom and Pop Mead—still looking at her, mystified. She smiled and put down the phone.

"We're going to win your case, Lill," she said triumphantly, hugging her friend. "And it's all because of Mom and Pop and this scrapbook. But you've all got to help. And we've got to act fast—superfast! So don't question why—just do your part. Are you willing?"

Three heads nodded enthusiastically.

"Good," said Cat. "Now here's what I want you to do. Pop, you need to go down to the Detroit Public Library and make copies of every newspaper and magazine article you can find about Congressman Williams returning the check to the Pentagon. Got it? Don't come back unless you're carrying a huge stack of paper."

Pop Mead started for the door. "No problem," he promised. "Bringing in the sheaves is what I do best."

"Lillian, I want you to get into those boxes of business materials you stored when you left Detroit. Search your father's papers and see if you can find any kind of government receipt that would verify that the check was returned uncashed. Okay?"

Lillian took her sunglasses out of her purse and made for the door.

"As for me, I'm going up to my room to call Drew. If he hurries, he can catch a taxi to the Pentagon before it closes. We need to put a tracer on that government check ASAP."

Cat turned to leave, but hesitated when she noticed Mom Mead waiting hopefully for an assignment. She smiled, walked over to the elderly woman, and kissed her soundly on the cheek.

"Mom, since you're responsible for keeping that scrapbook all these years, I've saved the best job for you. Are you ready?"

Mom leaned toward Cat to receive her instructions, then grinned when she heard Cat's directive.

"I want you to call the law offices of Smith and McKeand and tell them they're going to start earning their retainer," ordered Cat. "I want dossiers worked up on Roderick Davis and Paul Stattman and all the other key people who were with Michigan Technologies at the time of the takeover. Have them locate copies of M-T's annual reports for the past four years and see that they get delivered to me here tonight. And have them find out who bought the Parker family home when it went up for auction and what the price was."

"Yes, yes," Mom said, nodding as she quickly scratched out the orders on a notepad that had been next to the telephone.

"Oh, and Mom. . . ."

Mom Mead looked up. "Yes, dear?"

"This is no time to be gracious."

Mom reached for the Yellow Pages. "I hear you. Trust me, I'll have that office jumping in five minutes."

Thanks to a push-button phone, it only took her three.

CHAPTER 10

A soft knock sounded at the door of Juanita Martinez's room. Rosa Garcia arose from a chair in the darkened room and opened the door.

"It's nearly 4 o'clock, Rosa," said a young woman in a military nurse's uniform. "I've come to relieve you." She entered the room quietly.

Rosa nodded. "The prisoner is asleep," she said. "I gave her a heavy sedative. She should remain asleep until they come for her around nine this morning."

"Good," said the woman. "I think I'll lock the door and try to get a couple of hours of rest in the chair. I hate night duty."

"I'm sure you'll be able to sleep," promised Rosa.

And with that Juanita Martinez, hidden in the darkness, chopped the flat side of her hand sharply against the back of the nurse's neck. The woman instantly dropped to the floor.

"Quickly," said Rosa. "Take her clothes off. After you put on her uniform, we'll put her into the bed. I'll give her the injection that was meant for you."

The women worked rapidly and efficiently. They undressed the nurse and then pulled Juanita's hospital gown over her. Together they lifted the woman into bed, turned her face away from the door, and pulled the covers up to her chin.

"No one will know it's not you," Rosa whispered to Juanita.

"You're right. Now go, Mama," said Juanita. "You must. If you don't sign out, the guard will become suspicious. He'll come looking for you."

"Yes, yes, I'm leaving. I will leave the retreat center and go to the edge of the forest at the north of the compound. When your rescuers come, I will tell them where to find you. In the meantime, you must sit in the chair here and put a magazine over your face and pretend to be asleep. Keep the door locked."

"I know my part," said Juanita. She grabbed her mother's arm. "And remember, Mama: You *must not* come here with the rescue team. Stay in the forest where it is safe. We'll come back for you and we'll all leave together. Promise me you won't come here during the fighting."

"Yes, my dearest. I promise. And promise me that no matter what happens you will always remember your mama with love."

Juanita nodded. "Don't be pessimistic, Mama. We won't be caught. I know this will work. When you received the message back from Alma at Pedro Vargas' barbershop, I knew all was well."

"Yes. All is well. You will be safe, my Juanita. All will be well."

*   *   *

The *Winds of Windsor* dropped anchor two miles off the shores of Cuba and lowered three rubber rafts over her starboard side. Fifteen men with black outfits and grease-covered faces went rappeling down the ship's side on taut nylon ropes. Slung over their backs were M-16 rifles, grappling hooks, loops of rope, and bandoliers filled with percussion grenades and canisters of tear gas and phosphorus. Scott Parker dropped into the lead raft, grabbed a paddle and began to match rowing strokes with the other men. They had to hurry. If they didn't make it to the beach in half an hour they would be spotted by the Cuban shore patrol and peppered with bullets.

Scott pulled hard against the choppy water.

We're coming, Juanita. Just hold on. We're on our way.

*   *   *

When Rosa Garcia left Juanita's room, she walked through two hallways and came to the reception area of the retreat center. A handsome young soldier was seated behind a desk.

"Things quiet, Ramon?" she asked as she signed the night-duty roster.

"Yes, but I don't mind," the young man answered. "It's a lot better duty than what I had last year. I suppose our swamps and marshes must be guarded too, but, oh, the mosquitoes! Such torture."

"I can imagine," said Rosa with a sympathetic smile. "I left a small bag here at the desk when I came to work. Do you have it?"

Ramon reached under the desk. "This thing?" He extended a paper sack.

"Yes, thank you. My late-night snack."

Rosa started walking toward the exit. She paused, then turned back.

"Oh, Ramon, one little request. I left the prisoner sedated and I told Louisa she could just doze in the chair for the next few hours. You'll be quiet if you go back there, won't you?"

"Of course. In fact, if the prisoner is sedated, I won't even need to make my rounds, right?"

"No. No, I guess you won't," said Rosa, shrugging her shoulders. "Well, good night, Ramon."

*   *   *

In Washington, things were quiet in the Caribbean Command room. Alma Hammond sat amidst phones that were not ringing, teletypes that were not clicking, and computers that were not printing. The last relay of news from the Canadian freighter had come two hours earlier; it simply stated that things were on schedule. But now radio silence would be observed until the entire mission was over and Parker and the SEALs were either dead or back safely aboard the freighter.

As she sat alone in the silent room, Alma let her thoughts continually return to Gregor Kotusov. Why had he helped her that way? And what had he meant when he said she should *know* why he had done this for her?

Under other circumstances, if a man went out of his way to do something this special for a woman it would indicate his concern for her, even his affection. But, of course, that was impossible in regard to Gregor. He was merely her opposite number in the camp of the "enemy." They were sworn adversaries, despite their occasional efforts at cooperation for their mutual benefit.

No, it would be flattering to think that an intelligent and attractive man like Gregor Kotusov could be amorously attracted to her, but Alma knew that such thoughts were ludicrous. Of course they were, right? Oh, sure, Gregor had always been friendly . . . and, true, the other night at her apartment he had complimented her several times on her appearance. But . . . well . . . men do that. It never really meant anything. Surely not.

*   *   *

As soon as the raft hit the beach, Scott Parker was out and pulling it over the sand up to the rim of the vegetation. Serrated knives and hatchets were used to hurriedly cut branches and brush to hide the three rafts. Lieutenant Yake then gave a hand signal for his men to move inland.

Using a luminous-dial compass, Yake took a bearing and then set out in a northeast direction. His men used him as a reference point and followed closely behind, never saying a word.

The morning sun broke over the water and began to climb in the sky. Dawn's pinkness gave way to an early morning's glare. By the time the men reached the outskirts of the compound, it was becoming daylight. Rosa Garcia was standing in a small clearing that was surrounded by tropical trees. Lieutenant Yake approached her and exchanged code words. He signaled his men to secure a perimeter.

"Here is a sketch of the floor plan," said Rosa, giving Yake a paper with some pencil lines on it. "The retreat center has not been scheduled for use until Juanita is transferred. You won't have to worry about running into other guests or visitors. Juanita is here, in a room near the back of this second hallway. She's dressed in a military nurse's uniform. Please, now, I must talk to Señor Parker."

Yake shook his head. "First point out where the guards are stationed."

Quickly Rosa pointed on the floor plan where the lookout posts and patrol zones were located. Yake asked about the guards' weapons. Rosa knew nothing about armaments, but from the basic descriptions of what the "guns" looked like Yake determined that the internal guards were wearing .45 automatic pistols and that the two external lookouts were armed with high-powered Russian-made Salasnikov rifles.

Yake signaled toward the bushes. Scott Parker and two of the SEALs came out of hiding. Rosa stared at the men, wondering which one was Parker.

"We'll wait four more minutes until the sun crests over the roof of the retreat center," said Yake. "That will blind the lookouts for the time we'll need to dash across the lawn. Tony, you take Jonathan, Mike, and Tim with you. Go straight up the walls and eliminate the lookouts. No shots. Brad, you take Jason and Bud and hit the front door and side windows. Jump the guards simultaneously. Tie them up. Gags, too. Parker, you and I will go for the Martinez woman. Run as fast as you can down the hall. I'll watch right and you watch left. On the way back I'll go first and secure the route. You follow with the woman. Everyone understand?"

The men nodded. They turned to go back among the trees.

Rosa quickly grabbed Scott's arm. "You are Señor Parker? Please, one moment, I beg."

Parker looked at Yake, who nodded his approval. "Three minutes till we run," said Yake. "Make it snappy." He joined the others.

"I don't know who you are, lady, but I want you to know I'm in your debt," said Scott. "The woman we're coming to get is someone special to me."

"I know," said Rosa. "I am her mother. I know all about you."

Scott blinked. "Her *mother*?"

Rosa smiled. "Juanita can explain everything later. For now, I must talk. I know you are confused. I wish I had time to tell you more, but there's not a moment to spare. Juanita expects me to be waiting here when you come back. She wants me to go to America with her. I cannot. My husband is here and I love him. Juanita's love and devotion to you will eventually help her to understand my devotion to Ricardo. Besides, Cuba is my home. These are my people. They need my help. I am a nurse, and a good one, too. I hate what Communism has done to my country, but I can't change that. So I help my people try to cope with it. I do my part. I cannot desert my neighbors and friends."

"But . . . you'll be killed for helping Juanita escape," protested Parker.

"No, that's not a worry," said Rosa. "I signed out at the normal time more than an hour ago. Whatever happens now has nothing to do with me. I'm off duty. The woman who replaced me will be blamed for Juanita's escape. She'll accuse me of helping, of course, but no one will believe her. They'll assume she's lying to try to escape her own punishment. She'll be sent to prison. That's as it should be. She was part of a plot to . . . to . . . well, to do something horrible to my Juanita."

Scott bit his lower lip and nodded solemnly. "I know about it. You've saved Juanita from something worse than death. I wish I had some way to thank you."

"You are a Christian, is that right?"

"Yes," said Scott, slightly surprised by the question. "Yes, I'm a Christian."

"Then promise me with a holy oath that you will love and care for my Juanita. That's all the thanks I want."

"That's the easiest promise I've ever made," said Scott.

Rosa pulled Scott's face toward her and kissed his cheek. "I know you are a good man, Señor Parker . . . Scott. Help my Juanita to understand why I could not stay here to say good-bye. Tell her I love her and that I will go to the barbershop of Pedro Vargas each month for news from her. Oh—and give her this."

"A bag?" questioned Scott.

"Chocolate chip cookies," explained Rosa. "She'll understand."

*   *   *

Guadalupe Bentancourt had purposely left his bedroom drapes pulled open the night before. At dawn the sunlight of a new day awakened him. He smiled. Ah, morning. A lovely dawn. A fine omen for what was to be a wonderful day.

He left his bed and walked to the window.

"Good morning, World!" he said jubilantly. "This day is dedicated to the honorable Guadalupe Bentancourt, Ambassador-at-Large of Cuba. And, so, the day shall be spent in an appropriate manner. First, a long, hot shower. Next, an expansive breakfast on the terrace. Afterward, a manicure and haircut. And, finally, the donning of a flawlessly tailored suit, complete with the Order of Lenin—bulky weight that it is—pinned to the lapel. At 9:30 it's off to the Soviet Embassy for the award ceremony and what will obviously be a full day of fine food, good cigars, and celebrating."

Bentancourt looked at himself in the mirror.

"One day Fidel will step down, Guadalupe," he told his reflection. "Who better to succeed him? This country will need a touch of worldly sophistication by then. Yes, Guadalupe, your day is coming. And it will be those naive idiots the Russians who will make it possible for you."

* * *

The attack on the retreat center came so fast that Ramon had no time to think.

Crash! A body came breaking through the bay window in the foyer. *Crash!* A second body came smashing through the narrow glass window behind the registration desk.

"*Pare!*" yelled a third man who came running in the front door pointing a sawed-off shotgun at Ramon's head. "Freeze!"

Ramon froze. Only his eyes moved. Three men dressed in black outfits were converging on him, each brandishing a weapon. *Norte Americanos*, he thought. *But how? Why?*

Ramon's hands were pulled behind him roughly and were tied. A wide strip of tape was placed over his mouth. He was blindfolded and then his feet were tied. He was dragged across the room and dumped into a coat closet.

The three SEALs took position in the foyer. One laid flat on the tile, his M-16 rifle pointed down the west hall. Another crouched behind the reception desk, a pistol pointed toward the entrance door and a rifle pointed in the opposite direction toward the central hallway. The third SEAL put his back against the wall near the broken bay window. He watched the outside.

"Comin' in," came the voice of Lieutenant Yake from outside.

Yake and Parker entered the doorway. Yake carried a snub-nosed Uzi, the machine-gun pistol developed by the Israelis as an antiterrorist weapon. It could fire 60 rounds before needing to be reloaded.

"Bad news, sir," said the SEAL behind the reception desk. "Only the sign-in man was on duty up front here. He's locked in the closet over there. The other two inside guards must be somewhere at the back of the complex."

Yake grimaced. This would make it harder. Oh, well.

"Ready, Parker?"

"Yes, sir." Scott wrapped the sling of his M-16 rifle around his left elbow, put his left hand under the plastic barrel guard, and then put his right hand around the grip and the rifle's trigger.

"On three, then," said Lieutenant Yake. "One . . . two . . . three!"

Yake and Parker broke into a flat-out sprint. They kept neck and neck down the central hallway and rounded the corner in full stride. The moment they turned into the back hall, they were fired upon—single shots from handguns fired by poor marksmen.

Yake and Parker simultaneously dove forward onto their left shoulders, rolled, and came up firing. Parker's M-16 sprayed 20 rounds in less than three seconds. Yake rotated his Uzi in a wide circle and showered 60 rounds down the hallway. Parker instinctively pulled a fresh magazine from the side leg pocket of his fatigue pants. He reloaded quickly.

"*Nada mas, nada mas!*" called a desperate voice from the other end.

Yake yelled out in Spanish, "Throw out your weapons. Put your hands on top of your heads. Come out slowly."

Two handguns were tossed down the hallway. From behind a metal drinking fountain one guard slowly stood up. Another guard stepped into the hallway from the doorway of a room.

"Okay, Parker, go get the lady," ordered Yake. "I'll tie these two bozos together. Hurry up. If those shots were heard, we can expect visitors at any minute."

Scott was off instantly. He weaved his way through two short corridors and came to the room where Juanita was supposed to be.

"Juanita! Let's go!" he yelled.

Nothing.

"Juanita! It's Scott. Come out of there. Come on!"

Still nothing.

Why wasn't she coming out?

Scott banged the door. "It's me. It's Scott. Let's go!"

Cautiously the door latches and locks were clicked and the door was opened a fraction of an inch. Then, suddenly, the door was pulled open wider. Then, to their mutual surprise, all Juanita and Scott could do was stand and stare at each other. They were shocked.

So many changes had taken place.

Juanita was so thin and haggard-looking, thought Scott. Her once-beautiful black hair was now matted and twisted. Her cheeks were hollow, her eyes sunken. She appeared so frail and weak and vulnerable. She was certainly not the woman he remembered from a year ago.

Changes *had* taken place.

Scott was so muscular and firm, thought Juanita. His eyes were clear and his face was full and healthy. His hair was thick and cut very stylishly. Even with camouflage paint across his nose and forehead, he was strikingly handsome.

They stood gawking.

"I . . . I couldn't even recognize your voice," she stammered. "It's . . . it's so much stronger than . . ."

"Oh, Juanita. It's me. It's *me*. I'm here."

From some distance a frantic call arose from Lieutenant Yake. "Move it, Parker! Where are you? Let's get out of here."

Scott responded immediately. He stepped forward and kissed Juanita. He squeezed her close to him.

"Your barge awaits, Your Highness," he told her. "Ready for an ocean cruise?"

Juanita wrapped her arms around Scott. "Take me home. I can't stand it here any longer. Please! Take me home."

*   *   *

At 10 o'clock that morning Guadalupe Bentancourt was received by the Soviet Ambassador to Cuba. Bentancourt was elegance personified. His mustache was perfectly trimmed, his shirtsleeves sported gold cufflinks, and his Gucci shoes were buffed to a dazzling gloss.

To Bentancourt's pleasant surprise, the room was filled with far more dignitaries than he had anticipated. Politicians, generals, and statesmen from both the USSR and Cuba were on hand. My, this really was going to be something special, he determined.

"Ambassador Bentancourt," began the Soviet Ambassador, "you personally were in charge of the arrest and interrogation and imprisonment of the American spy Juanita Martinez?"

Bentancourt tried to appear humble. "Yes, Excellency, I have handled those matters by myself."

"And you were aware that this woman had tried to compromise the security of our embassy, and that she had for the past year or more been reviewing secret Cuban and Russian documents? You knew she was an incredible security risk, yet you chose to be personally responsible for her?"

"There are crucial decisions one must make in our line of work," said Bentancourt with some swagger, "and from time to time responsibilities one must accept. I think I handled the Martinez situation in an appropriate way."

The Soviet Ambassador stared hard at Bentancourt, then moved his glaring look around the room from the face of one official to the next. Finally he came back to Bentancourt.

"In that case, I now place you into the hands of Colonel Mendoza of the Cuban Peoples Army, who will arrest you for dereliction of duty, breaching national security, and violation of established government procedures. In case you haven't heard as yet, the American spy escaped from Cuba at dawn today. Your incompetence has set our Caribbean operations back ten years. If I have anything to say about all this, you'll be shot before the week is over."

Bentancourt's face went ashen. For a moment he was numbed, then his stomach wrenched into a knot. His legs became jelly. Had his arms not been immediately grabbed by two embassy security men, he would have fallen to the floor.

"No . . . no . . . it's impossible," he said weakly. "She's at the retreat center."

"How much verification do you need?" insisted the Soviet Ambassador. He snapped his fingers.

To Bentancourt's horror, Captain Reyes was suddenly brought into the room. His face was bruised and swollen, his nose broken.

"They made me . . . tell everything," said Reyes, coughing. "When I went to get the prisoner, she was gone. The Americans came for her."

Bentancourt's eyes widened in terror. *The Americans!* But they *couldn't* have rescued Juanita. Not unless the Russians had helped arrange it. But if that was so, then . . . then . . . *the Russians knew everything.* They didn't just know about this incident with Juanita. They knew everything. Somehow they had found out about Parker . . . and the escape from Vietnam . . . and the secret deal with the CIA. . . .

Bentancourt looked at the Soviet Ambassador. The Russian gave him a slow, satisfying half-grin, as if to confirm that Bentancourt's worst suspicions were correct. They *did* know everything. And they weren't anywhere near as naive or stupid as Bentancourt had supposed them to be.

Methodically the Soviet Ambassador walked up to Bentancourt. He reached forward and seized hold of the Order of Lenin in Bentancourt's lapel, then yanked. The ribbon on the medal was protected by the Ambassador's grip, but Bentancourt's lapel was torn completely out of his coat.

*   *   *

"You're so thin—eat another cookie," urged Scott, offering the bag of chocolate chip treats that Rosa had baked.

Since they had boarded the Canadian ship two hours earlier, Scott had not left Juanita's side. Still, they hadn't been alone. A medical officer had interviewed Juanita, asking her dozens of questions and jotting down the responses on a clipboard. Alma Hammond had insisted on a thorough medical debriefing to determine if Bentancourt's strategy included any slow-acting poison that could have been administered during the shifts when Rosa was off duty. Alma knew Bentancourt well enough to suspect he had a sinister backup plan. Although he had authorized surgery to incapacitate Juanita's mind and memory, he might have prescribed additional medication to assure that, if rescued, she would be muddled in giving any information.

"Actually, you're in amazingly good condition," the doctor assured her. "Underweight, of course, and weakened by the lack of activity, but your reflexes are good." True to his profession, he made notations on his pad in obscure scribbles that only he could decipher. "Do you recall being given any capsules or pills on a regular basis?"

"Vitamins," Juanita replied.

"*Vitamins?* You're sure?"

Juanita smiled at the doctor's response.

"Absolutely. They were the same kind my grandmother used to send me when I was in college. Chewables. The night nurse at the hacienda took very good care of me, although you might not have approved of her methods, Doctor."

"Oh? Why not?"

"She didn't follow orders very well. Thank goodness."

The doctor looked puzzled, but Scott laughed.

"Inside joke," Scott explained. "How many Communist agents do you know who would conspire to free a prisoner and would even pack chocolate chip cookies for the getaway trip?"

At that the doctor gave up, released his notes from the clipboard, and inserted them into an oversized envelope stamped "Top Secret." He started for the door.

"I better file my report with Washington," he said, "although they're never going to believe this one."

The door quietly clicked shut, leaving Juanita and Scott alone for the first time in more than a year.

"Tired?" asked Scott. "Maybe I should let you sleep for a while. I'll go find Captain Duhamel and see about getting you some warmer clothes. He said you could stay here in his cabin until we make contact with the submarine."

Scott got up and began to explore the tiny compartment. He quickly located an adjoining shower stall, one of the modest perks afforded the captain of the ship.

"I'll tell you what," he began. "Why don't you take a hot shower and stretch out on the cot for an hour or so? By the time you wake up I'll have scrounged up a sweatshirt and some fatigues for you. Can't guarantee they'll fit, but at least you'll be warm."

Juanita looked frightened. "Please don't leave me," she implored.

Scott hesitated, taken aback by her sudden mood swing. A moment earlier she had been joking with the doctor; now she seemed close to tears. What had Bentancourt done to her? She was so unlike the Juanita he remembered, who had helped nurse him back to health after his release from the POW camp. A year ago she had exuded confidence and strength. Now she seemed vulnerable and almost childlike.

The ship lurched to the left and Scott nearly lost his footing. He steadied himself by holding onto the back of a chair. Before the cabin righted, he sank into the sofa next to her.

"What's wrong? Is it the storm?" he asked kindly. "It'll blow over soon. The captain says it's just a squall. Not uncommon for this time of year. It's going to delay our rendezvous with the sub for awhile, but there's nothing to worry about." He playfully chucked her chin. "Before you know it, we'll be on the sub headed for home. *Home*, Juanita. Think of it! Finally you'll meet Mom and Pop Mead, you'll see the mission, we can spend some time in Austin and we'll. . . ."

She was crying now.

"What's the matter?" he asked. "Am I pushing too hard? Expecting too much? I don't mean to, honestly. It's just that I've waited so long."

He reached out for her, gently inviting her into his arms. Her cries became sobs as she buried her face in his shoulder.

"Tell me what's wrong, Juanita. I can't help you if I don't know what's happening."

She shook her head, struggling to put into words the emotions that seemed so contradictory.

"I don't mean to seem ungrateful," she whispered. "It's not you. I've waited for this a long time too. It's just that . . . that . . . why can't anything ever be easy?"

He offered her a tissue, then used his index finger to stop a tear that zigzagged down her cheek.

"All my life I've wondered about my mother," she explained. "When I was a little girl I used to fantasize about what she might look like, how she might dress, what her voice might sound like. Finally, after all these years, I've met her, and she's even more wonderful than I had dreamed."

Scott held her close and stroked her long, tangled hair. He said nothing, preferring to let her talk out her pain.

"We were so close those three nights in the hacienda, Scott. She told me about my father and about my Grandmother and Grandfather Martinez. I told her about how you and I met and about how we fell in love when I was assigned to escort you back to the States."

She brightened.

"We even laughed about 'dear' Señor Bentancourt. She dislikes him almost as much as we do!" She pulled away and faced him squarely, her eyes large with wonderment. "What was really amazing was her attitude toward him, Scott. Even though Bentancourt had treated her very badly, she had a sort of tolerance for him. It was almost as if she had forgiven him for all his cruelty over the years. We prayed together every night and she always asked a blessing for Bentancourt. I'm afraid I wasn't that charitable."

Scott smiled. "Your mother is a Christian," he said. "I think she and I are going to get along very well."

"But that's just it," replied Juanita. "We'll probably never see her again. I almost wish I hadn't found her. At least then I wouldn't hurt the way I do right now. I . . . I miss her . . . so much."

The cries began again, softly this time, and barely audible to Scott, who lovingly cradled her in his arms while gently brushing his lips over her hair. He understood even better than she realized.

"Remember, Juanita," he began, "your mother, at this very minute, is probably feeling the same emotions that you're feeling. She's thinking about you, even crying for you, and she's being held and comforted by a man who loves her very, very much."

"Like you're comforting me?" asked Juanita.

Scott nodded. "Exactly."

"I don't know Ricardo Garcia," he continued, "but I think I understand how he feels tonight. He's probably glad to have the woman he loves home safely, but he probably has some guilt at knowing that her pain is caused by her choice to be with him. He's probably as determined as I am to someday, very soon, bring about a reunion."

The tears stopped now, and Juanita lifted her face to Scott's. As strong and deep as their feelings were, they seemed content to savor the moment, neither one wanting to hurry the kiss they had played and replayed in their dreams so many times.

CHAPTER 11

"They look like guns," whispered Mom Mead, looking around the courtroom at the semicircle of cameras, mounted on tripods, aimed directly at the judge's bench and witness stand.

Judge Slater had decided during the pretrial hearing to allow all proceedings to be filmed and photographed. Smith and McKeand had been delighted with the decision, knowing that Cat would dominate most of the film footage aired on local television and that she would most likely be included in any still photos published by the newspapers. A rumor even persisted that *Time* magazine was planning to send a reporter and photographer to cover the story.

"There are twice as many journalists here today as yesterday," noted Cat.

"What do they want?" asked Mom.

"Us," answered Cat.

Mom looked confused. "What do you mean?"

"Word travels fast," explained Cat. "The media people think we've lost our case. They want to be here to write the eulogies."

Cat looked nervously at the clock. The judge would be announced at any moment, and Lillian still hadn't arrived.

"She'll be along directly," assured Mom, anticipating Cat's concern. "She had to answer the phone just as we were leaving. Charles told me to come ahead and bring the newspaper clippings you wanted. He and Lillian can drive over together as soon as she gets finished talking. Charles knows all the shortcuts across town."

Mom Mead hesitated, wondering if she dared ask the question that had been on her mind since she and Pastor Mead had arrived in Detroit the day before. She didn't want to pry, of course, but she couldn't help but notice that Cat looked pale in spite of her perfectly applied makeup. Her face appeared gaunt, although there was a slight roundness to her usually svelte frame. Other clues were evident too: Cat hadn't eaten any dinner last night, had declined Mom's offer of coffee from the downstairs vending machines this morning, and was now unwrapping a roll of antacid tablets.

"This is a hard time to be away from Drew, isn't it, Cat?" Mom began carefully.

Cat shot her a look. Did she know?

"I won't say anything, but if I can help in any way . . . ," said Mom. "Restaurant food can be a bit heavy sometimes. I could get you some fruit or saltines. Carbonated soft drinks settle the stomach, too."

Yes, she knew.

Cat smiled and sank into the chair next to her elderly friend. It felt good to share the secret, especially with someone who would not judge her or make her feel guilty for leaving Washington and her husband at such an important time in their very young marriage.

"Is it obvious?" Cat asked.

"Not really. At least not yet. Everyone is so preoccupied with the trial and with Scott that they haven't even noticed."

Cat frowned. "With Scott? Scott Parker?"

Mom was spared a reply by Lillian and Pop Mead, who entered the courtroom and quickly threaded their way through a tangle of reporters. Although questions were fired at them from all angles, Lillian and Pop merely smiled. No comment.

"Did you bring it?" asked Cat as they quickly huddled at the plaintiff's table.

"It's right here," replied Lillian as she produced a yellowed receipt indicating that the U. S. Government had accepted the uncashed check for Scott Parker's death benefits more than a decade earlier.

"Good. I'm going to find Smith and McKeand and update them on our game plan," said Cat. "Give me about five minutes."

Lillian nodded and took her seat next to Mom Mead.

"Tell Mom the news," urged Pop Mead, standing between the two women, his arms draped protectively around their shoulders.

"It's not good," began Lillian, lowering her voice to a whisper. "The call that came in as we were leaving the hotel was from Alma Hammond. The rescue went off without a hitch."

Mom put her hand to her chest and breathed a long sigh of relief. "Praise God," she said softly.

Lillian waited, knowing that Mom's joy would be short-lived when she remembered how Lillian had prefaced her report.

"But you said the news wasn't good," recalled Mom. "I don't understand. If the rescue was successful . . . ?"

"Scott and Juanita boarded a Canadian freighter off the coast of Cuba," explained Lillian. "They were headed back toward Miami and were supposed to meet an American sub once the freighter entered neutral waters."

"And?"

"There was a storm last night in the Caribbean. It prevented the Canadian ship from making it out of the coastal waters controlled by Cuba. When the storm cleared, the Cuban coast guard dispatched gunboats to halt and search all foreign vessels. A massive search has been going on ever since Juanita's escape was discovered. The vessel search is just part of the total operation."

"But what if they find them?" asked Mom, fearing the answer.

"I don't know," admitted Lillian. "Alma says the men Scott went with to rescue Juanita are expert fighters, but they don't have the kind of weapons needed to hold off the huge guns on the Cuban gunboats. Besides, the Canadians are unarmed civilians. They can't be of any help. We can only pray that Scott and Juanita won't be found if the ship is boarded and searched."

Mom began to wring her hands. "Lillian, I think Cat should know about all this. We're not being fair to her. She has no idea Scott is alive. Why are you girls deceiving each other?"

Lillian turned questioningly. "Deceiving each other? What? Is Cat not telling me something I should know?"

The conversation was cut short when the bailiff announced, "All rise," and Judge Slater entered the courtroom. Cat scurried back to the table and offered a thumbs-up indication to Lillian and Mom that Smith and McKeand had approved her plan of offense. She winked at Pastor Mead and whispered, "Ready, Pop?" Pop nodded confidently, then asked for one of Cat's antacid tablets.

"Mrs. Sanders, you may call your first witness for today," said Judge Slater.

"Thank you, Your Honor. I would like to call the Reverend Charles W. Mead to the stand."

The strategy was simple. Any of J. J. Parker's friends could testify about his resistance to the Pentagon's declaration that his son Scott was dead. However, none would be more convincing than the kindly preacher who had served Detroit congregations for years and then had retired to a mission in Appalachia. Cat had delicately suggested that Pop Mead should look, well, *pastoral* for his appearance on the witness stand. Pop had responded by wearing a clerical collar and a slightly rumpled black suit that had seen many a wedding and pie social. When Cat complimented him on his choice of clothing, Pop's eyes had twinkled. It was the only suit he had brought with him on the trip, he assured her.

"Reverend Mead, how would you describe your relationship with the late J. J. Parker?" asked Cat, slipping on her tortoise-shell eyeglasses as an indication that she was ready to get down to business.

"He attended my church . . . not regularly, mind you, but whenever the spirit moved him," replied Pop. Members of the jury caught the pun and smiled. "But more than that, he was my friend. I spent a good deal of time with him when he was troubled about his son's disappearance in Vietnam, and again later when his wife was diagnosed as having cancer."

Cat paused, letting Pastor Mead's testimony register fully with the jury.

"What kind of man *was* J. J. Parker?" she asked.

Roderick Davis sprang to his feet. "Objection, Your Honor. Do we really need to hear this man's assessment of one of his closest friends? As admirable as Reverend Mead may be, can we assume that he will be objective when describing a man he obviously cared for a great deal?"

Judge Slater nodded agreement. "Sustained. Mrs. Sanders, you will please refrain from this line of questioning."

Cat smiled sweetly.

"Pastor Mead, according to government records, Sergeant Scott Parker was reported missing in action on September 25, 1971. Is that correct?" asked Cat.

"Yes, ma'am."

"He was listed as an MIA for several years before the government decided to proclaim him officially dead. Correct?"

"That's right."

Cat hesitated, as if to frame her next question as carefully as possible.

"Without letting any of your personal feelings interfere," she said, eyeing Roderick demurely, "could you tell us how J. J. Parker reacted to the government's decision to declare Scott Parker dead after all those years?"

Pastor Mead cleared his throat. "J. J. was angry. No, furious would be more like it. And he went public with his anger—he challenged the government to *prove* that Scott had been killed. He refused to accept the check that the Pentagon sent. Instead, he went to the newspapers with his story. His timing was perfect because by then everyone was questioning the logic of our involvement in Vietnam. J. J. became something of a hero, a man willing to take on the whole bureaucracy. The government, offering money to a grieving father, was made to look like some kind of mustache-twisting villain."

Cat nodded thoughtfully, as if she were hearing the story for the first time. "And the check? Did J. J. Parker finally give in and cash the government's check?"

Pop shook his head negatively. "Never. In fact, he returned it to the Pentagon . . . hand-delivered by Congressman Williams."

Cat turned and faced the jury, although her words were directed to Judge Slater.

"Your Honor, I offer as evidence the receipt issued by the U. S. Government when the check for Scott Parker's death benefits was delivered to the Pentagon by Congressman Anthony Williams. I also have copies of more than 30 newspaper and magazine articles which chronicled the event. The government promised to reinvestigate the case."

Roderick was standing again. "Point of order, Your Honor. Could counsel please explain the significance of this testimony? If the purpose is to portray J. J. Parker as an object of pity, I concede. But could we get on with the business at hand? Could we return to less emotional, more current, and more *pertinent* issues?"

Judge Slater rapped the gavel. "Mrs. Sanders, the point made by defense counsel is well-taken. If there is a purpose to all this background information, please enlighten us. Otherwise, I'm going to have to sustain the objection and ask you to move on."

Cat bowed her head slightly in deference to the judge.

"May I assure you that there is a purpose to this testimony."

Again she faced the jury as she addressed the bench.

"Scott Parker was never officially declared dead by his family or by the government. It's true that the Pentagon attempted to issue death benefits, but when those benefits were refused by the family and when the government accepted the return of the check, Sergeant Parker's file remained open. He was missing, yes, but he was not officially dead."

The courtroom was silent. Cat paused to let the drama of the moment build.

"Prior to J. J. Parker's death, he bequeathed a sizable block of Michigan Technologies' stock to his son, Scott. It was placed in a holding trust for Scott, pending his return to America. My client, Lillian Parker Thompson, also owned a sizable amount of stock. Her stock, however, was co-owned by her and her father because it was purchased when she was a minor. When J. J. Parker died, he left a very large debt. Lillian's stock was liquidated to pay her late father's debt because that stock was also legally owned by J. J. However, because the lawyers for Michigan Technologies *assumed* that Scott Parker was dead, and because they *assumed* that his property would revert to his father's estate, they also liquidated Scott Parker's stock and used the funds to help pay off J. J.'s debts."

Cat walked to the jury box, placed both hands on the railing, and addressed the members face-to-face.

"I maintain that no one had the right to sell Scott Parker's stock because Scott Parker was legally alive. I maintain that in Scott Parker's absence, an attorney should have been appointed by the court to represent him during the stock liquidation by Michigan Technologies. I maintain that Michigan Technologies acted improperly, unethically, and illegally. At a time when Lillian Parker was grieving the loss of her father, alien forces within the corporation were attacking J. J.'s honor, fleecing his daughter of her position, and stealing his son's inheritance."

The rumble that erupted across the courtroom indicated that Cat's statement had hit home. Even Roderick looked shaken by her logic and presentation. Even so, it took only a moment for him to regain his composure. He signaled his objection.

"Your Honor, Mrs. Sanders' version of the Parker family saga is wonderfully melodramatic," he began. "It has all the elements of a daytime soap opera . . . but now I think we need to get back to the real world and start looking at the cold, hard facts of this case."

The jury members straightened in their chairs, duly recalled from the emotional scenario Cat had presented.

Roderick continued. "J. J. Parker was a brilliant but eccentric man . . . a modern-day Quixote. He took on city hall and, in a sense, he won. He kicked up a fuss and grabbed his share of headlines for a few days. The government, already suffering from image problems with an unpopular war, decided to accept the check rather than to continue to battle such a vulnerable and popular public figure. Sure, the check was taken back, but not because anyone in Washington, D. C. believed that Scott Parker was alive, but because no one wanted to cause any more grief to a man who already was distraught, despondent, and perhaps even deranged. Whether the check was cashed or not, the government knew Scott Parker was dead. Everybody knew it—everybody except J. J. Parker."

Lillian's eyes flared, but she bit her lip and said nothing.

"Your Honor," interrupted Cat, "I am in the process of tracing the Pentagon's file on Scott Parker. I have every reason to believe that the file will support my statement that the government has never reached a final decision on his status as an MIA or a KIA. And if he hasn't been officially killed in action. . . ."

"Your Honor," insisted Roderick, "I find this whole discussion ludicrous. Scott Parker is not alive."

"Neither is he dead," retorted Cat.

The gavel dropped with a sharp smack.

"Both counsels will refrain from bickering with one another," ordered Judge Slater. She smacked down the gavel again to underscore her authority. Roderick grimaced and Cat retreated a step or two.

"In order to resolve this case," began the judge, "the court obviously must determine whether Scott Parker is alive or dead. However, to provide documentation that he is not dead, Mrs. Sanders, is not the same as proving that he is alive. Do you follow me?"

Cat dutifully lowered her eyes in agreement.

"And to claim that no one believes Sergeant Parker is alive is not the same as proving that he is dead. Is that understood, Mr. Davis?"

Roderick nodded reluctantly.

"Very well then. I see no alternative other than to give both counsel for the plaintiff and counsel for the defense exactly two days to conduct research, scrutinize government files, and then return with conclusive evidence that Scott Parker is either alive or dead."

Both Cat and Roderick opened their mouths to object to the impossible challenge, but they were immediately silenced by a final resolute whack of the gavel.

Court was adjourned.

* * *

Juanita smiled when she stretched herself fully awake and noticed a small mound of carefully folded clothing on the captain's chair by the door. *Fatigues and a sweatshirt*, she thought. *Just as Scott promised.*

She had taken his advice: She had showered, washed her hair, and stretched out on the cot for what she had insisted would be only an hour's nap. Now she reached for her watch to confirm her suspicions: 5 A.M. No wonder she felt so rested!

She shivered when her bare feet touched the floor. She wouldn't complain about the temperature, though; at least the violent thrashing of the ship had ceased during the night. The storm had passed, as Scott had said it would, and now the freighter rocked rhythmically, almost cradle-like, inviting her to slip back between the sheets for an extra few minutes.

She was tempted, but the voices outside told her that the crew was up and working already—at 5 A.M.? *What a bunch of apple polishers!*—and the noise, to say nothing of her pride, would never let her sleep. She needed to show Scott she was the same strong woman he had fallen in love with a year ago, and not the confused, frightened girl he had held and comforted last night.

The fatigues fit remarkably well, but the sweatshirt was enormous; *St. Louis Cardinals, World Champs* it bragged in oversized red letters. And she, coming from Austin, had always been a Texas Rangers fan. Oh, well. She wondered if Scott liked baseball, and which team he favored. They had never had the time to talk about such routine matters. It would be fun, after their lives were more settled, to take in a game or two. Unless, of course, he liked the *Yankees*.

The knock on the door was insistent. Before Juanita could call an enthusiastic "Good Morning!" Scott had stooped quickly to enter through the tiny cabin portal.

"Shhh," he cautioned, holding one index finger to his mouth. He closed the door and hurried over to where she was applying her makeup.

"Wash your face," he ordered.

"What?"

"Wash your face," he repeated. "Take off your makeup and tuck your hair under this hat." He pulled a small knit seaman's cap from his back pocket and handed it to her.

She looked bewildered.

"Are you always this cheerful on Saturday mornings?" she deadpanned, hoping for a smile, if not a kiss.

He looked around the cabin, scrutinizing every piece of furniture, every corner, every built-in shelf. He spotted her discarded clothes—the nurse's uniform she had worn during her escape from the hacienda—and hurried over to them.

Hide these things in the duffel," he said, pulling out a canvas bag from the footlocker. "The makeup goes, too." He motioned for her to scoop up the modest assortment of foundation cream, blusher, eyeliner, and lipstick and deposit it into the duffel bag.

She stared at him, growing increasingly confused and angered by his brusqueness. The evening before he had been kind and solicitous; now he was ordering her around as if she were his dutiful handmaiden. Well, she didn't like it. Not one bit.

"Look, Scott, I don't know what's going on," she began. "Is this your way of telling me we've made contact with the submarine and it's time for me to pack my things for the trip? Pardon me if I don't snap to attention, Sergeant, but these last few weeks have been a little tough."

He looked at her and smiled in spite of himself. He had forgotten how spunky she was.

"I'm sorry, Juanita. Really I am." He reached out to her. She shook her head, then gave an "I-give-up" gesture and snuggled into his arms.

"I wish I could tell you that's all it is . . . that the sub is waiting for us," he whispered softly. "But, like you said last night, things are never easy for us." As an explanation he took her hand and led her toward the door. "We can't be seen on deck together, but we can walk to the top of the stairs and take a quick look around. Stay behind me and keep your hat on, okay?"

Baffled, she followed him through the door, up the stairs, and into the cold dampness of the early-morning air. When they reached the top of the short stairwell Scott moved to the left so she could take a sweeping glance of the ocean. She gasped in surprise, then quickly regained her composure.

"Who are they?" she asked quietly.

The stark horizon was dotted with sinister-looking gunboats, squatty vessels of blue-gray steel all nosed straight toward the freighter.

"Cubans," he replied. "We were blown off course during the storm last night. Somehow we drifted back into Cuban territorial waters."

Juanita nodded. "What do they want?"

He hesitated.

"Us."

CHAPTER 12

Alma Hammond grabbed the phone on its first ring. It was Gregor Kotusov.

"I called your apartment. No one answered."

"I spent all night here at HQ."

"I should have guessed that," he said.

"About last night . . . the call . . ." she struggled.

"Later," he interrupted. "This is business. Bentancourt has been dealt with. My people in Cuba, and in Moscow, are 'grateful.' We can't intervene officially, but we can make a suggestion." Alma grabbed a pen and some notepaper. "I'm listening."

"It would seem an expedient move to have the captain of the submarine waiting in the Atlantic change his location to something a lot closer to Cuba."

"The rendezvous sub? Why?"

"I'm afraid 'El Presidente' went a little berserk when he got the news this morning about Bentancourt and about the escape of the Martinez woman. Castro wants them all shot. He's in a wild man's fit."

"You mean that if the Canadian freighter is searched and Juanita is found, she'll be shot on sight? No arrest?"

"Not just the woman," said Kotusov. "They'll *all* be shot— the woman, Parker, the SEALs, and the Canadian crewmen. Everybody. Castro is outraged at the way he's been duped. He wants a vicious retaliation."

"Is there any chance your people could . . . ?"

"Out of the question," insisted Kotusov. "The Cubans are our allies. This call is our only intervention into this matter. And that's only because we owe you one for Bentancourt. Now we're even."

179

"Not yet," said Alma. "Moscow and Washington may be even, but not you and me. We still have a lot of settling to do. Personal matters."

There was a short, quiet pause. Then Kotusov said, "We'll talk later."

*   *   *

Lieutenant Stan Yake, Scott Parker, and Juanita Martinez were all on the bridge of the *Winds of Windsor* when its captain took a telegraphed message from the radioman. He passed it to Yake after he scanned it. Scott and Juanita read it over Yake's shoulder.

> TO CAPT DUHAMEL . . . WINDS OF WINDSOR
> . . . INSTRUCT YAKE . . . RESIST BOARDING . . .
> NO COOPERATION WITH CUBANS . . . SUPPORT
> COMING . . . (MESSAGE ENDS).

"Well?" asked Scott.

"You read what it said," Yake said flatly. "*No cooperation with Cubans.*"

"They can sink us," interjected Captain Duhamel.

"Not if we stall long enough," said Yake. "I've been expecting something like this. I've got a few ideas we can try."

"This is a commercial vessel," insisted Duhamel. "It has no defense weapons."

"No obvious ones, perhaps," mused Yake. "We'll use what we've got. Parker, you go below and tell Tony to get my men armed to the teeth and to position them on deck. Juanita, you stay on the bridge and keep me informed of any new messages. I'll also have a long one for you to dispatch in about five minutes."

"What about me and my men?" asked Duhamel as he watched Scott leave.

"I want every man to be at his normal post," said Yake. "If one gets hurt, I want someone ready to step in immediately. I also want your fire-fighting crew ready to use blast hoses to repel the Cubans when they try to board. And have the engine room build steam to full power."

"Full power? But we're surrounded. We can't head out to sea. They'll shoot armor-piercing shells at our waterline and our heavy cargo will pull us under in minutes."

"That's why the timing has to be perfect," said Yake, completely serious. "Now, listen to the plan and get your men ready."

*   *   *

The Director of the CIA entered the command room of the Caribbean Section.

"Status, Alma?"

"The last we heard it was still a standoff, sir. We received a message from Lieutenant Yake. He's a very resourceful man. We were going to send four F-16's from Florida to hit the gunboats. The jets could have been there in 11 minutes."

"The Cubans would still be able to scuttle the freighter," said the Director, frowning disapproval. "Four jets can't take out a dozen gunboats simultaneously."

"That's why Yake's plan is better," argued Alma. "It's a reverse squeezeplay."

"Oh? How so?"

"The Cubans have encircled the Canadian freighter so that it can't escape to the open sea or circle the island and reach Guantanamo," explained Alma. "Yake believes the Cubans will only be bullies-of-the-waves so long as they are convinced they have superior firepower. Tip the scales, and Yake believes they'll run. I agree with him on that."

"So how will you try to tip the scales?"

"By shifting the center," said Alma. "We're going to have the nuclear sub *Amend-All* come topwaters from the open sea directly toward the Cuban gunboats on the ocean side of the *Winds of Windsor*. Simultaneously we're going to have Cobra helicopters from our base in Guantanamo come overland until they approach the gunboats from the island side. The Cubans will be caught like books between bookends. They'll be even more in the middle than the *Winds of Windsor* because they'll have Yake and the SEALs shooting at them too."

Alma waited to receive the Director's go-ahead for the plan. She watched as he mulled her words for a few moments. His eyes narrowed at last and he nodded affirmatively.

"I'll inform the President," said the Director. "Let's hope the Cubans show their usual good form and turn tail at the first sign of a real conflict. We may get out of this without a shot being fired."

*   *   *

The first volley of gunfire against the *Winds of Windsor* took out the glass windows on the bridge, the radio antenna, the radar disc, and the staff holding the Canadian flag. A second series of shots reduced two lifeboats to splinters.

Captain Duhamel had started his ship moving forward at slow speed just as the Cubans had been ready to scale the sides and board her. This had angered them, and the trigger-happy sailors had opened up with warning shots designed to show they meant business.

As soon as the shots were fired, Lieutenant Yake appeared on deck. His men watched him for orders, but he neither waved nor called any instructions. Instead, he leaned backward and fixed his eyes on the top of a smokestack where one of his men was holding the top of a ladder and staring out to the sea with binoculars. The man turned suddenly and looked downward. He spotted Yake.

"The *Amend-All*, sir, coming head-on at flank speed," yelled the lookout. "Range . . . 2000 meters and closing fast. Deck guns appeared manned."

Yake pumped his fist up and down twice as a signal he had understood.

"Captain Duhamel! Full speed and left full rudder now!" yelled Yake.

In an instant the ship began to respond. The sudden surge of new speed and the unexpected turn of the large freighter into the midst of the shoreside gunboats served to thoroughly confuse the Cubans. Yake capitalized on this by signaling the fire-fighting crews to begin dousing the Cubans. In the pandemonium, one of the plywood gunboats crossed the bow of the freighter. The snap and pop of crunched wood proclaimed its destruction.

Yake knew his only hope was to maintain the chaos until the submarine could get within accurate firing range.

"Take out the two boats astern now, Tony," called Yake.

Yake's assistant squad leader and five other SEALs popped up at the back of the *Winds of Windsor.* Each was holding an M-50 grenade launcher, similar in appearance to a sawed-off shotgun. Almost in unison they fired at the two Cuban gunboats that had been assigned the duty of closing the imprisonment circle at the back of the Canadian freighter. The six lumpy shells of the grenade launchers thudded against the plywood hulls of the gunboats and instantly exploded upon impact. The damage was not great, but the element of surprise and the incredible noise caused panic among the Cubans. Several jumped overboard and began to swim for the shore, assuming the boats were about to explode.

The six SEALs at the stern reloaded rapidly, but this time with phosphorus and incendiary shells. They fired again at the two now-deserted gunboats. The shells hit their marks but made only small detonation sounds. Mostly they fizzed, hissed, and spewed sparks and smoke. Their fires spread rapidly; eagerly the blazes fed on the plywood, ropes, and fresh paint of the gunboats. Yake watched approvingly, knowing that the rising smoke from the burning boats would make it harder for Cuban snipers to shoot at the Canadian seamen and Yake's men.

"Right full rudder," yelled Yake through cupped hands to where the broken windows of the bridge were. Apparently his message was heard, for the ship began to reverse course and turn to the open sea.

Suddenly a heavy shower of machine-gun fire burst against the metal hull of the freighter. The noise climbed up until the bullets strafed the deck. The Cubans had overcome the temporary distractions initiated by Yake. Several boats were now firing in earnest on the *Winds of Windsor*.

Lieutenant Yake wedged himself between two metal girders. He looked up and saw Seaman Josh Watson hanging limp on the metal ladder attached to the smokestack.

Yake reached beneath his heavy sweater and withdrew a flare gun from his belt. He took a quick step into the open and fired it. Whether the lookouts on the *Amend-All* saw the signal or not, he couldn't tell. He quickly retreated to the safety of the girders.

Heavy gunfire continued to pepper the freighter. Yake's men were using M-16 rifles set on semi-automatic to return fire against the gunboats, but they were greatly outclassed.

Yake scooted down the girders and stretched himself flat on deck. He low-crawled toward his men at the stern of the ship.

"Tony!" he yelled. "They got Josh. I'm going to go up and try to bring him down. He may still be alive." Tony waved both hands frantically. "It's suicide, Lieutenant. Forget Josh. You've got bigger problems right here. Look!"

Yake's gaze followed Tony's nod. The three gunboats on the ocean side were no longer shooting their machine guns. Instead, the crewmen were pulling canvas off the barrels of the bow cannons. These three crews were out to sink the freighter before it could make it to the deep water and high waves.

The gunboats were too far away to be hit by anything but rifle shots. Yake looked around in desperation for any kind of bazooka, mortar, or anything with heavy firepower. There was nothing. All he surveyed were the brave men of the Canadian freighter working to put out fires or care for the wounded. Good men to sail with, Yake thought. They performed well.

"We're going to have to snipe the gunnery men," said Tony. "There's no other way for us to keep those cannons out there from being fired."

"Fat chance," said Yake, "but better than none. Give me one of those M-16's."

Tony threw a rifle, then three magazines of shells to Yake. "Make 'em count, sir. That's pretty much all that's left."

Yake and Tony took aim. Before they could fire, a huge explosion went off behind them. Within seconds another explosion was heard from the same area.

For a moment everyone was confused by the noise and flying debris. Had the helicopters finally arrived? Yake checked his watch. Impossible. At top speed it would still be another five minutes.

"The gunboats," yelled Tony. "The two in the stern. We hit them with phosphorus a few minutes ago. The fires must have reached the gas tanks and spare fuel on board."

As though in retaliation for the destruction of two of their companion boats, the Cubans fired their first cannon shot. A second and third followed soon thereafter. Unlike Duhamel's prediction that the Cubans would know how to sink the freighter by firing at the waterline, the cannon shots were directed toward the smokestacks and bridge of the ship.

"High rounds," said Tony. "Are they that stupid or just testing for range?"

"Doesn't matter," said Lieutenant Yake. "Either way, they'll start hurting us badly now. Start firing at their decks. Maybe a ricochet will get someone."

"Look!" cried Tony. "I don't believe it. He's crazy!"

Yake rolled onto his back and looked up. There on the metal ladder attached to the smokestack was Scott Parker. He had made it to the top and was now wrestling to drape the lookout, Josh Watson, over his shoulder so he could carry him down.

"Give him some cover fire," called Yake, rolling back into position and firing at the three distant Cuban gunboats. Tony needed no encouragement. He was already drawing a bead on the nearest boat and firing at it.

When Yake's clip was empty, he rolled over and replaced it. He stole a look at Parker working his way down the ladder.

Bullets were hitting all around Parker and Watson as though they were targets at a turkey shoot. At this rate Parker would be dead within five seconds. Yake didn't want to watch it. He rolled over and started firing again at the Cubans. He couldn't tell if he was hitting anything out there or not. The cannon fire was continuing. There was no hope.

"I'm out of shells," said Tony. "So are the other guys. That's it."

Yake, on impulse, flipped his rifle onto automatic and squeezed the trigger. His last five rounds blitzed out the barrel in less than a second.

"Yeah," said Yake. "That's it."

It was then that a new explosion was heard. This one was in the water. A large shell had hit between two of the oceanside Cuban gunboats.

Yake jumped to his feet. "It's the *Amend-All*. She's in range for her deck guns. Come on, men. We've got to help Parker."

The SEALs ran in crouched positions to the metal ladder. Yake went up to help Parker traverse the last six rungs. Together they passed Josh Watson down to the reaching arms of the other men.

"Look over there," Yake said, slapping Parker's leg. "Air support."

Scott saw four Cobra helicopters swoop over the water like huge metallic locusts. They unleashed their rotor machine guns in the small waves around the Cuban gunboats.

"They don't want to kill them," said Yake, "just scare them off."

Scott smiled with relief. "It seems to be working."

*   *   *

When Alma Hammond looked at her watch to see the time, she actually had to think for a couple of seconds whether it was 10 A.M. or 10 P.M. She had been at work so many hours that the day had all run together.

Finally she decided for sure that it was 10:00 on Saturday morning. She needed rest and a meal—real body nourishers, not just a 20-minute nap in a swivel chair and a candy bar from a vending machine.

But a promise was a promise. So she dialed the phone.

"Hello?" said a deep voice.

Alma was surprised. "Reverend Mead? I'm sorry if I woke you. I was calling Lillian."

"Miss Hammond . . . Alma," said Pop. "You didn't wake me. We're used to early hours at the settlement. I'm glad you called. Lillian was so exhausted that she fell asleep at our motel room last night. I left her there with Bea. I came here in case you or her husband Dave called. And, fact is, Dave just called too. I convinced him to come on up here."

"Oh? Any trouble?" asked Alma.

"Yes, I'm afraid so," admitted Pop. "But first tell me about Scotty."

"He's safe. So's Juanita. I'll give you the details in a minute, but first tell me about the trouble."

"It's looking bad for Lillian's case in court," explained Pop. "The judge threw out Cat Sanders's original line of evidence, claiming it wasn't reliable. Cat then found out from my wife that the government had never declared Scott officially dead. She tried to convince the judge that Scott was alive—at least on paper—so no one should have sold his stock in Michigan Technologies to pay off his father's debts."

"What happened?"

"The defense attorney said Cat was trying to win the case on a technicality," answered Pop, "so the judge ordered a recess from noon yesterday until Monday morning. By then, if Cat cannot prove that Scott is alive, the Parker case will be settled forever. Scott and Lillian will lose their stock, Lillian will be strapped with heavy court costs, and the Parker name will have been dragged through the mud all over again. You've got to do something, Alma. You're the only one who can help. Where's Scott now?"

"The final report came in just a few minutes ago," relayed Alma. "The Canadian freighter was rescued after its siege by the Cuban coastal patrol. There was some serious fighting, but miraculously no one was killed. Four men were wounded seriously, but they seem to be stabilized now."

"Was Scott hurt in any way?"

"He's fine," Alma promised. "Scott and Juanita and the SEALs weree transferred to the U. S. S. *Amend-All*, the rendezvous sub, and so were the wounded men. They'll be docking in Virginia on Sunday night."

"But he absolutely *must* be here at 9 A.M. on Monday," said Pop, not hiding his anxiety. "Can't you arrange that? Please, Alma. It's his whole future you're dealing with here. Lillian's, too."

"I can't promise you anything," said Alma, sounding purposely professional. "And I hope I don't need to remind you of the importance of secrecy in all this."

"I don't need a reminder," Pop retorted. "We haven't even told Cat Compton the truth about Scott. Here the poor woman is doing everything possible to save Lillian's case by arguing about a technicality . . . and we can't even tell her that the so-called 'technicality' is a *fact*. Scott's alive. Why can't you just announce it?"

"Because it's a matter of national importance," said Alma, "and that takes priority over any one family's personal problems. When the President says Scott Parker can be announced, then he'll be announced."

"But why wait?" Pop argued. "Juanita is safe, you've completed the taped interviews with Scott, and now Scott's health is back to normal too. He's ready to come out of hiding."

"I'll see what I can do," said Alma. "But don't get your hopes up. I'm not making any promises. After all, first I'll have to convince my Director, and then he'll have to convince the President. That's a lot of convincing."

"No problem," said Pop. "You've got all weekend."

CHAPTER 13

"I've never been to church in a hotel room before," said Cat. "I wasn't sure what to wear."

Lillian eyed Cat's plaid tent dress curiously. It was the third day in a week she had worn it. "You look lovely," she said. "As always."

They had debated about church. They had hoped to visit Pastor Mead's former congregation near Rochester, but after Friday's debacle in court they had decided against it. The local TV stations had featured lengthy segments on Pastor Mead's testimony and the judge's ultimatum to either prove or disprove Scott Parker's existence. Both city newspapers had devoted several columns to the story and had included photographs of Cat, Roderick, and Lillian. As interest in the case had increased, so had the number of phone calls from the media.

"I know this is a bit unorthodox," admitted Pop Mead, "but there are a couple of aggressive reporters stationed downstairs in the lobby just waiting for you girls to make an appearance. Bea and I could probably get past them, but not you two. With what's ahead of you in court tomorrow, I felt you deserved some peace and quiet today."

Bea Mead nodded agreement. "Besides, we'd cause too much of a stir in Rochester," she said. "There'd be such a commotion that folks wouldn't appreciate Pastor Tim's message." She shook her head as if to indicate disapproval. "Personally, I don't like all this attention. I'm too old for such hoopla. The only stars in my eyes are from all those flashbulbs popping."

Cat walked to the window. Although still early, people were trickling out of nearby apartment buildings and hotels to enjoy what promised to be a beautiful day. Cat watched a jogger run in place as he waited for a traffic light to turn green. Two couples with strollers paused to peek at each other's babies, and an elderly woman meandered through a park with a pair of French poodles on matching leashes.

"It's as if we're being held hostage," she said softly. "Now I know how it feels to be part of a sequestered jury." She sighed, almost in submission to their predicament, before taking her place next to Lillian on the couch. "We don't have to sing, do we, Pop?"

It felt good to laugh. With the tension relieved, they bowed their heads and prayed. When they were done, Pastor Mead reached for his wife's hand on his left and for Lillian's on his right. Cat joined in and the circle was complete.

"Tomorrow may be one of the most difficult days we'll ever face," Pop began earnestly. "We'll be challenged, tested, and judged. But whatever the circumstances, we'll face things together. With God's help, we'll have the strength to endure whatever Roderick Davis has planned for us."

He squeezed the hands he held, and the gentle pressure was passed around the circle. He smiled first at Lillian and then at Bea, but paused at Cat. Because it was Sunday and because she had known they wouldn't be leaving the hotel, Cat had put on very little makeup. She looked scrubbed, pale, and tense.

"You've been given the toughest task of all, Cat," acknowledged Pop kindly. "You have to stand in front of all those people and all those cameras and fight Roderick head-on. But God hasn't sent you into the battle without equipping you for it. I believe He's given you the wits and the words to convince the jury of the terrible injustice that's been done to Lillian and her family. He's given you the opportunity and the means to right the wrong."

Cat's eyes filled with tears. She felt so pressured, so insecure about her ability to represent Lillian. She wanted to respond but didn't trust her voice. Bea Mead squeezed Cat's hand to reassure her and to signal that she had something to add.

"Whatever happens tomorrow, I think we've already won a lot," Mom ventured. "I know the lawsuit is important, Charles, but what's really important is how much these girls have matured since this whole ordeal started. Can't you see the difference? For someone who had no courtroom experience, Cat has turned into a regular Clarence Darwin!"

Mom was so intent on making her point that she was oblivious to the smiles her remark prompted.

"As for Lillian," she continued, "why, Charles, do you remember two years ago when she left Michigan Technologies, how we worried when we helped her pack for her trip to the mountains? We prayed for her all night . . . not that she would get her job back or her title, but that her faith in God and her confidence in herself would be restored."

Pop Mead, serious again, nodded at the recollection.

"Dave helped restore Lillian's beliefs," Mom reminded the group, "and tomorrow the court will decide whether or not to restore her job and title. But, Lillian, your confidence returned the day you decided to come home to Detroit and face your past. That took courage."

Pop squeezed. It was his turn again. "Bea's right, Lillian. It would have been so much easier for you to stay in Compton Gap and leave all those questions about your father unanswered. But Christians don't retreat, and they don't always take the easy road. Even if the case is lost in court tomorrow, you will have found your answers days ago. Whatever Roderick says or the jury decides, you now know that your father died an honest man. Knowing that, you can put the past aside and go back to your future." He grinned at the familiar sound of the words. "Hmmm, sounds like a good title for a movie."

Cat sensed the mood lighten and she feared that the time of sharing was nearly over. She tightly gripped the hands she was holding as if to alert the circle that she too had something to contribute.

"I . . . I'm not sure how to explain this," she began shyly, "but I want you to know how I feel right now. I'm . . . well . . . grateful. These have been some of the hardest days of my life, yet I'm grateful for them, and I'm indebted to you for giving them to me." She shook her head in frustration. She wanted her friends to understand her feelings, yet words seemed to fail her.

"You see," she began again, "I've never felt so much a part of a group before. Even though I'm worried I may have let you down, you keep saying thank you to me. And even though I don't think I've done a very good job, you keep praising me. Even now, while I'm concerned about tomorrow because I have nothing new to bring to court, you're telling me it doesn't matter. To you, we've already won. You've given me so much love and trust."

She was crying now, but she wouldn't let go of Mom Mead's hand long enough for Mom to reach into her purse for a tissue.

"Just one more thing," Cat said, giving Mom's hand a final squeeze. "I know real friendships are based on honesty, and I haven't always been known for my honesty. But at least my motives for deception are better these days." She smiled at Lillian. "Forgive me, Lill . . . I have something wonderful to tell you. I only hope you'll understand why I waited so long to share it. It will explain the way I look, how I've been feeling, and even this awful dress I keep wearing."

Lillian nodded. "And I have something wonderful to tell you too, Cat. It's about Scott, and even though I've promised to keep it a secret, I think you have a right to know."

Pop hurriedly handed Mom Mead a pair of sunglasses and clipped a set to his own bifocals. "Excuse me, girls," he said, "but if Bea and I hurry we can sneak past the reporters and be in Rochester before the processional."

*　*　*

"You want Scott Parker in Detroit before 9 A.M. tomorrow? Don't be ridiculous."

The Director was irritated, first by Alma Hammond's phone call to his home on Sunday morning, and second by the audacity of her request.

"But surely the President will understand the importance of . . ." began Alma.

"The President is at Camp David for the weekend and is not to be disturbed," said the Director coldly. "Besides, he plans personally to announce the Parker return when it is most advantageous for his reelection campaign. He was thinking about the end of the month, during the opposition's nominating convention in Chicago."

Alma bristled.

"Sir, I don't know how much longer I can keep a lid on this thing," she said. "The government has raised havoc with Parker's family ever since the Pentagon went head to head with old J. J. Parker in 1976. They fought that battle on the front pages of every newspaper in the country, and if you recall the clippings I sent you, sir, the Parkers won."

The Director paused, a sure indication to Alma that she had made her point. Encouraged, she continued.

"J. J.'s gone now, of course, but his daughter is leading the crusade with the help of Senator Sanders' wife and two of the most respected lawyers in Detroit. They've even been endorsed by an old-fashioned aw-shucks type of pastor who has married, counseled, or baptized practically half the population of Michigan. Right now the Parkers are getting more ink in the area papers than the Tigers . . . and the Tigers have a shot at the pennant."

The Director exhaled loudly. "All right, all right, Miss Hammond, your concerns are valid. "I'll put in a call to the President. But even if I reach him and even if I convince him to step up his plans, the time frame you want is still impossible. Absolutely out of the question."

Now it was Alma's turn to sigh. She would have to try a different tack.

"May I have your permission to go to Detroit, sir?"

"I beg your pardon?"

"Detroit," she repeated. "Perhaps I could somehow stall the court proceedings. You know, I could buy a little time until you get clearance for Sergeant Parker to resurface."

A long silence followed. Alma waited nervously, wondering if she had gone too far and asked too much.

"I couldn't possibly authorize such an activity," said the Director. "Really, Miss Hammond, I'm surprised you would even ask."

Alma felt her face get very hot. Yes, she had gone too far. How presumptuous of her to suggest such a departure from protocol. She knew better.

"Of course, we do owe you some compensatory time for all the extra hours you've put in on the Parker-Martinez case," continued the Director. "Monday is usually a good day to be away from the office. Everyone is catching up on corrrespondence and not many meetings are scheduled. As far as where you spend your vacation, well, that's entirely up to you."

"You mean . . . ?"

"Goodbye, Miss Hammond."

*   *   *

"Hello? Who's there?" asked Cat nervously. She had fallen asleep on the couch during the 11 P.M. news and now awoke to the irritating hum of a test pattern and a rap at her hotel room door. "Lillian, is that you?" she said.

As if in answer, a thin red-white-and-blue mailing envelope was slipped between the door and the carpet. Cat smiled. Federal Express. *Thank you, Drew!* Somehow her husband had convinced the clerks at the Pentagon to search their files over the weekend, locate Sergeant Scott Parker's folder, and make him a copy of its contents. He must have then phoned the Fed Ex office and arranged for a pickup to assure overnight delivery to Detroit.

She ripped open the package and looked at the paltry assortment of papers it contained. There was a letter from Representative Anthony Williams berating the U. S. government for causing Mr. J. J. Parker "extreme and unnecessary mental anguish'" a note from J. J. Parker reaffirming his belief that his son, Scott, was alive; a copy of the check offered by the government to Parker in payment of Scott's death benefits; and a curt reply from a military attaché accepting the return of the check with a notation that "Sgt. Parker's file will remain open pending further investigation." It was dated October 8, 1976.

Cat looked at her watch. 5:50 A.M. Since Detroit and Washington were in the same time zone, she could awaken Drew before the alarm clock did if she hurried. Better to catch him before he began his morning ritual of exercise, shower, newspaper, and orange juice. She began tapping digits on the push-button phone.

"Hello?"

"Good morning, darling."

"Catherine?"

He sounded sleepy. Cat closed her eyes, cradled the telephone between her head and left shoulder, and tried to imagine Drew squinting slightly at the clock radio on their bedstand.

"It's not even 6 o'clock," he groaned.

"You didn't complain the *last* time I woke you up before the alarm went off," she teased.

"That was different," he said. "You were here then. And you didn't wake me up with a ringing phone, either."

"I sure didn't, did I? Ain't marriage fun, bud?"

Drew laughed in spite of himself. "So what's up? Not bad news, I hope."

"I wanted to say thanks for the file. You're a sweetie. At least now I won't go into court empty-handed."

She could hear Drew shift his weight to his other side and pictured him stretching his arm to shut off the snooze alarm.

"I'm glad you got the package," he said. "Sorry I couldn't come up with anything more substantial. What's your strategy for today? Are you going to put Pastor Mead back on the witness stand?"

She shook her head even though she knew he couldn't see her. "I wish I *had* a strategy," she confessed. "My only plan is to delay and hope for the best." She lowered her voice. "Drew, if I tell you something, will you promise not to repeat it?"

"Of course. Haven't I kept secret what went on the *last* time you woke me up at this hour?"

"Be serious, honey."

"Okay, I promise. What's the big secret?"

"Scott Parker is alive."

"What?"

"It's true," said Cat. "Lillian and the Meads told me the whole story yesterday. He's been in the States for a year, first recuperating and then being debriefed by the CIA. There have been all sorts of complications . . . some of them still haven't been resolved, but the most important thing is that Lillian's brother is alive! Isn't that wonderful?"

Drew was curiously silent. When he finally spoke, Cat was surprised by the edge to his voice.

"You mean Lillian and the Meads have known this all along and they never told you? They let you go through the trial without even giving you all the facts? Catherine, you've been under incredible stress, and in your condition! I know they don't know about the baby, but—"

"They do now," replied Cat. "Yesterday we told each other everything. It felt so good to be totally honest. It's not like I had lied to Lillian, but I certainly hadn't gone out of my way to tell her the truth. I never realized what a burden a secret can be. I think Lillian felt the same way. She hadn't told me about Scott because the government ordered her to keep it a secret. But she decided she trusted me enough to go against the orders. I've never had a friend like that before, Drew. Isn't it wonderful?"

There was a long pause. "I think *you're* wonderful," Drew finally said. "A lot of people would have never forgiven a friend for not sharing news like that. And a lot of lawyers—including me—would have walked out on a client for withholding such important information. You're extraordinary, Catherine . . . as a woman and as an attorney."

Cat blushed at the compliment before coming back with a quick retort.

"A regular Clarence Darwin, huh?"

*   *   *

"So, where's Washington's answer to Perry Mason?" asked Roderick sarcastically. "Is she having her hair done for the benefit of the cameras? From all the coverage she's been getting, I wouldn't be surprised if she didn't nose out Cosby in the ratings."

Lillian made no reply, but smiled placidly as Roderick brushed past her on his way to confer with several of Michigan Technologies' top executives.

"Where's Cat?" whispered Pop Mead, greeting Lillian with a quick hug. "It's after 9."

The bailiff entered the courtroom and began chanting his customary announcement of Judge Slater just as Cat hurried through the back door and took her place next to Lillian.

"Sorry. I thought if I came late the judge might call a recess for an hour or two," said Cat. "Looks like she was late too." She quickly pulled the Federal Express package out of her briefcase, then searched her purse for her glasses. "Any news from Scott?"

"Not a word."

Cat shook her head, discouraged. "I don't know how long I can stall for time," she said.

Judge Slater sharply rapped the court to order.

"Mrs. Sanders, when we recessed on Friday it was for the express purpose of gathering definitive evidence on the whereabouts and condition of Sergeant Scott Parker. Are you ready to present your findings to the court?"

Cat rose slowly. "Yes, Your Honor."

"Then proceed."

Cat smiled at the judge, then turned and addressed the jury. "Perhaps it would be appropriate first to review last Friday's testimony by Pastor Charles Mead," she began.

"Objection!" bellowed Roderick authoritatively. "I think we can assume the members of the jury are capable of recalling events that occurred last Friday."

"Objection sustained," ruled the judge. "Proceed, Mrs. Sanders. And that means go *forward*."

Cat extracted Scott Parker's file from its cardboard mailer and carried it to the bench.

"Your Honor, I have here a copy of the Pentagon's DD214 folder on Scott Parker. I would like to read its contents to the court."

"Objection!" said Roderick. "In the interest of time, couldn't counsel merely enter the file as evidence and give us an abbreviated version of its contents?"

"I agree," ruled the judge. "Objection sustained."

Cat attempted to collect her wits. She looked at her watch: 9:10 A.M. Her stall strategy was proving to be a disaster. Surely if Scott Parker had been given permission to appear in court he would have alerted someone to the plan by now. She was clearly on her own.

"Your Honor, I believe the most important information in this file is contained in a letter addressed to Mr. J. J. Parker and signed by the military attaché assigned to the case. Would counsel for the defense allow me to read just one tiny sentence?"

Laughter erupted. Roderick's face flushed with color.

"The letter to Mr. Parker is dated October 8, 1976. The key sentence reads, and I quote: 'Sgt. Parker's file will remain open pending further investigation.' Unquote."

Cat offered the evidence to Judge Slater for her scrutiny. The judge quickly perused the document and handed it back to Cat with a look that seemed to say, "So . . . ?"

"As you can see," continued Cat, "the Pentagon has never closed its file on Scott Parker. No further mention was found in any other correspondence to indicate that a settlement was reached."

Roderick tapped his fingers on his desk to demonstrate impatience. Finally he stood up.

"Is that it?" he asked. "Is this the definitive proof of Scott Parker's existence that the court requested?" He chuckled as he approached the judge's bench.

Cat turned to look at him, but her gaze was distracted by a woman attempting to gain entry to the courtroom. A guard, stationed at the back door, was indicating with a sweep of his arms that all the seats were taken. Still, the woman was insistent. Cat looked at Lillian and nodded toward the woman. Lillian turned, recognized Alma Hammond, and flashed a thumbs-up signal to Cat.

"Your Honor, may we have a one-hour recess?" asked Cat. "A key witness has just arrived and I would like time to confer with her."

Roderick exhibited obvious displeasure. "Your Honor, the court generously gave counsel two days to prepare for today's session. Is it necessary to grant an additional hour? My clients are anxious to bring closure to this case. Contrary to the plaintiff and the counsel for the plaintiff, my clients have other business to attend to."

Judge Slater tapped the gavel.

"If that comment was offered as an objection, Mr. Davis, I will sustain it," said the judge. She looked at Cat. "Mrs. Sanders, the court believes you have been given sufficient time to prepare your case. Please proceed."

Cat hurried to the desk and took a piece of scrap paper from Lillian. Haltingly she said, "Uh, we wish to call . . . uh, Miss Alma Hammond to the stand, Your Honor."

Alma made her way forward.

Cat listened as the witness was sworn in.

"State your name."

"Alma Hammond."

Cat and Lillian exchanged glances. So this was the woman Lillian had described as the CIA section head who had been instrumental in getting Scott back to the United States. But how much information could the woman reveal to a court-room filled with reporters? Cat was unsure of the questions she should ask the witness. What was Alma Hammond willing or authorized to tell about Scott Parker? If only they could have had five minutes of conversation! Cat decided to feel her way through the interrogation cautiously and just let the witness lead her.

"Miss Hammond, you are a resident of . . . ?"

"Washington, D. C." answered Alma.

"And your employer?"

"I work for the government."

Cat sensed an unspoken warning. *Back off*, it seemed to say. *Don't pursue this line of questioning.*

"Miss Hammond, please explain to the court your relation-ship to the plaintiff, Lillian Parker Thompson."

Alma cleared her throat and looked squarely at the jury. Although her arrival had been unannounced and her entry to the courtroom had been somewhat breathless, she looked calm and in control.

"Actually, my relationship with Mrs. Thompson is an indi-rect one," she explained. "I've spoken with her on the telephone, of course, and I've seen her several times in the past year when I've been in Appalachia to visit her brother, Scott Parker. But my acquaintance has been more with Scott than with Lillian."

Gasps of surprise filled the courtroom, causing Judge Slater to soundly smack the gavel to her desk.

"Am I to understand that you've *seen* Sergeant Parker within the last year?" clarified Cat.

"That's correct."

"When was the last time you saw him?"

Alma pursed her lips and looked down, as if trying to recall the exact date.

"It's been several days," she answered. "Sergeant Parker has been on special assignment and has been out of the country."

Cat felt a certain hesitancy on the part of the witness and interpreted it to mean she should not explore the "special assignment" remark any further. Again she switched directions.

"There are some people who would have us believe that Sergeant Parker is dead," said Cat, shooting a glance at Roderick. "Could you comment on his condition?"

Alma smiled. "Sergeant Parker is very much alive. In fact, I would venture to say he feels happier and healthier today than he's felt in years."

Cat was uncertain whether to ask Alma to explain her observations. She assessed the jury and decided she had already achieved the reaction she wanted. The impact of the testimony had been phenomenal. In spite of the number of people jammed into the courtroom, total silence prevailed. Cat chose not to break the mood.

"No more questions, Your Honor."

Judge Slater nodded. "Mr. Davis?"

Roderick rose and walked confidently to the witness stand.

"You say you work for the government, Miss Hammond," he began. "So do hundreds of thousands of other people. Exactly what do you do? Are you a clerk? Postal worker? Secretary?"

"My position is classified," said Alma. "I'm not at liberty to discuss it. However, I would be happy to show the court my identification."

Roderick held up his hand in mock protest. "Not necessary, Miss Hammond. We'll take you at your word." He turned and walked toward the jury as he continued his rapid-fire questioning. "If we can't talk about your assignment, perhaps we might talk about Sergeant Parker's. Where is he? What is he doing? And, most importantly, why hasn't anyone seen him for more than 12 years?" Roderick wheeled around to face the witness.

"I'm sorry, but much of that information is classified," said Alma. "I can say that both Mrs. Thompson and I have seen Scott Parker several times this past year. He is alive. Mrs.

Thompson could not testify to this because the government had told her it was classified information. No one was authorized to discuss it."

Roderick snickered as he addressed the jury.

" 'Not authorized to discuss it,' " Roderick repeated sarcastically. "Your Honor, forgive me for sounding unpatriotic, but all this 'classified' information has me confused. I feel as if I'm shadowboxing with some phantom dressed in Army fatigues."

"I can understand your frustration, Mr. Davis," said the judge. "Miss Hammond, although counsel has declined your offer to show your government credentials, the court would be remiss in not reviewing them. May I . . . ?"

Alma opened her purse and pulled out a small leather folder. She handed it to Judge Slater.

"Also, I brought with me a copy of the voucher that Scott Parker signed a year ago when he collected his back pay from the Army," said Alma. "As you can see, its sizable sum suggests that he was a prisoner of war for several years."

The judge carefully read both documents. Finally she passed the voucher to the bailiff to be entered as evidence and handed the identification folder back to Alma.

"The court recognizes Miss Hammond's position to be one which would give her potential access to information about Sergeant Parker," said Judge Slater. "Mr. Davis, you may continue."

Roderick looked bewildered.

"Continue what, Your Honor? Continue to ask questions and be refused answers? Continue to be assured that Scott Parker is living, although no one knows where? Continue to accept on faith the testimony of a woman whose classified job makes her above reproach and cross-examination?"

Roderick shrugged dramatically. "I'm used to dealing with more substantial evidence, Your Honor. When you told us on Friday to prove or disprove Scott Parker's existence, I attempted to do just that. I contacted the Vietnamese Embassy in Paris and received a sworn statement from the ambassador denying that Scott Parker was ever held in a Communist POW camp. I have a copy of the check issued by the U. S. Government to the Parker family to cover Scott Parker's death benefits. I have personally spent the weekend calling Scott Parker's friends, classmates, and former neighbors in the Detroit area to determine if they have had any word from Parker. The message they gave me was loud, clear, and unanimous: *Scott Parker is dead!*"

Roderick sat down in resignation. Members of the jury looked at Cat, then at Alma, then at Judge Slater. No one spoke. Finally the judge indicated with a nod that Alma could step down from the witness stand. More silence followed as the judge wrestled with the options.

"We seem to have made little progress since Friday," she concluded. "The only difference is that both counselors now have located documentation to support their respective positions. On the one hand, we have a foreign ambassador who says Scott Parker was never detained in a POW camp; on the other hand, we have a representative of our government saying that Scott Parker was issued back pay for all the years spent in a POW camp. Which piece of paper has more credibility? It is the court's belief that we need something more conclusive than documents and opinions."

Judge Slater shook her head. "I see no alternative but to recess until 9 A.M. tomorrow. At that time, Mrs. Sanders, you will either present Sergeant Scott Parker *in person* or I will dismiss this case."

Still shaking her head, the judge stood up and began to walk toward her chambers. As if in afterthought she turned back to the bench and cracked the gavel.

"Court adjourned."

*   *   *

Roderick Davis was shaken by the phone call he had received and was nervous about the call he had to make.

Paul Stattman had always been his friend, or at least Roderick had thought of him in those terms—that is, until the telephone call. Five minutes of conversation had changed everything. Stattman had insisted that he was just doing his job. He was calling Roderick merely to pass along some information . . . info that Roderick needed to know before tomorrow's session in court.

But Roderick recognized a threat when he heard one; he had heard enough of them during his 11 years as an attorney. None, however, had ever been delivered by a friend, and none had ever carried such serious consequences. Roderick's reputation, his career, his *future* were at stake.

The message was simple: Certain executives at Michigan Technologies—executives present in the courtroom during Alma Hammond's testimony—were becoming increasingly uncomfortable at the direction the case was taking. Surely Scott Parker couldn't be alive . . . could he? they asked. Surely Parker wouldn't resurface after all these years and begin probing the circumstances of his father's exit from the company . . . would he? Surely the conspiracy to oust Lillian from her job and the strategy to liquidate the Parker family assets were not about to be revealed . . . were they?

Stattman's ultimatum was delivered quickly. Roderick was to do anything necessary to assure the absence of Sergeant Scott Parker from the courtroom on Tuesday. In addition, he was to guarantee that *Lillian Parker Thompson vs. Michigan Technologies* would be dismissed permanently.

And if he failed in either duty? Roderick had asked Stattman.

"*You'll* be dismissed permanently," Stattman had answered flatly. "M-T will drop you as the company's chief legal counsel. And since you were hired by your law firm because of your link with M-T, you'll be out on your ear there, too. It'll all be over for you, Rod. Word will travel fast. Not just in Detroit, but everywhere. You'll never get another shot at the big time."

Roderick had protested, of course. He had argued that he knew too much about the takeover of Michigan Technologies;

he threatened to tell everything about the plot against the Parker family. He promised to name names and give dates. He could ruin them, he had boasted.

Stattman had laughed at Roderick's counterthreat. "You forget, Rod, that if Scott Parker comes back the damage will have been done. My bosses will already be ruined. Besides, to implicate them you'd also have to implicate yourself. And you'd never go that far."

It was then that Roderick realized he had to make the second phone call.

*   *   *

"This better be good," warned Cat, slipping into the booth at Casey's All-Night Diner. "I was getting ready for bed when you called. If you hadn't threatened to come to my room and beat on my door I would have hung up on you."

Although it was after 10 P.M., she was wearing sunglasses and a wide-brimmed felt hat. To hide her pregnancy she had put on slouchy pleated slacks and an oversized Liz Claiborne shirt.

"You must have been anxious to see me," quipped Roderick. "You didn't take time to change from your pajamas."

"Very funny," replied Cat.

Roderick ordered two black coffees and asked the waitress if she had any bagels. "Aren't I thoughtful?" he said to Cat. "I remember how much you like bagels and cream cheese."

Cat chose not to answer, but after the waitress had withdrawn she leaned across the table. "What's this all about, Roderick? I don't like risking being seen in your company."

"So that explains the glasses," said Roderick. "Okay, Cat, I'll give it to you quick and straight." He took a deep breath and lowered his voice. "My clients at Michigan Technologies aren't very pleased with what went on in court today. They feel confident we're going to win all right, but they don't like the way the case is dragging on ad nauseum. They say it's bad for business and for employee morale. Just when J. J. Parker's supporters are starting to make peace with the new regime, the lawsuit forces everyone to choose sides and start fighting again."

Cat doffed her hat. The coffee and the company were making her uncomfortably warm.

"Please get to the point. I'm waiting for a call from Washington."

Now it was Roderick's turn to feel uncomfortable. He wondered if the expected call had anything to do with Scott Parker.

"Okay, okay," he replied. "While my clients haven't liked your case, they've been impressed with your presentation. They've authorized me to extend to you a very lucrative business offer."

Cat took off her glasses to better read Roderick's expression. "What?" she asked incredulously. "Michigan Technologies is offering *me* a job?"

Roderick mistook her surprise for excitement. "Great, isn't it? And that's not all. They're willing for you to stay put in Washington and be a liaison on government contracts. The retainer will be unbelievable . . . probably a lot more than your husband makes in the Senate."

Cat shook her head as if trying to comprehend Roderick's words.

"And in return?" she began. "What does Michigan Technologies want from me in return?"

Roderick looked down, not wanting to meet Cat's gaze.

"My clients want the Thompson case dismissed," he said simply. "They're willing to give Lillian a cash settlement that will equal the current market value of the stock she lost. In addition, they'll give her a title; it won't be director of sales, of course, but she'll be listed as some kind of marketing consultant. That should satisfy her pride, don't you think?"

Cat hadn't blinked since Roderick had begun to outline the offer.

"Incredible," she said. "I can't believe it."

"I knew you'd be pleased."

"Pleased? I'm flabbergasted." She looked at him with compassion. "Roderick, you don't understand me at all, do you? If you did, you'd never suggest such a deal." She attempted to lean closer so no one would hear her. "Let me try to explain something," she said. "I know we didn't end our relationship on very good terms in Nashville, and we haven't talked for a long time. I need to bring you up to date on my life. There have been some big changes."

Roderick sniffed. "I can read, Cat. Along with the rest of the country, I followed the Sanders-Compton romance in the newspaper gossip columns. You really outdid yourself, luv. I had barely made my exit before you nabbed yourself a U. S. Senator. Not bad. I understand he's very rich, not to mention handsome and ambitious."

Cat's eyes glistened. "He's the kindest, most honest man I've ever known. But best of all, he's a Christian. Do you know what that means?"

Roderick rolled his eyes back to indicate exasperation. "Spare me any sermons, okay? This is good old Roderick, remember? Of *course* I know what a Christian is. We're all Christians—or at least most of us are. This is a Christian country, so I'm a Christian and you're a Christian. We've all done time in vacation Bible school and sung in the church choir."

Cat shook her head. "Being a Christian is so much more than that," she explained. "Before I asked Jesus into my life I was restless and dissatisfied. I didn't know what I wanted—I only knew I wanted a lot and I wanted it in a hurry. I played acquisition games; I hurt people; I was selfish. . . ."

"Yeah, I remember," said Roderick with a laugh. "Two peas in a pod. We were made for each other, weren't we?"

"I've changed," insisted Cat. "And if it happened to me, it can happen to you too."

"But there's one difference, Cat."

"Oh?"

"I don't want to change." He looked at her and grinned, but then became serious as he watched her take out her wallet and extract a one-dollar bill. She tucked it under her coffee cup.

"Hey, where are you going?" he asked. "What am I supposed to tell my clients?"

"Tell them court convenes at 9 A.M. Sharp."

CHAPTER 14

At dawn on Tuesday the big-bellied Huey helicopter circled Langley Field in Virginia, then set down. Its bay doors were slid aside and immediately people started jumping to the concrete. First was Lieutenant Yake of the Navy SEAL team, then his assistant squad leader Tony, and then Scott Parker. They helped Juanita down next. Instantly a medical team came running forward to help unload the wounded men from the helicopter.

Scott and Juanita hastened away from the helicopter in order to let the medics do their work.

"Welcome home!" came a shout above the noise of the rotors.

It was Alma Hammond.

"So you were the one who arranged this special ride from the sub!" said Scott as he, Alma, and Juanita went from handshakes to hugs.

"Couldn't wait to see you," said Alma, leading them to an office in a nearby hangar. "You look better than I expected. Especially you, Juanita. Come on in. The coffee's hot. How're you feeling?"

"I may cry," said Juanita, "but for joy. Last week I thought I'd never get back again. It may be a cliché, but there's no place like home. Now I really know how Scott felt when we brought him back from Vietnam."

"Yeah," said Scott, "this is like déjà vu for me. Didn't I just go through this about a year ago?"

Alma smiled. "I guess bad habits are hard to break. No more foreign adventures for you anymore, though. Here, have some coffee. It's Mexican-grown by the way, not Cuban."

They shared a laugh.

"I talked with Lieutenant Yake while you were still aboard the sub," said Alma. "He told me you saved the life of one of his men. He wants to recommend you for a medal."

"Medal?" mused Scott. "I'd rather have my discharge papers. Did you bring them as I asked? Juanita and I want to get married and then lose ourselves for about 50 years in the peaceful Appalachian Mountains."

"Can't say I blame you," said Alma. "But first you've got to help your sister."

Scott looked anxious. "My sister? What do you mean? What's wrong with Lillian?"

"Physically, she's fine," promised Alma. "Emotionally, she's in pretty bad shape. It's the court case. The evidence her attorney had that was supposed to make it an open-and-shut case was ruled unacceptable by the judge. The strength of the case shifted to the defense attorney. You know the guy . . . Roderick Davis. He put your sister on the stand and tore her to shreds."

Scott's eyes narrowed and he clenched his fists. "For two cents I'd—"

"But then your sister's attorney tried a new approach," continued Alma. "She argued that since your family had refused to accept the death-benefits claim for you, and since the Department of Defense had kept the investigation of your alleged 'death' open, you were legally entitled to the shares of Michigan Technologies stock that were liquidated to help pay your father's debts after he died. Of course, if that was so, you Parkers would have real company power again."

"What did the judge say?" injected Juanita, becoming caught up in the story.

"The judge decided that Lillian's attorney had to *prove* that Scott was alive."

"And did she?" asked Scott.

"She tried," said Alma, "but it didn't work. I got on the witness stand and swore that I had seen you alive. I offered your signed pay voucher as further evidence. But the defense attorney showed a list of a zillion people in Detroit who had known you years ago and were positive you had never come home from the war. There also was a document from the Vietnamese government saying you were never a POW."

"But this is ridiculous," protested Scott. "I *am* alive. And I'm here in America. I'll testify to my own existence if I need to. Let's go to Detroit. Now!"

He rose from his seat.

"Whoa!" cautioned Alma. "It's not that easy. You can't go anywhere until the President authorizes it. My Director is trying to convince him to let you go to Detroit. Believe me, he's insisting it's urgent."

"Urgent? Why so urgent?" asked Scott. "I mean, I'm anxious, but . . ."

Alma averted her eyes. "I'm afraid today is the final day of the trial."

Scott was amazed. "You're kidding. The trial ends today? Already?"

"There's nothing more for them to debate," explained Alma. "If you're alive and can prove it by being in court at 9 o'clock this morning, Lillian will have helped you win back part of the family honor and your stock holdings. If you're not there . . . well . . . you're 'dead' in more ways than one."

"But that's only four hours from now. Why can't I just call the judge?"

"She said, 'in person, in the courtroom.' Sorry. A call won't do it."

"Then that does it," said Scott angrily. "I'll have to sign my discharge papers and go. Juanita will give you her resignation notice. We'll fly to Detroit as two civilians. You can't force us to stay here against our will."

Alma lifted her eyebrows.

"Calm down, Scott. Don't talk so foolishly. Of course I could hold you here against your will. I could even have you gagged and tied, for that matter. Wake up to where you are. You're in no position to try to call the shots around here. That's all beside the point anyway. Even if I would let you go, you'd never make it to Detroit in time. Not by commercial air travel, you wouldn't. Your only hope is to get clearance from the President . . . who also happens to be the Commander-in-Chief. He can put military aircraft at your disposal. Then you'd make it on time."

"Well, why doesn't he give us the clearance?" Scott demanded.

Alma glanced at her watch.

"Because he probably hasn't been reached by his most important consultant yet. I just called him a few minutes before you landed. He'll be trying to get through to the President about now."

"Who? The Secretary of State?" asked Scott.

"No," said Alma. "The President's campaign manager."

*   *   *

"Room service" came the voice outside Lillian's hotel room door.

Everyone looked up.

"I didn't order anything," said Lillian. "I'm too nervous to eat."

Cat, who had spent the night in Lillian's room, shrugged. "Me? Breakfast? Just the thought of bacon makes me—"

"Uh, I ordered some coffee," interrupted Pop Mead from a corner chair. He put down his newspaper. He and Mom had come to the hotel at 7 in order to ride to the courthouse with the girls.

"I'll get it," said Lillian. "Stay where you are, Pop."

Lillian flipped the locks, turned the doorknob, and pulled open the door.

"Dave!" she almost shrieked.

"Checking up on you," he joked.

Lillian lunged forward and threw her arms around her husband. She squeezed him fiercely. "Oh, Dave . . . Dave . . . darling, I'm so glad you're here."

Dave Thompson lifted his wife into his arms and kissed her.

"I couldn't wait another day," said Dave. "I told Phil Compton I was coming to Detroit. Know what? He offered to put in a good word with Mayor Young if you and Cat were still having problems here. I can't figure out how he knows Coleman Young. . . ."

"I heard that," said Cat, coming to the door. "Sounds just like daddy. Hi, Dave. Come in, come in. Pop told me about your call, but I didn't want to ruin the surprise for Lillian."

Dave gave a casual glance at Cat, then did a doubletake. For someone like Dave, who had known Cat for so many years, the woman now appeared to be . . . different.

"I'm pregnant," she explained with a smile. "But don't tell my folks until the trial is over. They'd panic."

"Your dad is going to be so proud," said Dave.

"We *all* will be," said Pop. "Good to see you, Dave. You're just in time. We're going to have a brief prayer time and then drive to the courthouse."

"Any specific requests?" asked Dave.

"Just one," said Pop. "A phone call."

"Call?"

"Alma Hammond of the CIA said that if she could get Scott back to Detroit in time to testify, she would call us. If we don't hear from her, we're on our own."

"When is she supposed to call?" asked Dave.

The room went silent. Finally Cat spoke.

"Ten minutes ago."

*   *   *

Gregor Kotusov rapped sharply on the office door of his

superior at the Russian Embassy in Washington. A voice said for him to enter.

"You requested my appearance at 8:00 this morning, Comrade Ambassador?"

"Come in, Kotusov. Yes, yes. I'm glad you are prompt, my boy. I have important news for you. Please, sit down. Be comfortable."

Kotusov accepted a chair, but sat erect and respectful. The man across from him was past 70, stocky, thick-lipped, and gray-haired. The old regime—out of step with contemporary policy changes, yet too well-connected to be removed from his post. He would probably die in office.

"Everything you said about that situation in Cuba has proved to be right, my boy. The turncoat Bentancourt has been dealt with and the American spy . . . the woman . . . has been removed from her sensitive position. The Americans came for her, just as you predicted they would. It was best to let her go. We had Bentancourt, our big fish."

Kotusov nodded. "I'm glad we were able to flush out the traitor."

"Not *we*," corrected the older man. "*You* did it, Kotusov. How you discovered all this is still a mystery. But that does not matter. In our work, secrets are to be respected . . . protected."

"I just did my duty, Comrade Ambassador."

The old man grunted. "Our superiors in Moscow think it was more than that. They are extremely impressed—not only with the exposure of Bentancourt, but also with the help you arranged from the American scientists. You're being called home, my boy."

Kotusov looked shocked. "Home?"

"Indeed! A medal awaits you, and a promotion. No more living abroad for you, Gregor. You've been named the new commercial attaché to the Finance Ministry. You're going to be a political analyst for the bankers. It's a plum of a job. A car, a beautiful apartment, a good salary. And, best of all, you get to stay in Moscow on a permanent basis."

"But . . . but my work here in America . . . ?"

"Your work here is over," said the Ambassador. "You are a hero. Go accept your rewards."

Kotusov slowly rose to his feet. "Do I have some time? How soon must I go?"

"Now. Tonight. You are to leave immediately, as soon as you can pack and arrange a flight."

The old man came forward and kissed Kotusov on each cheek.

"What you have done, Kotusov, has brought glory to our entire embassy here. I am grateful to you for the mutual prestige we are enjoying. Go now. And good luck at your new assignment."

Kotusov turned and left the office. He walked slowly down the hall. When he turned the corner, he paused.

Standing alone, he whispered, "Oh, Alma. What have we done? What *have* we done?"

*   *   *

By 8:15 A.M. they decided to leave Mom Mead in the hotel room just in case Alma might still try to call. Cat, Pop, Lillian, and Dave rode together to the courtroom.

"What can we do without Scott?" Lillian asked Cat.

"I can stall for a little while," said Cat. "I'll try to put you and Pop back on the stand, and now Dave too, and have each of you say under oath that you have seen Scott alive during the past year. That may help, but it still won't prove that Scott is alive now. And that's what really counts. Oh, how I wish Alma Hammond could have brought just *one* of those classified videotapes you said she made of Scott last year! Maybe seeing Scott and hearing him tell his own story would have influenced the jury."

Suddenly Dave brightened. "Videos? Hey . . . you want to see Scott? I can show you Scott."

"What are you talking about, Dave?" asked Lillian.

"Our wedding," said Dave, pulling out his wallet. "I'm still carrying that wedding picture we made of you, me, Scott, Cat, and Pastor Mead. You know, the group shot we posed for at the altar. It's just a snapshot, but Scott's in it. Here it is. What do you think?"

They bunched their heads over the photo. The focus wasn't clear and the camera angle was lopsided, but Scott Parker's face was visible and recognizable . . . at least, to those who *knew* Scott Parker.

"It's not a great photo," Dave admitted. "Alma and that bodyguard Kent saw us forming up to take photos and they put the kabosh on it. My cousin took the picture anyway and no one knew. He later gave it to me."

"I always wondered why we didn't take many photos at that wedding," said Cat. "And to think that I had seen Scott Parker myself. I wonder if the judge would let me put myself on the stand."

"I'd worry more about Roderick Davis than the judge," said Pop, who was driving. "You offer that photo as evidence and he'll put six people on the stand from Michigan Technologies who'll swear it isn't Scott. And they'll think they're telling the truth. After twelve years as a POW, Scott's appearance has changed a lot."

Cat shook her head. "Pop's right. The only thing that will help us is Scott Parker. Where *is* he?"

*   *   *

Kotusov hung up the phone. "Where *is* she?" he wondered aloud.

No one knew where Alma was. He had tried to reach her at her apartment, at her office, even at the naval base where he knew the *Amend-All* would eventually be putting into port.

Kotusov checked his watch. 8:40 A.M. He had to finish loading things from his office into boxes and then race back to his apartment and pack his clothes and leave. It was all so fast.

Too fast. There was so much that he would have liked to have said to Alma . . . discussed with her . . . explained to her. But now there was no time. No time at all.

As Kotusov hastily emptied his file cabinet of personal items and left instructions on how to have the remaining materials sent to him, he tried to think of a way to get a final message to Alma. It would be too risky to send her a letter or a cassette tape. Yet he somehow had to let her know that he cared for her and that he was sorry he had not been able to say goodbye before going back to the USSR.

Then an idea struck him.

His eyes scanned the book collection in his office. He searched a moment and then located the book he wanted. He pulled it from the shelf, took it to his desk, put it in a large mailing envelope, and addressed it to Alma. He put no return address on the outside and he inserted no written message inside. She would understand. After all, who else ever gave her Russian novels as gifts?

Just before sealing the envelope, Kotusov withdrew the book and looked at its cover once more. Yes, he told himself, Alma would understand the secret message.

*   *   *

"What kind of a secret message is this?" asked Cat as she read a piece of paper which a courtroom clerk had handed her as she arrived for the trial.

"That's the message verbatim," repeated the clerk. "A woman named Mrs. Bea Mead called here five minutes ago and said to tell you this message just as soon as you arrived. She said it was absolutely essential that you be told it immediately."

Cat read the paper again and just shook her head. "What's it mean, Pop?" she asked, turning to Reverend Mead. "It just says 'John 11:44.' "

Pop thought a moment, then began to smile broadly. "Ha! It's great news. Great news!"

"What? What does it mean?" asked Lillian as she and Dave moved within whispering distance of Pop.

"It means Alma has called," explained Pop. "She and Scott must be on their way. We've got to stall long enough for them to get here. Bea wanted to get the news to us without tipping anyone else."

"But how can you be so sure that it's about Scott?" asked Dave.

Pop grinned. "Elementary, my dear Thompson. John chapter 11 is the story of Lazarus. Wait here a second." Pop approached the bailiff and asked to borrow the Bible used for swearing in witnesses. He came back thumbing the pages.

"Yep, just as I thought," he said. "Scott's definitely on his way here."

"You can tell that from reading the Bible?" asked Cat somewhat dubiously.

"Sure can," promised Pop. "Listen to this: John 11:44, 'And he that was dead came forth. . . .' "

Cat dropped into a chair. "Hallelujah!"

*   *   *

"I still can't believe that the President sent Air Force One for us to use," said Juanita. "How did you ever manage that, Alma?"

Alma leaned back in the cushioned chair. "I told his campaign manager that Scott wanted to deliver an endorsement speech for the President while all the news people would still be on hand to cover the big court case. That *was* all right with you, wasn't it, Scott?"

"Listen, if this plane gets me to Detroit in time to help my sister, I'll deliver a very eloquent endorsement. After all, I'm technically still in the Army, and he is my Commander-in-Chief."

"That's what I like about you, Scott," said Alma. "You're always so willing to cooperate, just as long as everything is going your way. Fasten your seat belt. That's Detroit outside your window."

"It's already time for the trial to begin, though," said Juanita.

Alma winked. "Trials don't start until the judge arrives. And something tells me our judge may be a bit tardy today."

*   *   *

Paul Stattman leaned over the banister that separated the first row of visitors' seats from the table and chairs reserved for the defense attorney.

"What's the story here?" Stattman barked at Roderick Davis. "It's 9:20 and still no judge."

"Something about papers to sign in her chambers," said Roderick. "The bailiff won't say any more. We're supposed to wait."

"Our people don't like it," said Stattman. "They want this wrapped up now. Remember: Your neck is on the line, Rod. When the judge does arrive, you'd better come out swinging. End this mess. Now!"

Roderick started to respond but was cut short when the bailiff ordered "All rise." After the standard ritual of proclamations, the judge rapped the court session in motion.

"Permission to approach the bench, Your Honor?" said Roderick immediately.

"Granted."

Cat and Roderick moved to the judge's bench.

"Your Honor, I can anticipate that counsel for the plaintiff will attempt to drag out these proceedings again today," Roderick lamented. "My clients have been more than tolerant thus far, but since this case now hinges on whether or not Scott Parker is alive, I would ask the court to let us focus solely on this one matter. If counsel can show Sergeant Parker to the jury, we would like that to occur now. If not, then we would like an immediate dismissal of charges."

"The court empathizes with your concerns," said the judge. "But the court also wishes to show complete fairness." The judge glared sharply at Cat. "There seem to be many people who are very anxious to *make sure* that the court shows every courtesy possible to Mrs. Lillian Thompson and her attorney."

Cat looked baffled by this remark. She knew Drew would never use his influence as a Senator to try to put any sort of pressure on the judge. Who then. Alma? The CIA? The President? Cat looked at the judge. Whoever it had been, the message had been clear. Cat would be allowed to present her case without undue pressure.

"Mrs. Sanders, I will allow you 30 minutes this morning to present any new evidence relating to the case. By 10 A.M., however, if you do not produce Scott Parker, I will have to give my instructions to the jury members and send them into consultation chambers. Are we clear on that?"

Both attorneys nodded their understanding. They returned to their tables smiling.

Roderick leaned over the banister and whispered to Stattman, "Good news. We've won. The judge told them to produce Parker by 10 A.M. or it's over."

Across the room, Cat leaned next to Lillian and whispered, "Good news. We've won. The judge is going to let me kill time until 10 A.M. so that Scott can make it here."

*   *   *

The two motorcycle police officers kept their sirens blaring as they escorted the car carrying Scott, Juanita, and Alma. Taking the shortest route, they moved rapidly through Detroit traffic toward the courthouse.

Cat had used the extra half-hour to put Dave, Lillian, and Pop Mead on the stand for brief testimonies. All had sworn they had seen Scott Parker alive during the past year. Dave showed his snapshot of Scott, and Pop offered to send to the hotel for Bea Mead to come and testify that she too had seen Scott. Roderick immediately objected and the judge told Pop to step down from the witness stand.

At precisely 10 A.M. Cat was reminding the jury of the original pay voucher. Roderick rose to his fee and interrupted.

"If the court pleases, Your Honor, it's 10 o'clock and we wish to point out that all evidence thus far has been either hearsay, biased, or unsubstantiated. It is altogether obvious that Scott Parker is not alive."

"Says who?" a voice suddenly boomed from the back of the courtroom.

All eyes turned. All cameras, too. Chatter rose to meet speculations. The judge rapped for order.

"Scotty!" screamed Lillian, leaping from her chair and racing to meet her brother. A volley of camera flashes followed her.

"Hey, Lill," said Scott. "Hope I'm not too late. Is it my turn yet?" He hugged his sister.

"Order, order!" demanded the judge. "Do you wish to call this witness, Mrs. Sanders?"

Cat looked at Roderick. His mouth was open, his face was white. Absolute shock was written all over him. Cat turned to the judge.

"Yes, thank you. We wish to call Sergeant Scott Parker to the stand, Your Honor."

Scott came forward, paused at Roderick's table, and said, "What's the matter, bud? You look like you've seen a ghost."

As Scott was being sworn in, Alma stepped out of the courtroom and located a telephone down the hall. She phoned the Soviet Embassy and asked for Kotusov.

"Comrade Kotusov has been given a new assignment. May I connect you with someone else?"

"New assignment?" echoed Alma. "Where? When?"

"I'm sorry. That's not for public release yet. Can someone else help you?"

"No . . . only Gregor." She hung up, then dialed Kotusov's apartment. No answer. He was gone. Vanished. How was that possible? They had talked the day before. Now he was out of her life? And without even saying goodbye.

Alma felt tired. She also felt sad. More than anything else, she felt alone. Maybe it had been silly to grow fond of a man with whom she knew she could never have a serious relationship. But everyone needs someone to care for. And she had begun to feel that Gregor really cared for her. It was becoming special. And now he was gone.

Alma walked slowly back to the courtroom. She entered and sat at the back in a seat that Kent had found for her. Up front, Cat was finishing her questions.

"For the sake of summation, your story is that you were a POW until last year," Cat said to Scott, "after which you returned to America. You've been in Appalachia since then, being debriefed by the Central Intelligence Agency."

"Yes, ma'am, that's right."

"And so," continued Cat, now looking at the jury, "since you *weren't* dead, and your family *said* you weren't dead, and the government still had its file *open* on you, how do you feel about the fact that the directors of Michigan Technologies sold your private shares of stock while you were away in the service of your country?"

With no hesitation Scott answered, "I feel angry. My stock was stolen from me and that's all there is to it."

Roderick Davis buried his head in his hands. Behind him Paul Stattman was whispering, "Do something! Do something!" But there was nothing Roderick could do. Scott Parker was not only alive, he was here. And he was mad.

"One final question, Sergeant Parker," said Cat, returning to the front of the witness stand. "In obedience to our government, you did not come forward before now to claim your stock shares. We understand from your story how important it was to keep your whereabouts a secret this past year. But now that this is over, have you considered what would be a fair compensation for your mistreatment by the directors of Michigan Technologies?"

"Fortunately for them, that's not up to me," said Scott. "We had ways of dealing with traitors and liars in Vietnam. If it were up to me, I'm afraid that's the kind of compensation I might ask for."

Cat nodded her understanding. "No further questions."

"Your witness, Mr. Davis," said the judge.

Roderick, too weak-kneed to stand, simply responded, "Nothing."

*   *   *

A security room was provided for Scott, Kent, Lillian, Pop Mead, Alma, Juanita, Dave, and Cat while the jury was in seclusion. In the hall a mob of reporters was awaiting the outcome of the trial and the chance to interview America's longest surviving POW of the post-Vietnam era.

Cat, confident of victory, was huddled in a corner working with Lillian on a statement for Scott to read after the verdict was announced. Alma and Juanita were using the time to talk in some detail about Juanita's last week of imprisonment in Cuba.

Scott signaled to Pop Mead that he wanted to talk. They pulled two chairs into a corner near a clanking window air conditioner.

"Lillian told me about how supportive you've been through all this, Pop. I'm really grateful."

"Nonsense," said Pop. "Bea and I were ready for a trip back to Detroit anyway."

"Sure. No doubt."

"That little gal of yours is really sweet," said Pop, changing the subject. "If you two are going to be needing a preacher soon, I could certainly use the work."

Scott smiled. "That's why I wanted to talk to you. We want to be married, that's for sure. But we want more. If your offer is still open to live and work at the mission settlement, we'd like to take you up on it."

"Are you serious? But if you get your stock back, you'll be a rich man."

"I already *am* a rich man," countered Scott. "I've got Juanita back and I've got my friends at the settlement. I've got Lill and Dave, and you and Mom, and I've got a chance to serve God in a way that will justify all those years I spent in Vietnam. If I get the stock, we can use the money to build the mission work. So how about it—will you take me back?"

"As far as I'm concerned, son, it's as if you never left."

*   *   *

During the time the jury was out, Paul Stattman had stood toe-to-toe with Roderick Davis in the parking ramp next to the courthouse. The words they exchanged were vicious, threatening, and laced with a combination of panic and arrogance. Roderick had dropped the ball on this one. Stattman told him to wrap up the case and get out of town. Roderick told him that he wouldn't take any directions from a flunky of Paul's stature. He knew too much to feel threatened. No, he was staying and he was going to hold onto his positions at M-T and at the law office.

Roderick came back into the courthouse, fought his way through the throng of reporters, and made it to his table just as the jury started to return. The judge asked the foreman to read the verdict.

"We find Michigan Technologies guilty on all counts of illegal stock usurpation and misuse of stockholders' funds. We recommend that the plaintiff be awarded the largest settlement permissible by law."

Lillian hugged Cat. Scott and Dave shook hands. The courtroom was instantly abuzz.

Judge Slater called for order.

"In light of the jury's rulings, I now order the following procedures in this case: First, Michigan Technologies will return to Scott Parker the full number of shares that were taken from him; second, all accrued dividends and stock splits which have been paid or directed since the liquidation of Scott Parker's stock shares shall be tabulated and appropriate compensation shall be awarded to Scott Parker; and third, Michigan Technologies shall be fined 10,000 dollars for improper business practices as outlined in a summary I shall prepare as a supplement to this ruling. Court is adjourned."

A final rap of the gavel made it official.

CHAPTER 15

True to his word, Scott had spoken briefly to reporters after the court case. He credited the President with his safe return to America from Vietnam and endorsed him for reelection. He then announced that a formal press conference would be held in the ballroom of the Waverly Hotel at 7:00 P.M. that night. Then, with Kent's help, Scott Parker and his entourage vanished from public sight for the rest of the day.

Roderick Davis was also confronted by reporters on his way out of court. He had planned to make several grandiose statements about appealing the ruling, but he never had the chance. The reporters had all been informed by Paul Stattman that Roderick Davis was no longer the legal counsel for Michigan Technologies. The questions from the reporters focused on whether or not Roderick had another job lined up, where he planned to live, and how he personally felt about so humbling a defeat. Roderick stammered for a moment, then began to mumble, "No comment, no comment" as he edged his way to his car.

Roderick drove to his office, where the humiliation continued. He immediately noticed that his name was in the process of being removed from the roster of partners listed in the law firm's waiting room. He headed toward his office and discovered his secretary, Jennifer Wilkinson, packing his personal belongings into boxes.

"What are you doing?" Roderick demanded.

"I'm . . . I'm sorry, Mr. Davis," Jennifer answered, "but Mr. Ranes told me you were . . . uh . . . no longer with the firm. He told me to get your things for you to pick up."

Roderick set his briefcase on a chair and went storming down the hall to the plush office of Harold Ranes, senior partner in the firm. Without knocking, he went in.

"What's going on here, Harold? What are you trying to pull? My secretary tells me you ordered her to clear out my things. Have you forgotten that I'm a *partner* in this firm?"

Ranes looked squarely at Roderick Davis. He spoke to him in even tones. "You were a *junior* partner in this firm, Roderick, and that only due to your connection with Michigan Technologies. But now you've lost the account. You have nothing of value to offer us anymore. Even worse, you've suddenly become a serious liability. The members of the M-T board also sit on other corporate boards, and unless you go, they plan to withdraw those accounts from us as well. We can't allow that. So we had an emergency meeting and voted unanimously to drop you from the firm."

"That's unreasonable," Roderick protested. "How was I supposed to know Parker was still alive?"

"That's why we receive generous retainers," said Ranes. "We're supposed to know everything. You messed up, Davis. You're history. Get out."

"I *own* part of this firm."

Harold Ranes lifted his eyebrows at that remark. "Ah, yes. That reminds me." He pulled a sealed envelope from the briefcase lying on his desk. "Here's a check for your share of the business. It's not much . . . but then, neither are you. Take it."

Roderick flinched at the sight of the envelope. It looked exactly like the payoff envelope he had forced on Lillian Parker the day he had broken off their engagement and told her she was fired from Michigan Technologies.

"I don't want your check," said Roderick. "I want my job. I'm a good lawyer. Everyone knows that. I want to stay here."

Ranes approached Roderick and stuffed the envelope inside his inner suit pocket. He then walked to his office door and opened it.

"If you're not out of here with all your things in 15 minutes, I'll call the security people and have you thrown out," said Ranes.

*   *   *

Kent had arranged for a private suite to be secured at the Waverly Hotel for Scott and his party. When everyone arrived, Mom Mead was already there waiting. She hugged both Scott and Lillian, then kissed Cat and offered her congratulations.

"It's been on every TV station," Mom told them. "You've all been shown. Even you, Charles."

Pop Mead scowled. "Whatta ya mean *even* me? Why, I ramrodded this whole shebang."

"Of course you did, dear," agreed Mom. "By the way, did you remember to put my scrapbook back into the car? You know the one I mean—the one with the articles about J. J. and Scott . . . the articles that turned the whole case around?"

Pop nudged Juanita and with a wink warned, "Get used to that sort of barbed comment. Mom has never learned to respect the clergy *or* her husband."

Cat began rapping a pen against a glass in order to get everyone's attention.

"I know you are all ready to celebrate Scott's homecoming and our court victory, but I'm afraid we still have a lot of work to do before the press conference tonight."

A collective groan arose.

"Come on, come on," admonished Cat, "none of that. We've come too far to back off now. We've got momentum and public support on our side. Let's use it."

"For what?" asked Lillian. "We've already won Scott's stock back."

"That's not what you came to Detroit to accomplish, Lillian," said Cat. "We still haven't cleared your father's name. That was your real goal, remember?"

Lillian and Scott exchanged looks.

"She's right," Lillian said. Turning to Cat, she asked, "But how?"

"I've got two ideas," explained Cat. "Even though the court would not accept the file that Walter Hadley discovered in the computer data base as evidence, now that the case is over we can turn those records over to the media. I'm convinced the public will accept them as valid."

"What good will that do?" asked Pop Mead.

"It will give us public support for the second phase of our operation," said Cat. "Tonight we will announce that Scott is going to use his shares of company stock to call a special board meeting of Michigan Technologies. The purpose of the board meeting will be to nominate and elect Scott as a board member. Once on the board, Scott will spearhead a complete investigation aimed at clearing J. J. Parker's name."

"Do I actually have enough stock to elect myself to the board of directors?" asked Scott.

"Alone, no," admitted Cat. "But with public support strongly behind you, we can secure enough proxies from other stock-holders to give you a majority vote. And with that same public support, we can intimidate the other board members: If they try to vote against you, the public will begin to dump M-T stock shares and the entire company will suffer. We'll force them into a corner. They'll have to elect you."

"Ha! I love it," said Scott. "Suddenly the tail is wagging the dog."

"And all brought about by a Cat," answered Pop.

*　*　*

After returning to his apartment and fixing himself several stiff drinks, Roderick Davis began to make phone calls to everyone he knew in a position of authority at Michigan Technologies. No conversation lasted more than 30 seconds. Panic was reigning at the company, and the less that people communicated with the man who had caused it, the better.

Roderick's hands began to shake. The liquor hadn't helped. He knew he needed to get control of himself. He took several deep breaths and then walked into the bathroom. He plugged in his electric shaver and spent five minutes giving himself a shave and sideburn trim. He then brushed his teeth and rinsed his mouth with a mint-flavored mouthwash. He put some eyedrops into each eye and then neatly combed his hair. He cinched his tie into a firm knot.

Gradually his hands stopped shaking. The pretend game was working. Life was fine. He was in control.

He went to his work area in his den and opened his brief-case. Methodically he sat down and prepared a bank deposit slip for the check that Harold Ranes had given him. He placed the check and the deposit slip into a prestamped bank mailer. He then wrote checks for all his bills for the month—credit cards, rent, tailor, utilities, racket club membership, car lease—and put them in appropriate envelopes. He affixed stamps. Yes, things were routine, normal—just the same as always.

He went to the mail drop in the lobby of his apartment building and mailed the envelopes. He was feeling better now. He was in control.

As Roderick returned to the elevator, Gordy Smith, the maintenance man, spotted him. Roderick smiled, but Gordy looked anxious. Roderick entered the elevator, but Gordy stayed in the foyer.

"Hello, Mr. Davis. I seen ya on TV. Too bad."

"About what?" asked Roderick lightly.

"That case," said Gordy. "And your job. I feel sorry for you, sir."

Roderick was immediately incensed. "You? Feeling sorry for me? Don't be ridiculous. You're a janitor and I'm a lawyer."

"Maybe so," said Gordy, "but I got a job and you ain't."

The elevator doors closed.

*   *   *

Alma Hammond had been in touch with Camp David. The President was so pleased with Scott's post-courtroom talk with the press that he scheduled a White House visit for Scott the following week. Alma confirmed the arrangements with Scott and then announced to everyone that she was going home. Everyone tried to convince her to stay for the big party they were going to have after the evening press conference, but Alma hinted at some work that had to be done.

On her way out, Juanita spent a moment with her.

"You okay, Alma? You haven't said much all afternoon."

"Just tired, I guess," said Alma. "And a little moody. I'm losing you and Scott after today . . . and another friend apparently has moved on, too."

"Someone special?" asked Juanita.

Alma shrugged. "I must have misread the signs. I thought it was someone special. But right now I feel a little silly. Two days ago I began to think I was stupid for not realizing this man cared for me, so I started to give my heart a little slack. Now he's gone, and I feel embarrassed for letting my imagination get out of control. Aren't we silly at times?"

"I guess so," agreed Juanita. "But I'd be silly 100 times over again if it meant getting a guy like Scott. It's worth some risk, Alma. Don't give up on your man yet. There's always hope."

"You've proved that, haven't you?"

"And I'll be proving it again someday," said Juanita. "One day my mother and I are going to be reunited. I just know it."

Alma smiled. "If you can be that optimistic after all you've been through, I guess I shouldn't get depressed over one forgotten phone call. Thanks, Juanita. Goodbye."

*   *   *

The very idea of a common custodian feeling pity for him

had so enraged Roderick that he had raced back to his apartment and spent nearly two hours calling every lead in his "networking" card file. He was determined to find a new job. He would not allow those jackals at Michigan Technologies to toss him off as if he were a nobody.

But two hours of having people hang up on him proved that he *was* a nobody. Yesterday's golden boy was today's tarnished relic.

Well, he would not go down alone. Stattman had warned that the only way Roderick could bring the other board members down would be by incriminating himself. *And you'll never do that*, Paul had said.

But Paul was wrong. The only thing Roderick had left was revenge. His career was over. His prestige was lost. His money would soon be spent. And then, while he was wandering aimlessly and pennilessly through life, his former confederates would be spending J. J. Parker's three million.

No. No way. One good toss to the wolves deserved another. He would get them—every one of them. He knew where each skeleton was buried. He would show that the computer file which Cat had tried to introduce as evidence was real, that old J. J. had not embezzled three million from M-T but just invested it in stocks with coded entry names in the computer's memory. Roderick could explain in detail how the five chief officers at M-T had secretly contrived to liquidate those stock holdings as they simultaneously embezzled equal monies from other corporate accounts; the bottom lines of the balance books always looked accurate, so no one ever knew about the thefts.

Roderick had invoices and memos and letters and canceled checks that would show how—acting as a legal liaison for the various M-T board members and officers—he had arranged a mock auction of J. J. Parker's estate in which the furnishings, home, cars, property, and art works were purchased at depressed prices before any bidding ever began.

They didn't think he had the nerve to turn them in. Well, they would see.

Roderick pulled a cassette tape player close to him and pressed the record button. He began to speak.

"My name is Roderick Davis, and this is my full confession of how I consorted with four executives at Michigan Technologies to rob the company of three million dollars and frame the late J. J. Parker for this crime."

He pressed the pause button. Was he really this desperate? Was he?

He released the pause. "I am making this confession of my own free will, fully knowledgeable of the fact that what I say here can and may be used against me. . . ."

He hesitated a few seconds.

". . . and used against those I am implicating as my accomplices in a court of law."

*   *   *

An hour before the press conference was to begin, Cat sneaked off to a side room in the suite and phoned her parents with the big news—not about the courtroom victory, but about the pregnancy. Phil and Hattie Compton, on separate phone extensions, both began trying to talk to Cat at once. Cat was laughing and attempting to get a word in edgewise and thoroughly enjoying herself. In the midst of this glee, Lillian and Mom Mead burst into Cat's room without knocking.

"Hang up that phone and get in here quick!" said Lillian.

"Hurry up!" urged Mom, waving frantically. "It's Roderick. He's giving a statement to the press . . . from police headquarters."

Cat dropped the phone receiver on the bed and hurried into the next room. Mom Mead stayed behind to finish the call to the Comptons.

"This is live," said Dave Thompson as Cat drew near the TV set.

On the screen was a close-up of Roderick's face with a dozen microphones held near him. Two Detroit Metropolitan

234   The Caribbean Conspiracy

Police officers could be seen over his shoulders in the background.

"That's correct," Roderick was saying. "This afternoon I mailed a 90-minute cassette tape to the City District Attorney giving information about the embezzlement of three million dollars in funds from Michigan Technologies. I am now here to surrender myself to the police. I am seeking a plea-bargain arrangement by which I will be granted a reduced sentence in exchange for my testimony against those who perpetrated this crime."

A question was called to Roderick out of camera and microphone range. He nodded his understanding of what had been asked.

"Yes, that's exactly right," confirmed Roderick. "J. J. Parker did not embezzle any money from Michigan Technologies. He was used as a scapegoat. I have proof that Mrs. Lillian Parker Thompson, and now her brother Scott, are entitled to reclaim all of the shares of stock formerly held in Michigan Technologies by J. J. Parker."

In the hotel suite gasps were followed by outbursts of *"Did you hear that?"* and *"I can't believe we're seeing this!"* and *"Do you have any idea what this means to you, Scott?"*

Lillian was so shocked that she had to sit down. Scott, however, grabbed Juanita in his arms and began to twirl her around. Pop hurried into the side room to relay the news to Mom. Dave let out a war whoop and then opened the hallway door to tell Kent, who was on security duty, the sudden development.

Only Cat remained staring at the television. She continued to stare at Roderick until he finally turned and walked away from the cameras. He had tried to put up a good front, but Cat had seen how broken a man he was. He had bitten his lips several times as he had spoken. His hair had been mussed. His shirt collar had been wrinkled and stained from perspiration.

She had come to Detroit to face Roderick, and she had wound up destroying him. Her victory in the courtroom this afternoon had led to the complete eradication of Roderick's hopes, dreams, and goals for the future. She had ruined the career of the man she had once hoped to marry. And no matter how appropriate her actions had been, and no matter how Roderick had deceived her and given her cause for embarrassment, she now took no delight in seeing the devastation she had brought upon this man. The "old" Cat would have relished Roderick's agony; the "new" Cat found herself actually feeling sympathy for him.

"You can handle the press conference on your own," Cat told Scott. "It's your show from now on anyway. I've got one stop to make, then I'm going home."

Scott looked genuinely surprised. "What? You're kidding! First Alma, now you. No way. You said it before yourself: We've just begun to fight. I need you to stay on and represent me when Lill and I go back into court to claim our father's stock."

Cat grabbed her handbag and sweater. "Thanks, but no. I told Lillian I'd help her exonerate your father. Roderick's now done that for us. My duties are finished here. I need to go home and get a nursery ready."

Lillian hugged Cat. "We love you," she said. "You made all this happiness possible. I never would have survived without you. You're the most wonderful friend I've ever had. How can I ever thank you?"

"Just be there," said Cat. "As always . . . just be there."

CHAPTER 16

"Who's there?"

Roderick Davis had fallen asleep on the shabby couch in the waiting room of the minimum-security detention center. He had been assured that he would be released on his own recognizance just as soon as the necessary paperwork could be prepared. The investigating officer had seemed embarrassed about reading him his rights. After all, everyone knew Roderick was an attorney . . . at least until the state bar association reviewed his case and took steps to revoke his license.

He sat up, rubbed his eyes, and squinted at his Rolex: 8:35 P.M. He shifted his attention to a woman standing in the doorway, a woman who looked very much like . . .

"Cat?"

"Hello, Roderick."

He stretched his cramped legs in front of him and slipped his feet into his Gucci loafers. He stood up and attempted to brush the wrinkles out of his slacks. It was then that he noticed the small piece of carry-on luggage she was holding in her right hand.

"Ah-ha! I get it," he began. "You're on your way to the airport and just stopped by to gloat. You're all heart, Cat." He stooped over and snapped on a light. "Take a good look, luv," he said with an exaggerated bow. "I concede defeat. If I had known you were coming I would have arranged for a white flag."

She sat down. "I don't have much time . . ."

236

"I know, I know, you've got to dash," he said flippantly. "Well, don't let me hold you up. We wouldn't want to keep the limo waiting."

Cat leaned forward, determined not to let his words affect her. "Listen to me: I'm here to help. You're going to need an attorney . . . a good one. And when you get out of this mess, you're going to need a job. With your permission, I'd like to talk to Drew about that. I can't promise anything, of course, but he knows a lot of people. It would mean you'd have to relocate, but. . . ."

Roderick sank down into the couch. He looked beaten.

"Why are you *really* here? Why are you doing this?" he whispered, a choke in his voice.

"Because you need a friend," she answered. "Tonight, when you made your statement to the police, you turned an important corner. I know your motives weren't right, but what you did was on target. It could be the start of a whole new life for you. If you can only shake off the idea of revenge and concentrate on starting over. . . ."

Even though his eyes were fighting tears, Roderick didn't turn away from her. His bravado was gone. "I'm so mixed up," he whispered. He shook his head and rubbed his bloodshot eyes. "You're sure right about a couple of things, though; I could use a friend. And a good attorney. And a job."

She smiled. "One at a time," she said. "On my way in I stopped at the front desk and made two phone calls. First, I talked with Smith and McKeand. They're supposed to be the sharpest law team in the city, and I think it's time they proved it. They'll be here any minute."

As the reality of her words and the sincerity of her purpose sunk in, Roderick could only whisper a soft thank you.

"And then I called Pop Mead," she continued. "I was fortunate . . . the press conference had just broken up and he was in his room packing. He promised to come right over."

Roderick nodded. He didn't need to ask the purpose of Pastor Mead's visit. Again he whispered, "Thank you."

Cat looked at her watch and quickly gathered up her purse and her carry-on luggage. Roderick remained on the couch, his head in his hands. She walked over to him and lightly touched one of his shoulders in a gesture of goodbye.

"As far as the job goes, I'll talk to Drew about it tonight," she said. "When I'm home. At last."

After a moment's hesitation Roderick reached out to her, but she was gone.

*   *   *

When Alma Hammond arrived at her apartment in Virginia, she saw a large envelope stuffed inside her mailbox. She used her key to open the mailbox door and yanked hard to pull out the envelope. It felt heavy. There was no return address. She decided to open it before going up to her apartment.

She tore loose the end flap and tilted out the contents. A hardbound book came out. Alma turned it over and read the title:

WE
by Yevgeny Zamyatim

Alma hugged the book tightly to her chest. She instantly knew who had sent it and why.

Oh, you were so right, Juanita, Alma thought. *We must always have hope.*

She looked down again at the book.

"Yes," she whispered, "we must always have hope."

HARVEST HOUSE PUBLISHERS

For The Best In Inspirational Fiction

RUTH LIVINGSTON HILL CLASSICS

Bright Conquest	$5.95
The Homecoming	$5.95
The Jeweled Sword	$5.95
Morning Is For Joy	$5.95
This Side of Tomorrow	$5.95

JUNE MASTERS BACHER
PIONEER ROMANCE NOVELS

Series 1

Love Is a Gentle Stranger	$4.95
Love's Silent Song	$4.95
Diary of a Loving Heart	$4.95
Love Leads Home	$4.95

Series 2

Journey To Love	$4.95
Dreams Beyond Tomorrow	$4.95
Seasons of Love	$4.95
My Heart's Desire	$4.95

Series 3

Love's Soft Whisper	$5.95
Love's Beautiful Dream	$5.95

MYSTERY/ROMANCE NOVELS

Echoes From the Past, *Bacher*	$4.95
Mist Over Morro Bay, *Page/Fell*	$4.95
Secret of the East Wind, *Page/Fell*	$4.95
Storm Clouds Over Paradise, *Page/Fell*	$4.95
Beyond the Windswept Sea, *Page/Fell*	$4.95
The Legacy of Lillian Parker, *Holden*	$4.95
The Compton Connection, *Holden*	$4.95
The Caribbean Conspiracy, *Holden*	$4.95

PIONEER ROMANCE NOVELS

Sweetbriar, *Wilbee*	$4.95
The Sweetbriar Bride, *Wilbee*	$4.95
The Tender Summer, *Johnson*	$4.95

Available at
your local Christian bookstore